D0984988

MADCHILD RUNNING

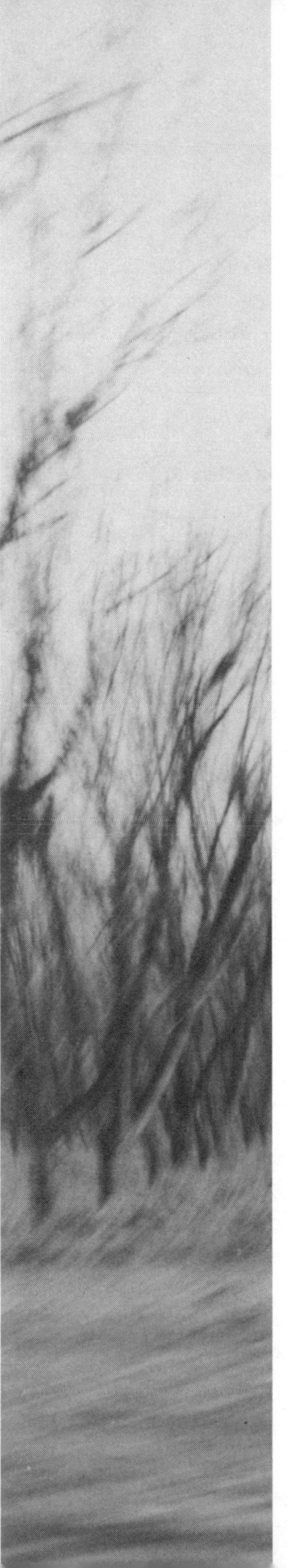

MADCHILD RUNNING

A NOVEL BY

KEITH EGAWA

RED CRANE BOOKS
SANTA FE

First Edition
Manufactured in the United States of America
Design by Beverly Miller Atwater
Cover Photograph by Joseph Morris

Library of Congress Cataloging-in-Publication Data
Egawa, Keith, 1966–
Madchild running : a novel / by Keith Egawa.
p. cm.
ISBN 1-878610-72-4
1. Indians of North America—Fiction. 2. Social workers—United States—Fiction.
3. Teenage girls—United States—Fiction. I. Title.
PS3555.G2968 M34 1999
813'.54–dc21
99-050154

Red Crane Books
2008-B Rosina Street
Santa Fe, New Mexico 87505
1-800-922-3392
publish@redcrane.com
www.redcrane.com

Dedication

Thanks to my family, their belief and their mettle
Friends and their endurance
The inspiration of the little girl who is grown and living
The inspiration of you who have gone away
For the strength and vulnerability of you all

Prologue

Coyote ran. Out from the frozen cattails and reeds he ran. I had fired my Remington; twice I squeezed the trigger, sending bird shot into the air, trying to scare up the ducks that were out of range across the frozen lake, floating in thawed patches. The reports leaped from hillside to hillside, sounding like the flat smack of wooden beams being beaten together.

Coyote appeared suddenly, running from the sound, out onto the ice, his paws punching holes without sound in the layer of snow that hid the frigid water. His body was unlike those of his brothers in the city. His was healthy and wild, with only a slight but bewildering sense of the bounty on his spirit.

Coyote ran, bounding at an angle adjacent to where I stood on a ridge, ten feet above the ice with my shotgun and duck vest, my breath coming in sharp, frosty clouds. Confused, he began to turn; gradually and gracefully he curved, striding toward the shore, toward me. I could clearly see the pointed muzzle of his cunning face with the keenness and fine edge of the natural world, in his copper eyes the tempered alertness of being unbroken and free. Thick silver fur with streaks of rust blew back along his entire body with the breeze of his movement as he made a skillful arc on the slickness of ice, leaning and stretching out along the shoreline, twenty feet from where I stood. His head just barely moved, quickly from this side to that, not looking at me but beyond for his escape to the distant marsh grass and the fields.

Coyote passed and in seconds was gone, but I had seen a piece of his spirit emerge from his proud body, and he had looked confused and frightened. And he was running.

1

Washington State is home to twenty-nine federally recognized tribes of American Indians and a number of others that missed out on the title when it was being granted. The title was an allowance made by the newborn United States government, still teething on the eternal bounty of God's country—deeded to it by God to do with what it willed. For the federally recognized tribes, this title ensured the contained security of a reservation, along with permission to harvest fish and game from the "usual and accustomed places," or at least those places that had not been industriously covered with farms and houses and towns. Included in this title were painfully small incentives, positive points in the terms of surrender, promising the recipients that they would forever be considered Indians, the natives of America, who had settled on these terms to avoid losing everything. It was in those days that a generational division in the continuity of Indian tradition began to occur. On this side of the great gap, among the more recent generations, began a new progression, fueled by anger and born of ruin.

Anger is passed on as easy as eye color. It is passed on through learning, through example, through recognition of the reasons why it is burning in your mother's eyes—simple history. Anger comes without effort. Sadness turns to anger, loss turns to anger, shame turns to anger, and hate makes it bearable for those volatile moments. And when anger burns itself out on its own huge appetite, it reverts back to these quieter qualities of the wounded spirit, gathering strength to blaze again. Booze, drugs, and anger—all amount to measured suicide when craved by the wounded spirit. The wounded spirit wants to hide out wrapped in a comfortable blanket of deception, while just beyond this blanket of illusion pulled tightly about the head and face is a knowledge of the necessity to venture out and recover what was taken. You know that your survival depends on recovering what was forced from the grasp of an old woman and man, before you were born to have any say in the matter, as though you would have had some anyway. The truth is that what was taken can be recovered now, although many are afraid of journeying out and reclaiming what was lost, a path whose end disappears in the distance like a highway in the desert, a task that seems too daunting to face.

Many Indians leave the reservations, briefly or forever, and sometimes they come to Seattle. If those Indians are dragging their devils in tow, then they might walk through the doors of a place where I once worked—the Urban Native Support Services.

The main offices of the Urban Native Support Services, or U.N.S.S., overlook a lake, although most of the lakeside windows stare into the living rooms and kitchens of the condos just between the building and the water. The window I looked out when I was there is on the opposite side, facing the street. Nestled in a neighborhood of middle-class homes, in between the University District and downtown Seattle, U.N.S.S. is one small piece of "the system." It's the piece for Indians, with counselors and caseworkers waiting for referrals from Child Protective Services, tribal social programs, and the Washington State Court System. Pleas from the displaced and desperate come over the phone lines, and people come walking through the front door with a lot of pain but little to say.

When I arrived there, after graduating from the University of Washington with a degree in sociology, we had a staff of about eight who worked in offices furnished by Saint Vinnie's and donations, evincing humility and limited funding. Black coffee percolated furiously from eight to five, with the hiss of steam and the smell of burnt Folgers. The sound of electronics hinted at an industrialized environment of high-speed office performance, with ringing phones, a beeping switchboard, clicking keyboards, a droning fax machine, laser printer, and photocopier. But the people I encountered there were laid-back individuals, working on scars that seemed to be almost genetic—day after day, family after family.

The services provided—anger management, domestic violence

treatment, drug and alcohol aftercare, sexual abuse counseling, and talking circles—whether court ordered or voluntary—offered a shot at rehabilitation and survival. Wilma, the boss, started me out running errands and attending various trainings. Then she gradually assigned me some heavier stuff, like interviewing new clients, administering intakes, and writing up reports. I talked with kids and played the role of a positive Indian male role model—as the organization saw me—scribbled on my notepad, and always showed only my mask, everything else held tightly beneath the collar, buttoned up to the neck. All my efforts were funneled into one purpose: to divert Indian families from the clutches of the system, and if they got in it, then help get them out. When I began work there, I was idealistic; I wanted to be there trying to help individuals, I wanted to learn and understand. I was airtight, sucking it all in. And so it remained—for a while.

One typical day I looked into the bathroom mirror at the end of the hall, studying my features, the color of my eyes and hair. My hair, which I always kept short, was black, and my eyes dark brown, though my skin was fair. Alone I looked as pale as any white person, but when I saw myself with white people, like in pictures with friends, I was different. I was darker, my hair coarse and straight, my face more broad, more flat.

A blend of two different Coast Salish tribes and Flathead, I didn't grow up on a reservation and was never enrolled. According to my father, from whom my sister and I inherited our Indian blood, we did not meet the blood quantum for any one nation. While growing up, we never questioned this. Then when my father left the family while I was in grade school and never came back, a large part of being Indian left with him.

My dad had lived on the reservation from birth through high school, and though he wasn't a big man, he was always able to hold his own physically and came to be a dominant force in small town athletics. After high school he took a step down from running a football through the backwaters of northern Washington, left the reservation, and became the head sugar man in a pickle factory, measuring and mixing sugar for the brine. This was one piece of family history that made my mother smile when she referred to it, for this was when they had met. I never asked her what had attracted her to him, aside from the allure of his job. After a couple years of being ribbed by his peers, he became a pipe fitter.

We grew up in the suburbs of Tacoma, Washington, where Tia and I continued to live with my Irish and Scandinavian mother, Teri Shea. Tia and I took my mother's surname after my dad deserted us. By way of explaining my father's departure, my mom said he went out to get a gallon of milk and never came back, although that wasn't exactly how it happened. She just thought it was more colorful to tell it that way, and important to give it a humorous spin to emphasize the tragic irresponsibility of his action. In reality, he actually did leave for a gallon of milk and was gone for a week, but the pattern of disappearing and returning without forewarning or explanation grew in frequency and duration until one time he simply didn't return at all—like a pet pigeon flying a little further each day until eventually it forgets how to go home or no longer has sufficient feelings of attachment to care about returning.

Once Dad was gone, we experienced only occasional reminders of our Indian heritage, during visits to my grandmother on the Lummi Reservation or when the topic of Indians came up in school for an hour or so out of an entire semester in United States history. At such times I'd become alert with recollection, and the other kids would look at me as if I were going to take over the lesson.

Then our visits to the Lummi Reservation decreased drastically after my grandmother died. Following that my connections with my Indian heritage became tenuous or virtually nonexistent. So with a rudimentary knowledge of my ancestry, the black hair and dark eyes of my father, I took my job with the agency to hold hands and lock souls with people with whom I shared blood and history.

2

The Tall Fighters were battling over the front seat, Rosie, Amelia, and Johnny Tall Fighter. It was time again for an afternoon with their mother, Josie Tall Fighter, a monthly ritual that was drawn up in the case plan with the end goal of returning them to her care. Though sometimes unreliable, Josie was a quiet and likeable person, with a cooperative, slightly frightened demeanor, that made the situation that much more frustrating. Either she would show for the visit, or it would be yet another long ride back to the foster home, recycling excuses about Josie missing the bus.

Booze and vagrancy had washed the Tall Fighters from Montana to Seattle, with Josie seeking sanctuary and opportunity hundreds of miles from the place of her undoing, leaving the children's father behind where he could focus more fully on not being involved with his family. Josie had repeatedly tried and failed to stop drinking, until one day the worn-out troop was found taking shelter from the rain under an I-5 overpass in ripped jeans and sweat jackets with the sleeves stretched over their cold fingers. Child Protective Services, or CPS, was called, dependencies were filed, and into the system they went.

The family was Salish-Kootenai and Piegan. Rosie was the oldest at age eight, Amelia in the middle at seven, and Johnny was the youngest at six. They were all full of smiles and energy, everything still an adventure, the world still promising in its endlessness. Whether it was taking long rides over the plains and mountains of the northern states, chins resting on the windowsills of Greyhound buses, or using their small, fast bodies to get in and out of dumpsters to retrieve food, youth was protecting them so far. They had been in foster care while Josie took another shot at sobriety under the supervision of Luke Child, the foster care caseworker for our agency. Since I was the taxi, Luke kept me apprised of the family's progress, and after each visit he'd ask me if Josie had been drunk or sagging from a bender of the days before. "They're so bonded with her," he'd say each time. "She has just got to make a decision between them and the alcohol." But unfortunately she was making a decision, and so far it wasn't the right one.

Rosie was shouting hysterically, "It's my turn!" Pushing in front of her brother and sister, she got one foot in the front seat before Amelia grabbed her from behind.

As the oldest, Rosie was sometimes entrusted as the keeper of the lunches, and her heavy brown bag got hung up on the shoulder strap of the seatbelt. "Melia!" she screamed, jerking the sack from the vinyl strap, "Melia!"

Amelia pulled Rosie's kicking body back from the open door, digging in her heels like the anchor in a tug-of-war, while Rosie screamed through clenched teeth.

"Hang on! Hang on!" I said, holding Johnny back as he made his way towards the sudden opening. "Now everybody will get to ride in the front, but we have to take turns. Let go of each other!"

They stood in a row, fidgeting and waiting for the decision as I blocked the passenger seat. Amelia took advantage of the silence by saying, "It's my turn!"

Rosie kicked her foot into the gravel, spraying the side of my car with a shower of rocks. "You rode up front last time, Melia!"

"I think she's right, Amelia, you were the last one to ride up front. Now we have to take turns so everybody gets their chance. Today is Rosie's turn, and then on the way home it's Johnny's, then next time it's yours."

"But now I'm last," Amelia protested, sticking her lower lip out and frowning so intensely that her black eyes nearly disappeared under her eyebrows.

"No, Amelia, it doesn't work that way. You see, next time you're first and then Rosie, and then Johnny. See it goes in a circle, no one's first or last."

"Except today I'm last." She pushed her lip out a little further.

I put my hand on her head and gave it a light squeeze, trying not to laugh. "You're going to have to trust me on this one, Amelia. It moves in a circle, 'round and 'round, no one's first, and no one's last. Now let's hurry up or your mom's going to be sitting there waiting for us."

It worked. Amelia hurried into the back, Johnny followed, and Rosie scrambled into the winner's seat. I pulled a U-turn back onto the road and headed for the city.

In five minutes Johnny discovered the coins in the backseat ashtray—a handful of pennies, a nickel, and a dime. "What's this?" he asked, jingling the coins.

"You know what it is, Johnny."

"Whose is it?"

"Well, it's mine, but I'll tell you what, you can keep it if you promise to spend it wisely."

"But it's mostly pennies."

"Yeah, that's true, but those pennies add up to more nickels and dimes."

Rosie wrestled with her seatbelt until she was twisted all the way around. "Gimme some!"

Amelia's hand shot out for her fair share.

"He gave it to me!" Johnny defended, hiding his money behind his back.

"Johnny, you have to share with your sisters. I should have clarified that right off the bat, but knowing what a good kid you are I just assumed you'd spread the wealth."

"But there's only one dime and one nickel."

And so we drove along the waterfront, me looking for a parking spot and digging in my pocket, the ashtray, and the crack of the seat for enough change to pacify these shrewd kids. Finally, I found enough, announcing, "Now everybody here's got twenty cents except me." They found this acceptable.

I spotted a parking place across from McDonald's, where their mother was to be waiting. As I backed in, with the kids squirming, craning their necks, and shouting conflicting directions, I could see Josie a little way down the street heading for the rendezvous. I advised the kids on how to safely exit the car, and they poured out onto the sidewalk like fleeing rats.

They saw her on the other side of the street as they stepped into the crosswalk. Hands flew into the air, Johnny's pennies scattered, and a cacophony of elation rose from their mouths of missing baby teeth and crooked canines. With no means to stop them, I joined the charge, jogging at the rear of the pack. They latched onto Josie like merging droplets of water, arms and legs squeezing their bodies to hers, their cheeks pressing against her face in a communion of reassurance, confirming that they had come from her.

Josie was smiling and kissing them in turn, glancing over at me with a nervous laugh. "That's enough, that's enough," she said, prying Amelia off the fronts of her legs. "Levi here needs to talk to me before we go have fun, okay?" Josie had cut her hair since the last time I had seen her. It was leveled off just above her shoulders, the edge uneven all the way around like she had pulled it into a ponytail then lopped it off. The dark cast of her eyes moved out into the skin, right to the edges of her cheekbones in hollows of exhaustion and strain.

"How've you been, Josie?"

"I'm doin' okay. I start in-patient in one week."

"Alright! You finally got a space."

She smiled and looked down at her feet, then forced her eyes back up. "Do you want me to tell Luke or do you wanna?"

The children moved around me in a semicircle, their heads tilted up with anticipation, their soft, straight bangs laying against their foreheads. They looked like a row of carolers or trick-or-treaters.

"You better call him," I said. "I'll let him know you're starting treatment again, but you can give him the details—times, dates, place, all that stuff."

I could feel the heat rushing through the blood vessels in my face. Again—you're starting treatment again. You failed the first time, but I'm glad to see you're starting again, I thought to myself. The way I had phrased it was an accident—not cruel but insensitive-sounding. Sometimes she made me angry, but mostly she made me sad, the way her eyes were always on the ground, as though she could see the pieces of her life scattered there and she was preparing to make yet another attempt at gathering them together. I hoped she hadn't noticed the way I had worded my response.

"Okay," she said, nodding her head rapidly, "you let him know, and I'll call him soon as I can."

"Sounds good, I'll do that."

Amelia was wiping her nose on her sleeve. Rosie was rifling through the lunch bag. Johnny was digging in his pockets. The waistband of his jeans was too slack, and they sagged a little on his narrow hips.

"Well, I'll let you guys go, and I'll meet you here at 4:00."

"Could you maybe get them at the Greyhound station?" Josie raised her eyebrows apprehensively like she was taking some kind of gamble, afraid I might get upset. "Do you know where that is?"

"Uh, yeah, that's okay, 4:00 in front of the station."

"It's just that I planned on heading in that direction."

"It's no problem."

Before crossing the street, I waved to the kids, but they didn't see me. They were skipping along at their mother's feet, down the sunny waterfront, where pigeons took clumsy flight from the pavement before their approach.

At 4:15 P.M., I pulled to the curb in front of the Greyhound station, fifteen minutes late. The Tall Fighters were leaning against the wall and didn't see me pull up. When I got out of the car, Josie finally saw me and waved. Suddenly hurried, she busied herself wiping down Johnny's hands with a paper napkin. Rosie and Amelia were sitting hunched over, their backs to the wall, too intent on what they were doing to look up.

"It's time to go home," I said. I walked up to the little girls. "What you got there Rosie?" I squatted down to take a closer look at the thick glob of yellow substance quivering in her palm.

She produced a mini Ritz cracker and dipped it. "It's Cheez Whiz!"

They both had a gummy residue on their hands and the lower halves of their faces. Just as I was wondering what it was, Amelia fished out the last peanut-shaped marshmallow from a bag between her legs, thrust it in my face as if enticing me with something palatable, then popped the whole thing into her mouth with a frenzied laugh.

"I haven't cleaned 'em up yet," Josie explained, scooting up to my side and taking the empty bag from Amelia. She took Amelia's delicate little hands in hers and started rubbing on her fingers. The paper napkin stuck to them like flypaper.

"That's okay," I said, "Rosie, just scrape that cheese into the marshmallow bag."

"No! No!" She screamed and jabbed one last cracker into the blob.

"Yes, yes, Rosie," I said, guiding her hand into the bag, "this stuff will glue your insides together."

Finally I got them into the car, with Josie wiping at their hands and faces. They wriggled in their seat belts, with their hands pressed against the window, making collages of fingers and palms, while their mother waved and told them to be good. I stood on the sidewalk next to Josie to say a few words before taking her children away.

"How'd it go?"

"Good. They had fun, I think."

"Yeah, I'm sure they did."

"When I come out of treatment, I was wondering if there's any way you can help me get a place big enough for the kids to have overnights?" Josie was still looking in the car as she asked me for help. Then she glanced up at me. "Luke said that after some time I could, you know, keep them overnight."

"Yeah, I can do that. I can put in a word when you're on the list for Section 8 and I'll write a letter. I'll tell 'em it's an emergency. Sometimes things move faster if you lie a little."

She forced a laugh and looked away from me again. "Damn this is just weird."

"I know," I said. "It'll work out, though." We stared at the kids on the other side of the glass. "Well, I better get them back to the foster home. Just call Luke for the next visit, and we'll set up a time."

"Okay," she said.

I watched her walk away across the parking lot of the bus station, looking straight ahead, her hands in her pockets.

"Did you all have fun? What'd you do?" I tried to get their minds off the separation, make them go back to when they were with her, but it didn't work. They were so revved up from the sugar that their quiet, frowning resentment of times before was kicked into high gear. They rolled the windows up and down, swore undying loyalty to their "real" mom, and twisted out of their seat belts the whole way home. The worse they became, the more uneasy it made me. Sometimes when kids come home after visiting their parents they get so furious and wild that the caseworker stops the visits or restricts them to supervised visits in the office. One angry little guy got worse each time until one day he wiped shit on the walls, tried to kick the foster dad in the nuts, and bit the foster parents' baby. The visits with his mother went well; it's when they would come to an end that he'd fall apart. As a result, he was only six years old when he was placed in institutionalized care, where he spent many hours in the tantrum room, padded from floor to ceiling.

At times like this, I was reminded of my childhood separation from my own father. After my dad had abandoned our family, there were no visits, just one clean, heartless break. When he had been gone for a record amount of time, I stood on the bed in my bedroom and methodically pounded small circular holes in the wall with a hammer. My memory of this doesn't even seem like an angry one—just an image of a huge, passionless pattern of perfect holes. My mom broke into the room after about ten minutes and yanked the hammer out of my hand. She didn't yell, but instead cried, picked me up, and took me out of the room. The holes remained there for a long time, without my mother ever saying anything about them, just like they were invisible to her. She was a fastidious housekeeper, though she ignored that one wall in my bedroom. I suppose that either she wanted to leave the damage to remind us kids of how horrible our dad was for leaving, by contrast drawing attention to how loyal and responsible she was, or she could not face repairing the wall since it might open up the entire topic of our father's abandonment for discussion—something that we never did. Ultimately, when I was a teenager I filled the holes in with spackle and painted the room.

As I opened the car door in front of their foster home, the Tall Fighters scurried across the lawn. It was dusk, and they looked so small, their fast legs chopping through the high grass. The front door opened, and Rosie and Amelia pushed past their foster mother and into the house. Johnny stopped under the swing set and turned suddenly as if he had forgotten something important. Then across the lawn he came with his arms out in front of him, his feet almost falling back behind him in his hurry. But he regained his footing, and I knelt down as he dove into my arms, holding on tight with what felt like gratitude and reluctance, as if maybe I was becoming something consistent in his life—symbolic of a drive across town and sometimes a visit with his mom. And each time I left, in my absence was an empty stretch of time measured by uncertainty about whether I would return, and the possibility that he might never see his mother again.

He thanked me for the ride and followed after his sisters.

3

Here's the scoop, Levi. You need to make a drive. How's your car holding up?" Wilma had set down her sandwich and was scratching a phone number on a post-it for me. Her small office smelled like venison.

Wilma was a Blackfeet Indian and also part white, but hardly anybody ever says that, they just focus on what kind of Indian they are. It's nothing against whites; some people would claim instead that it reflects a complete lack of shame about being Indian; and besides, when a non-Indian finds out a person's Indian that's what they are called anyway till their dying day. Wilma was in her early fifties with a sense of humor that always got her through the worst of situations. Not that she didn't take things seriously; rather she had the strength to pull her staff through day after day and still simultaneously crack some good jokes, many of them unintentional. When she hired me, she talked at length about all the angles of the job, since I had no background in social work. She seemed confident in me, and I could see her excitement at getting someone young, Indian, and male to round out the mostly female staff, though she frequently ended her instructions and anecdotes with warnings.

"It's really no-host bar out there," she said, at the end of our first meeting, after telling me that I was hired. I wondered if she was making some obtuse analogy to the job and alcohol abuse when it clicked. "Do you mean 'no holds barred'?" I asked, wondering if it was a bad idea to correct the boss on day one.

"That's exactly what I mean," she said. "You'll do just fine."

While growing up, Wilma had played basketball and softball, touring Montana and the Pacific Northwest with other Blackfeet girls, challenging teams from various reservations. She would make references to being team captain, talking about clearing the bases as the team's heaviest hitter, and commonly shooting over twenty points per game. Wilma was fairly tall, though she also made a point of mentioning that she had lost at least an inch to the settling of the spine. Now in her mid-fifties, it was still evident that she was the jock she had claimed to have been. She moved with physical confidence and strength, walking from task to task with her arms swinging purposefully as if she were late for a bus, and heaving the cumbersome thirty-pound water bottles into the cooler instead of asking one of the men to do it. Wilma had lived in Seattle for seventeen years, but she and her husband returned to Browning, Montana, several times annually to visit the families of their three grown children, all living in various towns along the I-90 corridor between Spokane and Missoula. They always packed a huge empty cooler in the back of their station wagon, which on the return trip would contain thirty or forty pounds of deer and elk meat from relatives, enough to last them until the next cherished trip "home," as Wilma called it—the place of her tribe and her upbringing.

"My car's okay," I said. "Where am I going?"

"You know how to get to Kingston?"

"Yeah, I think so." Kingston was across the water from downtown Seattle.

"Well, good. This is the number to a youth home outside Kingston. It's not on the Suquamish Reservation, but it's right by it." She ran a finger down the scribble on her legal pad, found what she was looking for, and wrote down a second number.

"Six months ago a twelve-year-old girl was taken from her house by CPS because of domestic violence between her father and mother. They were drunk, and Dad beat up Mom. The girl, named Nicki Sanders, was standing out in the yard distraught and screaming at eleven o'clock at night. A neighbor called police after hearing sounds of violence in the house—breaking glass and screaming. Before the cops got there, the father came out, grabbed Nicki by the hair when she wouldn't go back in, and dragged her inside.

"The Sanders are a Suquamish family. The case was taken by the Tribal Court, and they put Nicki into temporary foster care for four months. The court saw fit to file a dependency, and we agreed to do a courtesy supervision. The father was ordered to attend anger management, and both he and the mother were ordered to do outpatient treatment for alcohol. They've both been coming here for their sessions. In fact, you've probably seen 'em around—Charles and Lydia Sanders. They kept in strict compliance, and at the review hearing yesterday the court gave back their daughter."

"Four months?" I said. "Isn't that a little soon?"

"Well, all parties involved, including us, agreed they were ready. If they're doing well, then you've got to give 'em the chance. And four months alone on a cot is an eternity for a girl her age. Also, the tribe has requested we continue courtesy supervision for a grace period of six months to make sure everything's goin' okay. Becky will be counseling Nicki here. Connie will be working with the parents, and sometimes all of them will work together. Luke will be doing the casework. We don't let go of cases that easily."

"Why am I getting her?"

"Just a courtesy, really. Her parents live on this side. Her dad works as a stonemason during the day, and her mom doesn't drive."

"They live here? So why's she so far away—Suquamish, I mean?"

"We tried to place her in a foster home around here, but there weren't any available. So the tribe put her in the youth home over there by the res. Her parents were supposed to visit her at least once a week."

"Did they?"

Wilma nodded. "They must have, or they wouldn't have been in compliance." Wilma handed me the post-it. "Here's the number of the youth home and her parents. Make a couple calls and get directions. The worker's name is Gene Pinkus."

I stuck the post-it to my clipboard. When I looked up, Wilma was smiling. "You'll be fine," she said. "Now go get that kid." Wilma rocked back in her chair and folded her hands together around the full curve of her stomach. She was a red meat eater, packing an extra thirty pounds from protein and macaroni. Then she picked up her sandwich, signaling me off with a dismissive wave of white bread and French's mustard.

About ten miles north of Seattle, I took the Kingston ferry along with retired folks and families going for a boat ride and drive on the other side of the bay. It was already warming up, so I took a cup of coffee onto the upper deck and stared across the water at islands and peninsulas I couldn't name. Further down the deck a flock of seagulls dove at the French fries a kid flung at them, while his friend used the dime telescope as a machine gun. The ride was short, and before I had finished my coffee the ship's horn right above me nearly blew the cup out of my hand. I checked my pockets to make sure I had the ferry receipt for reimbursement and went down to the car.

As Wilma had said, the youth home was just about a mile off the Suquamish Reservation. It was a rectangle of unpainted cinder block, too large for the number of children cycled through it, some Indian, some white. Although it had the capacity for about twenty, there were rarely more than ten kids there at a time.

Upon entering, I found myself in a large room with furniture focused around a television set opposite the entrance. The carpet was orange shag with a linty, blackish hue. There was only one kid in the room—a girl whose gaze was fixed on the television. I had just registered her presence when a man hurried out from a hallway and identified himself as Gene Pinkus. I couldn't tell for sure if he was Indian or just wished he was. He had a long, sandy-brown ponytail and a large turquoise rock with dangling silver feathers hanging from a leather cord around his neck. His shirt was a Northwest Coast formline of a killer whale. His face looked sallow and exhausted.

"You're Levi from Seattle," he said, making me sound somewhat infamous.

"Yeah, you must be Gene," I responded, resisting the temptation to say "from Kingston."

"Nicki's been watching out the window for you, but I think she's given up." He looked past me to the girl in front of the television.

She was sitting in a brown recliner, one of four mismatched chairs, tilted way back in front of the cartoons, her black hair pulled into a short ponytail. Her skinny forearms were draped over the swollen armrests that burst yellow foam out of random tears in the seams. Her legs were propped up on the chair's footrest, five inches of caramel-colored ankles sticking out of blue denim.

"That's her," said Gene, swinging his clipboard towards the chair. "Hey Nicki, it's time to go!"

Her face turned slowly around with bored, cat-like regard and distrust in her dark eyes. She looked like a mixed-blood, a breed maybe. Then, suddenly realizing what Gene had said, she grabbed the armrests, pushing herself up into a straight-backed position. Her eyes fell on me, shifted to Gene, then back to me. "I'm outa here?"

"You're outa here," I confirmed. Her face changed, becoming innocent and relieved as her defenses slipped, revealing how rehearsed her initial expression had been. Her smile rushed out at me from the dimness of the room, then she bounced out of the chair and hurried toward me. I offered her my hand, and she slapped it with enthusiasm, holding my gaze out of the corner of her eye as she slid past me and down the hallway. "I gotta get my stuff."

"My car is the orange Mazda right out front," I yelled after her. "It's unlocked, so you can go ahead and throw your stuff in the backseat."

"Orange?" she said, wrinkling her nose and walking backwards down the hallway, "Yuck!" She pointed a finger at me and told me not to leave without her, then she disappeared into one of the rooms off the hallway.

I turned to Gene as he fumbled through the papers on his clipboard. "How was her stay?" I asked.

"It wasn't too bad," he said, still flipping papers, his eyebrows crowding in toward the bridge of his nose. "I had some stuff to give you, but apparently I left it in the office. Let's go back there where we can talk. She'll find us."

I followed him down a narrow hallway to a cramped room with stark unrelenting white walls broken only by one window, which was nearly opaque with grime. A short sofa occupied one wall, a rack of books and papers filled another, and a desk was centered beneath the window. He poked around the magazines and newspapers crowding his desktop. "I was just looking at it, now where'd it go?"

He pulled open his desk drawer, and a bottle of Maalox and a tin of Altoids slid to the front with a few dozen unsharpened pencils. "Here it is," he said, pulling a brown file out of the drawer, "just where it doesn't go."

Gene removed a thin stack of notes fastened with a paper clip. "These are copies for you to take. It's stuff that happened while she was here. There's a part in there about her being suicidal," he said. "She told me and other staff, on a few occasions, that she wanted to die, and we caught her cutting a word into her forearm when she first got here. She also made a small cut across her wrist."

"Did you ever talk to her about the suicidal ideation?" I asked, using a term I'd heard a few weeks before.

"Yeah, of course. She said it was about punishment. I asked her who she would be punishing, and she said, 'Who's responsible for me sittin' in this dump?' She's very precocious. I don't think she's suicidal, just feeling betrayed and isolated. The sooner she's with her parents the better."

"What did she make the cuts with?"

"With a razor blade."

"Where did she get it?"

"I don't know, must have brought it with her."

"What was the word?"

"I don't know."

I wanted to inquire as to why he hadn't asked her, but I didn't feel like calling attention to his failure to do something so stupidly obvious. Instead, I asked him if it had been too illegible to read. Once said, this sounded even worse, but it didn't faze him. "She only got two letters finished," he said, "an A and a T."

"How bad was the cut?"

"Not bad. She didn't need stitches or anything."

"Oh. Anything else I should know?"

He thought for a moment, frowning. "Not really. She's a pretty good kid." Then as an afterthought he added, "She startles easy, I mean she reacts to loud noises—shouting, a dish being dropped, things like that. A guy came in here all pissed off, yelling about us not bringing his kid out for a visit that was never scheduled. When he left, I found Nicki standing in my office behind the door, big round eyes, clenched fists, really on edge."

"Did she say if her dad ever hit her?"

"No, unless there's any information about that on yer end, it was just Mom getting beaten as far as we know. It sounds like her parents clean up for a while then go on a bender, and its gets ugly. Then they clean up again, and on and on it goes. One of our accounts from CPS did say that he pulled Nicki into the house by her hair during one of the fights."

"Yeah, I heard that, too."

A child's scream erupted outside. Gene looked away from me, out the filthy window toward the noise. "But even if he didn't hit her, witnessing domestic violence is pretty traumatic," Gene said absently, preoccupied with the screaming.

I shuffled the papers and stuck them on my clipboard. Through the window I could see a small boy standing beneath the bars of a jungle gym, coarse hair on end and shimmering like a beaver pelt as his body vibrated, screaming like the world had ended. A young female staff member was trying to console him.

While I was scanning some of the documents, Nicki appeared at the end of the hallway. She was standing with a wide agitated stance and a black Hefty bag slung over her shoulder, looking like she was ready to jump out a window. "Car's full," she said.

I thanked Gene, and he walked us to the door. "Be good, Nicki," he said, patting her on the shoulder before she took the stairs three at a time.

"No way!" she said, without looking back at him. I could tell she was smiling. I could hear it in her clear, laughing voice. She stuffed her bag into the backseat, hopped in, slammed her door, and pulled on her seat belt. "You smoke?" she asked, composing her face as much as she could, prepared to pounce on an opening.

I shifted the car into reverse, navigating through a space in her heap of bags. "No. How long have you been smoking?"

She didn't say anything, but her face opened into an embarrassed smile, her lips tightening, trying to hide her square white teeth and failing. Her face was radiant and fascinating; she had flawless skin and black eyes with the unbridled expression of child-hood consuming the stimuli around her, still more powerful than the encroaching adult. Then a curious expression came over her barely detectable. Her expression reflected what I was feeling, a moment of mutual misgiving, and questioning—as though we had already known each other for a long time and now for an ephemeral moment hesitated on the threshold of something very grave. There was a brief pause as if to allow each of us one last opportunity to back out before going forward. Then she asked, "What are you starin' at?"

"You kinda look like my sister," I said, "when she was yer age I mean."

"Oh, your sister, huh? C'mon, let's get outa here." She looked back once at the youth home as we drove away, held up her middle finger to its receding gray walls, then exhaled heavily.

On the ferry we sat in the cafeteria. I had a cup of coffee, while she had a huge paper cup of ice and Pepsi.

"So what do you like to do in all your spare time?" I asked.

"Controlled substances," she said without a pause, as though it had been used for effect numerous times before.

I scoffed and looked down at the tabletop. When I looked back up, she was staring at me. "Naw," she said. "I like playing sports, mostly basketball. Sometimes I read if I'm bored and I got a book. I like to write, too."

"Do you like school?"

"You gonna tell me how important school is now?"

"Yeah," I said. "I guess I was gonna. But you screwed it up."

She laughed. "Sorry. Had to do it."

"Alright. What type of stuff do you write about?"

"Sometimes I write in a journal. But mostly I write poetry. It's pretty much poetry about things that happen, so it's kinda a part of my journal. You know what I mean?"

"Yeah, I think so."

"Teachers always say write about this thing or write about that," she said, tossing her head from shoulder to shoulder, "and that's kind of a bummer. But the stuff I write about has gotta come out, you know? Besides, what else are you gonna do when you're locked away starin' at the walls but read and write? Here, let me write you a poem!" She grabbed a napkin off the table and held out her hand for a pen. I found one in the inner pocket of my coat and gave it to her.

"Okay, silence now," she said, smoothing out the napkin several times, then tapping the ballpoint against the soft paper, thinking.

I stared out the window, sipping my coffee, pondering what my response would be if she handed me something like "roses are red, violets are blue."

About three sips of coffee later she slid the pen across the table to me.

"That was quick," I said.

She folded the napkin over as if the words needed to be concealed until I was fully prepared to focus on them. "It's a short one," she said.

I unfolded the napkin and read:

I'm out there, man.
Somewhere.
Looking for a place to stop.
Looking for a place to feel.
Looking for a place.
Somewhere.

I read the lines over about three times. "This is mine? I can keep it?" I asked.

"Yup, it's for you. It's not very good, just a quick one."

"It's very good. I like it." I folded the napkin and put it in my shirt pocket. "You're only twelve, right?"

"Uh huh."

"Well, keep writing, you got lots of time, and it's a great way to reach people."

"That's the nice thing about writing," she said. "No one can touch what I say. And when I drop dead all my bitching and moaning will live on to haunt the guilty."

"Oh yeah? So that's why you gave me this?" I reached into my shirt pocket like I was going to take out the poem. "Then maybe I oughta give it back."

She laughed, high and clear, shaking her head rapidly, her face flushed with embarrassment. "No, no, that's not what I meant!"

"Are you sure?"

"Yeah, I'm sure. You keep it."

"I wouldn't have given it back anyway," I responded. "When you drop dead in about a hundred years, it could really be worth somethin'."

She raised her eyebrows and clasped her hands together, placing them on the table. "Can I go outside?"

I had never had a kid as old as she ask me for permission to do something, and it felt strange. "Yeah, that's fine," I said. "I'll go with you."

She grabbed her cup of pop and slid off the bench. "You can make sure I don't jump."

"And you can make sure I don't," I said under my breath as I followed her out to the deck.

She heard me and laughed, her mouth full of ice. "Deal."

The wind had picked up, but it was warmer than before. The breeze occasionally swept her straight bangs completely off to the side. She had set her pop down next to her feet, and her hands were twisted up in the excess of sweatshirt in front of her stomach. The wind whipped the surface of the sound, tossing green swells and splashes of white foam. I watched her out of the corner of my eye as the sting of the breeze blurred my vision with a film of tears. Her gaze, glassy with an occasional slow blink of black curly lashes, swam far out into the bay and plunged away where my sight couldn't follow. I knew she was in her own world so I retreated into mine, a place of calm beneath the churning waves where there would be no thoughts of what to do about Nicki's life or concerns about the role that I might be called upon to play. We both remained silent, in our separate yet parallel realms, until the cruel blast of the ferry's horn.

Back in the city, cruising along the interstate, I set the clipboard across my legs so that I could see the directions to her home. "I can get us there," she said when she realized what I was doing. "Take the next exit." Her voice had become colorless and flat, and she watched the green flash of street signs as they rushed toward us and past, clicking off the increments to her home.

"Are you tired?" I asked, stealing a look at her immobile profile, the slight curve of her forehead and the small delicate nose, feeling a tug of apprehension without the power to intercede. Suddenly I fully realized that I had no more confidence in the future than Nicki had. I thought of my own father clutching a bottle and spiraling out from our family and into oblivion. From what I had heard of Nicki's parents, they needed to make changes at the very foundation of their lives, after which everything would be sober and strange. At that point, they might find that they didn't even know each other or how to behave, and that the horror of reflecting on the past would test their ability to fight a backslide. Because of my own family experiences, I already knew that big changes are hard won, and often can be little more than dreams and promises—shattering to increase the pain. I caught glimpses of the things Nicki might have to face, the dread of her future confirmed by her past, the promises she would have to accept until they were proven to be lies, again and again.

"Make a left on the next street," Nicki said.

The strongest link we shared as she pointed to her house was an unfocused helplessness. I was taking her home to test the waters, and in a matter of minutes I would pull away and leave her to her life.

"They're home," she said, looking up at the electric glow that illuminated the drawn curtains.

"Of course they're home. They're expecting you. They can't wait to see you," I reassured her. We pulled into the gravel driveway.

"Maybe I should have one last cigarette in the yard," she said, as if she needed to gird herself for the reunion.

I laughed and turned off the ignition. "No, you can't stand out here sucking down a cigarette, how would that make me look? You're home. It's time to settle in. Grab your bags."

We both crowded under the porch light with her bags in our hands. She set down her portable stereo and rang the doorbell, her finger holding the glowing button in for several seconds. The buzz of the doorbell was followed by a rustling inside, then the door opened wide, and Mrs. Sanders reached out with both hands to hold her daughter's face. She smiled with an expression of pleased discovery then led her inside by the hand. Looking up at me, a glimmer of discomfort flickered across her face with a weak smile. "Thank you for bringing her," she said, seemingly indecisive about whether to invite me in or shut the door with a relieved "good-bye."

"I'm Levi," I said finally, extending my hand without moving forward and encroaching on her decision.

She put her hand into mine, and I squeezed it lightly. The feel of her hand made me think of a warm, paralyzed bird. I glanced over at the couch, seeing her father facing the TV, his back to the door. He turned slowly, as if out of pure, agonizing obligation, a tough-looking guy with a brown bristling crew cut. He gave a quick sharp nod, offering a type of masculine approval for a job well done. His discomfort was more apparent than hers—reflecting guilt, corked, sealed, and confirmed in his silence and the way his eyes locked onto mine, holding for a half second of acknowledgment before darting away. His face was lined and weathered, not from age but from years of squinting under the harsh glare of life—turning his hands and heart to leather.

I began passing Nicki's things across the threshold to her mother. Nicki walked up to her father, stopping within ten feet of him, her feet shuffling and tentative as if waiting for a signal to go further. "Hi," she said.

"How are ya?" he answered, leaning towards her on the edge of the couch. "There's dinner in the kitchen. You hungry?"

"No, I'm fine."

"Well, I better get back on the road," I said, feeling just as awkward as the scene before me. "You'll be coming to see us, right, Nicki?"

She turned and smiled. "Yeah, I have to, don't I?"

"Absolutely," I said.

She started walking towards me, then stopped abruptly like she had bumped into an invisible glass pane between us.

I smiled at her mother and nodded at her father, immediately aware that I'd done the same thing as he. "Bye, Nicki. See you soon," I said, departing.

On the way back to the car, I patted my shirt pocket to make sure the poem was still there. I thought about what I had tried to push from my mind while standing next to her on the ferry. What role would I be called upon to play in her life, while she looked for a place—somewhere? And what role would she play in mine?

That night I had dinner and a battery of drinks with Don Boyd, a childhood friend. Don's family lived only a few blocks from mine. He had been adopted before his adoptive parents had two sons, both of whom Don took charge of through childhood and on into early adulthood. Don's birth mother, a relative of the Boyds, was fifteen years old when she had Don. No one knew who Don's biological father was except her, and apparently it wasn't worth going into, since the man had never expressed an interest in Don. During my childhood, the Boyd family was very poor, and my family was not well off either. Thus I performed many tasks—trips to the grocery store, walking my sister to her bus stop before heading off to school myself—because my mother was either working or sleeping in preparation for work. An underlying air of independence and misfortune made the blond Boyd boys and I gravitate toward each other. Don was a gifted but destructive child who took on a paper route as soon as he was old enough, as did his brothers, since they had to pay for all their clothes, carefully budgeting enough for all the sugar they could hold, especially Don. Since my allowance was barely above zero, once I witnessed the possibilities for excess provided by fifty dollars of my own at the end of each month, I followed suit, becoming an employee of the Seattle Times, and a participant in the junk food free-for-all, up and down the strip mall nearby.

Don was now an entrepreneur, struggling with his own small software and consulting firm in downtown Seattle, consisting of him and his two younger brothers, who were virtually enslaved in a small leased space, unable to shake the family hierarchy of childhood. Don's childhood hyperactivity and worse acne than the norm had since subsided, but his childhood identity, still existing, reflected in the way he sat at the computer chain-drinking coffee and making faces at the wall mirror behind his monitor, gobbling candy bars and donuts, and cussing out his brothers.

It was nearing 1:30 A.M., and the waiter hurried us another two bottles of beer, removed my half-eaten plate of pasta, then came back about four minutes later to tell us that we had to finish our drinks at once, mumbling something about the liquor control board cracking down. We gave him matching incredulous looks, sliding our bottles back out of his reach as if he were going to make a dive for them.

"Okay, I'll be back in one minute!" he said, flinging his wipe rag over his slender shoulder and strolling off.

Our water glasses were empty so we poured the rest of our beer into them. "Addiction makes a man very innovative," said Don, raising his glass and taking a sip. Then he suddenly added daringly, "Let's go to the mountains!"

I was getting tired and hoped he could be discouraged. "Sure, we'll plan a trip."

"Now. Right now! Tonight!"

I took a sip, sucking my beer through the watery barrier of ice. "You mean tonight?"

"It's great up there—totally bleak."

The waiter came back with the bill, along with my leftovers encased in aluminum foil that had been shaped into the likeness of a shiny bird. "I knew you could do it," he said, smiling and taking our empty bottles, oblivious to our glasses of yellow water. "I can help you up front when you're ready."

"Bleak?" I said. "Can't the mountains wait?"

Don smiled. "Absolutely not."

We paid the bill, and about 2:00 A.M. started for the mountains in search of bleakness. Don drove a blue Subaru family wagon, minus the family. His marriage of one year had ended abruptly, and he had recently finished tying up the loose ends of the divorce. Only two weeks before, his ex-wife had come into town while Don was out, armed with an apartment key and her mother. She had taken everything in the place, including food, leaving only his suits and an outrageous phone bill. The apartment manager who had witnessed the sacking of Don's apartment quoted the mother as saying, "We'll show him." Don had not remotely suspected any rifts in their marriage until he had found himself standing in the doorway of the apartment, his profanity echoing in the gutted space. "She was waiting for me to get rich," said Don, offering an explanation. "When I took too long, she panicked."

Interstate 90 was desolate at this hour. "We shouldn't have been drinking, not for this," said Don. "You gotta be sober to really appreciate it. I drove up into the mountains a few weeks ago, and I went up a logging road and pulled off to the side. In the woods I found an old-growth. You can't believe the feeling of standing next to one of those trees. I put my hand on it just to see how it felt to be touching something that old." Don was drunker than I had thought. Given the chance, he'd have cut down that tree and sold it to the Japanese in a heartbeat.

Climbing up toward the pass, Don snapped upright with recognition and jerked the wheel toward an exit. The car wobbled dramatically then straightened out. We turned onto a narrow road covered with a thin layer of ice and snow. Around and beyond the headlights was heavy blackness, night pressing against the back windows like a void closing in on the car, as if behind us nothing existed. The snow was getting deeper, and it put up a real fight before yielding to the car. We could hear it crushing against the undercarriage like cement being scraped.

Don was leaning out over the steering wheel. "Goddamnit! I wish we had a Suburban or a Landcruiser. This would be no problem, we could go all the way to the top."

We plowed ice for about another half mile until the sounds from below indicated the crumpling of an oil pan. Don stopped the car. "We can't go any farther, we're doin' damage."

"Yeah you're right, let's get out here."

Don shut off the engine, unplugging the audio for the whole

world. When we got out, there wasn't a sound. We walked a ways up the road and with no more than thirty feet between us and the car, I looked back to discover it had been eaten up by the black void. I stared as hard as I could, boring into the darkness, and could just barely make out the different shade of blackness that indicated the presence of the car, like a fingerprint left by its passing.

"Don," I said, "you can't see the car."

"Yeah, I know. There isn't any starlight because of the clouds."

"Well, this is bleak," I said.

"You gotta do stuff like this once in a while," he whispered. He had moved several paces away from me, and his voice had become disembodied. "It makes you realize that your job and your life back in the city don't matter all that much."

"Don," I said, "it sounds like you're gettin' away from bleakness out here. You know what I'm sayin'?"

"Maybe so," he agreed. Then he added, "Someday we'll have to quit drinking, you know?"

"Especially with my job," I said. "The two don't really jibe."

"There's no future in that job," said Don. "Nothing but grief. Why don't you come work for me?"

"Because I don't know shit about computers."

"You can do sales, you can learn enough to pull that off. That way you can keep boozin' for a while, too—drinking's acceptable in sales."

"I don't know. Besides, what would you pay me with?"

That offended him a little, and he didn't answer the question. Then he suddenly asked, "What do you do exactly? You work with abused kids and stuff, right?"

"Yeah, that's part of it."

"Why do you feel it's your problem?"

"I work in the Indian community," I said, thinking that this obvious connection would explain everything—that I had a duty determined by blood.

"And…?" He rebuked in an irritating manner, as if he were guiding me toward some obvious epiphany that would alter the foolish route I was on. "You didn't grow up in the Indian community," he said before I could answer. "You grew up with us."

Did he mean he and his brothers and our other friends from the neighborhood, or did he mean us whites? I wondered.

"We need to start duck hunting again," he said, retreating from confrontation and changing the subject like the solution was swarming upon him, "get out of the city more often."

"Yeah," I agreed. I was tired and wanted to sleep rather than think about my situation or the tedious human condition.

We stood there in the cold for a few minutes longer, I turning in slow circles looking up at the sky, the walls of shadows, and the utter expansiveness of the dark. On the way back home, I fell asleep, fighting it all the way to unconsciousness for the sake of fairness to Don. While I twisted around in my seat, slipping in and out of sleep, I saw Nicki's face, in only several silent seconds of rich color. Her black hair was glossy and pulled back from her face, and her skin and eyes shined. A man's hand was painting her face with bands of red, his long index finger drawing a line down the curve of her chin before withdrawing his hand. Then Nicki's face became frightening in its strength. The strength in her eyes was as unyielding as the blackness of an ocean current far below the surface; they were now eyes that knew everything, had seen everything. When the image disappeared, there were no more dreams. Only bleakness.

4

Luke Child, the foster care caseworker at the agency, shared an office with Victoria Sanchez, the foster care licensor, and together they comprised the foster care component of the program. Luke was a thirty-eight-year-old Sioux man, with short black hair—maybe a little too short for its strong, brush-bristle quality, which made it stick out above the ears where it was shortest. He stood a few inches over six feet, and although his tinted glasses made him look a little corny and mysterious he was a handsome man who had a broad face and youthful skin, somewhat how I remembered my father looking—in fact, he resembled my father more than I did. This made me like him right off the bat, or maybe it made me want to like him, a strange reaction either way, considering that it was an association that held little positive sentiment beyond the chromosomes that had contributed to my existence.

Luke frequently threatened to head east to deal black jack, though he didn't specify how far east; so far his own reservation in South Dakota didn't have a casino for him to flee to. Despite his threats, he'd been a caseworker for six years, which is pretty long for an Indian who's always talking about leaving.

Victoria was a Shawnee and Comanche woman from Oklahoma who described her status as Luke's cell mate. Vicki was several years younger than Luke, which was the most specific answer she gave regarding her age. But since the lowest number that several can be is three, before it becomes a couple, and since she would describe anything beyond three as ages, we figured that she was probably thirty-five.

Vicki was tough and seemed a little standoffish at first with a low-eyebrowed look of suspicion she'd fix on strangers, making you feel like you had to explain yourself and why you had entered her space. But this was short-lived, dissolving quickly when she laughed uproariously or gave you a long and throaty, "Ayyeee," which is one of the ways that Indian people let you know they're joking. Her toughness was the real thing, developed early in life for the usual reason—necessity—but then becoming a permanent character trait. As Vicki said telling one of her stories about being attacked eight years into her sobriety, eight years from tooth-and-nail fighting on the reservation in Oklahoma: "You keep it forever, locked away and spring-loaded. You think it's gone away after years of bein' sober and all touchy feely—you know, like in a place like this. But then sometimes out it comes. Like the time when I was jumped on a college campus by a guy askin' for the time." Then she went on to describe in vivid detail her resistance: "The first thing I could get in my hand was the ballpoint pen that I broke off in his face. In that instant I was scrappin' on the floor of a tav' in OK, bombed and toxic. I kicked and punched him enough to injure my tender, educated knuckles before I took off running. He wasn't going to get me down! That's the trick, you can't let them get you down."

Soon I remembered her enthusiasm waned, and she said, sadly, "Just like old times."

The office Luke and Vicki shared was two doors down from mine and served as the gathering spot where we could have a cup of coffee, listen to stories, or bitch about things that made our job difficult. The laughter often grew in proportion to the number of people present, pulling more and more staff out of their offices to catch a piece of levity.

I went to see Luke to tell him about the Tall Fighters' visit two days earlier, and to let him know that Josie would be calling him about starting in-patient treatment. When I walked in, Jones Percy, an Alaskan Indian and counselor, was in the middle of a story about a new client family of his and motioned me towards the only empty chair, near Vicki's desk.

"So anyway," he said, "the mother looks into the living room, and this supposed friend of the family is...well, he's having sex with their dog."

Three mouths dropped open.

"Wait," Jones urged, "that's not all. I shouldn't be laughing—hang on a minute." Jones leaned back in his chair and took a deep breath. "Okay, the mother gets the husband. So now they're both standing in the doorway watching this when all of a sudden they realize that their little girl has gotten out of bed and she's standing behind them. Now, the guy with the dog sees them, gets really pissed, runs to the garage, comes back with a baseball bat, and attacks the father."

Jones choked down a swell of laughter.

"C'mon," said Luke with morbid urgency, "let's have it."

"Okay, hang on." Jones's olive skin had gone red from chin to forehead.

"The dad takes the bat from the guy and beats him so bad he has to have his gonads removed."

I was certain I wasn't supposed to laugh; Jones was fighting it, so I figured I'd better try as well. Although I wasn't completely familiar with social worker etiquette, I assumed it consisted of the sincerest sensitivity, and laughter at something so twisted would be uncouth if not an outright violation of the code. But there was no hope of maintaining even a little composure—I was hysterical. Jones grinned at me, apparently relieved that he now had a companion to draw off some of the heat.

"Well, he won't be doing it again," Vicki said, laughing raucously like the bawdy screech of some large-throated jungle bird.

Luke just leaned back in his chair, his forearms folded up high across his chest, looking at us like we were all crazy. "I'll tell you," he said after some reflection, "if someone caught me with their dog, I think the last thing I'd do is get pissed off and grab a baseball bat. I think I'd probably go through the closest window and leave the state, aayyyee!" Luke began shaking in his chair, his shoulders bouncing in rhythm with his low chuckle.

"Imagine the contrast," said Jones. "One minute he's in the throes of passion, and the next he's having his testicles removed."

"Okay, look," said Vicki, forcing herself into a semblance of calm, "he wasn't in the throes of passion, Jones, he was with a dog for Christ's sake!"

"I know, I know, but from his point of view he's enjoying himself, right? Then the next moment he's...I'm just saying that he had no idea he'd be payin' such a heck of a price for a fling with the dog."

"Jones," I said, "how big was the dog? I mean, it must have put up a fight." Logistically the story was questionable.

"Oh no, it was really small."

"Well, then it must have made a lot of noise."

Jones frowned, his laughter momentarily stifled by the very relevant consideration. "Well, maybe he held its little mouth."

Vicki choked a couple of times, fighting for some dignity. Sweeping her hand towards the door, she said, "It's sick, and it's not funny! Now go before you all embarrass yourselves."

I glanced up to see that Luke was now more amused by my hysteria than Jones's unwholesome tale. I staggered out into the hall and off to the bathroom with images of the poor twisted bastard hopping around the living room in a naked panic, all that sickness culminating with emergency surgery, making the world a safer place for small dogs.

After about ten minutes I calmed down and went back to Luke's office, still smiling. "Josie starts treatment within a week, and the kids are doing fine," I said. "They had a good visit."

"Great!" Luke said pulling his clipboard on his lap. "Where's she goin' and when's she startin'?"

"I didn't get the details. I told her to call you."

"Oh, good. You won't need to transport for a little bit. I'll take care of it the next few times it comes up. I wanna see her and the kids myself before she starts treatment and after she's done. Thanks a lot, though, Levi. I appreciate it. Kids are doin' good you say?"

"Yeah, considering."

"Right. Well if she hangs in there this time..." He put his thumb up. "Thanks again."

"No problem."

"Not yet." He smiled at me then busied himself writing.

I stopped in the doorway and leaned against the jamb, looking up at the ceiling like something had just occurred to me. "You're doing the supervision for Nicki Sanders, right?"

"Yeah, I am."

"I took her to her parents the other day," I said. "Nice kid."

"Tough little customer," Luke said, smiling. "She told me that if her dad so much as raises his fist again she's gonna get some of her mom's relatives to give him a stomping."

"She said that?" I could imagine her face gathering into a tough, heavy scowl and delivering the threat.

"Is she the one you took out to Suquamish awhile back?" Vicki asked. "The one who ate the cookies out of your lunch while you were in the bathroom?"

Luke smiled. "Yeah, that's her."

"Sure Nicki said that," Vicki told me. "She's scared."

Sometimes I have questions while looking down at the blur of forms and the scratch of ink pens from faceless people scattered across the state, enclosed somewhere in little cubicles and hidden behind partitions, writing endless words, court orders, and case plans, piling into tons of paperwork and protocol and procedure, dumped onto desks in suffocating piles of formulated human beings—people transformed into words and orders and plans. And my own signature is mixed in with the heaps of narratives and faxes and ideas circulating from office to office, through the telephone wires and post offices and right over the lives of individuals cursively summed up and stamped in black print. Where do they go, and when does it end? Sometimes you can see the reams of effort touch a life or two, the ideas of the documents merging with the pulse of actual flesh, but usually the result amounts to only a scratch across the surfaces of the lives reflected in the pages. During weeks and months and years of supervision and intervention—tons and tons of paper and ideas are thrown at injuries rooted in history, back beyond ancestors dead before our birth and as close as our mothers and fathers. We were given a bureaucracy to cure injuries, so we use it and we fight, like a sapling growing from the scorched earth, galvanized in the wake of a savage fire; a salmon swimming against the currents of a circular river.

I had spent the morning writing up reports and quarterlies, some destined for Wilma and Luke, some for D.S.H.S. and the nonconfidential stuff for the accounting office. It was prematurely warm for June. The minute hand was entering the slow motion zone of the last twenty minutes before 5:00 P.M.—that zero productivity period of shuffling papers and organizing my desk.

At 4:55 as I was closing my office door, I saw two people pacing around in the lobby at the end of the building. The woman had her hair pulled tightly back into a bun, and her posture had a slight wilt to it, giving her the appearance of folding up, as if there was too much open space around her. She was wearing a thin white sweater with swirling lines knitted across the back and fronts of her shoulders like a cowboy shirt. The man had both hands stuffed partway into his back pockets, which were too tight to fit more than his fingers. I could see the raised veins in his toughened hands and the reddish hue of tiny broken blood vessels in his face. They were Nicki's parents, here for their weekly session with Connie LaForce. She was working with them while Becky Davies worked with Nicki, then periodically the family would meet for a talking circle. At the sound of my door closing, the Sanders couple looked over, Lydia offering a fleeting smile and a wave, her hand hardly passing waist level, and Charles giving the same quick nod as at our first meeting.

I began walking towards the front door, which was just around the corner from them. "How's Nicki?" I asked, digging in my pockets for my car keys.

Connie opened her door and leaned out. Their energy was torn between her and me, creating an opening for their discomfort to pour forth in the rush of answering my question and greeting Connie at the same time. "Good! Nicki's doing good!"

"I'm glad," I answered. "Tell her I said hi."

Connie winked at me. "How are the two of you?" she asked. "Come on in." She turned the sign over to "In Session, Do Not Disturb," and closed the door behind her.

I hadn't thought about Nicki for a while. I hoped she was really okay.

If you think about someone in the Indian community or mention their name, they appear without fail. The phone rings and it's them, or they come strolling into your office. Wilma pointed this out to me once, and thereafter it held almost disturbingly true.

So it was with Nicki. The day after I had seen her parents she came to visit me. It was the tail end of quarterly reporting time, and I had reports spread out all over my desk, the collating table, and the floor. She bounced in, careful not to plant her white nylon tennis shoes on the stacks of paper, and fell into the chair near my desk. She sat there smiling with her head tilted to the side, wearing a baggy, navy sweatshirt with the sleeves pushed up into piles of folds above her elbows and a streak of white paint across the shoulder. She was wearing the same jeans I had picked her up in. I remembered because they were too short.

"What's up?" she said, slapping her hand against the desktop.

"Take a look around you," I said, "chaos, mayhem."

"Uh huh," she said, nodding and looking around the office. "Looks like a regular old mess to me, but if this is a bad time?"

"No, it's okay. I'm glad you stopped by. How've you been?"

"Fine."

I looked closely at her eyes, watching for a glimmer of enthusiasm or passing shadows, but there was nothing. "That's good," I said. "Everything smooth sailing?"

"Uh huh, smooth sailing. My dad hasn't recovered from being an asshole, though—just kidding," she said, very matter-of-factly, as if reflecting back from middle age over something that she had accepted years ago. I noticed when we first met that she would suddenly fluctuate between the demeanor of a little girl and a young woman, switching back and forth years at a time with flashbulb spontaneity.

"Are you sure you're kidding?"

She bit her lip, thinking, now very much the little girl. "Naw, he's okay. You know how dads are."

"Yeah, I guess so. How are your visits goin'?"

"You mean my counseling? These are no visits, man, this is therapy. Crisis!"

"Right," I said, laughing. "I mean, how's your counseling going?"

She smiled coolly. "It's alright. I'm seeing Becky for counseling, and I'm visiting you." The little girl was gone again. "So," she said, "do I really remind you of your sister?"

"Yeah, a little bit."

After my dad left for good, after the incident with the hammer and my bedroom wall, I became really unaffected and cool about his absence. I took care of the yard and watched out for my sister. My mom worked as a legal aide for a couple of lawyers in the afternoons, and in the evenings she worked retail. She would prep our dinner before going to work, and there would always be a note of instruction for cooking whatever was in the kettle or Crock-Pot when we came home from school. When Tia turned thirteen, she decided it was high time to lash out, and began sneaking out of the house at night, smoking cigarettes and marijuana, and raiding the liquor cabinets of her friends' parents since our mother didn't drink. On many occasions, I covered for her, hosing her vomit off the driveway beneath her window before our mother woke up. Though by the time she wrecked our mother's car, after rolling it out of the garage, drunk at age fourteen, and put her friend's head partway through the windshield, hiding her behavior had become an impossibility. The phase played out fast and furiously, and by the late high school, Tia tired of making the innocent suffer, namely our mother. After that she became a good student and was ultimately accepted to NYU, about as far away as possible. Attending college there was for her a radical change of theater and a positive fresh start.

I asked Nicki if she was getting along well with Becky.

She offered a disinterested shrug. "Yeah, sure. This is only my third session, though," she said, as if there were still plenty of time for the relationship to fall apart. "I came to see you after my first session, but you weren't here, and I had to miss my second one."

"Well, I'm glad you're coming in. I saw your parents the other day."

"Yeah. They come at night. After my dad works—you know?"

"Right. Sounds like things are going pretty good."

Her eyes were scanning the pictures on the wall across the room, pictures of European landscapes left behind from the worker before me, places so far away they might as well have been photos of the moon.

"Sure, things are goin' good. That's why you brought me home, right?" she asked, watching for my reaction.

"You and your family are working together—that's improvement."

"Yeah, I know." She looked back up at the pictures, then down at the floor, then gave a bored nod. "Well, I'll tell ya, living in that youth home sucked. If things go bad again, I'll kill myself. I've tried it before—sleeping pills, I cut my wrist...."

She held up the underside of her forearm to show me her wrist. I could see the faintest traces of a thin white scar, like the stitching on a pant leg, so slight that segments of it had healed completely and disappeared. Then higher up her arm and just as faint, I could see an A and a T, each about half an inch high.

"I've almost left this world before," she continued with a magnified frown. "But someone's always been able to stop me."

"When did you take the pills?"

"Months ago," she said. "My parents were fighting, and I took a bunch of 'em—sedatives. All it did was keep me in bed for about fourteen hours. My parents were so hung over they didn't notice."

"When did you cut your wrist?"

"About a month later. My parents were fighting, and this time they noticed. It was the first time the CPS people came around, 'cause a teacher saw the cut. But I didn't say shit about nothin' when they interviewed me."

"Well, don't do any of it again," I said. "We all want you to stick around. I'll let you know when we've had enough of you. Don't hurt yourself because you're pissed at someone else—and don't hurt yourself to try and control your parents. Okay?"

"Good job," she said, "but you're leaving something out, Mr. Counselor—the end of pain. If you go all the way, then it's over. Then it doesn't matter what your parents do, no one's ever gonna piss you off again."

I wasn't about to tell her I thought that the things she had done to herself were expressions of anger, having little to do with a resignation to death. I sensed that this kid would take any doubts about her seriousness as a challenge to prove me wrong. "Just don't do any of that stuff, Nicki," I said. "If you ever feel that way again, come and talk to me or Becky, anytime, okay? No one wants you to hurt yourself. You're a buddy of mine now, and I'd be pretty pissed."

"Alright, alright," she said, squirming in her chair and grinning, her tongue and teeth purple with jawbreaker dye. She had been doodling on the post-it where I had listed phone numbers to call for the day. "Oh, was this important?" she asked, suddenly aware that she'd covered my phone list with graffiti.

"Actually, it still is important," I said, taking the pen from her.

"I'm sorry."

"No problem. Just don't let it happen again."

She popped up out of the chair. "I'm gone. But I'll be back."

"And I'll be ready."

She backed out of the office, waved, and disappeared. I had meant to ask her about the scars, the letters A and T she had carved in her skin. I was left wondering about their significance and the deeper wounds they symbolized.

5

In the apartment above me, lived a buddy of mine I had met during the latter part of my University of Washington days when I lived in a building next to the roar and carbon monoxide of I-5 with Don Boyd. His nickname was Arti-Boy, Arti being short for artificial, because of his penchant for junk food and those candies dyed with brilliant chemical colors that target two year olds in eye-level supermarket dispensers.

Arti used to show up at our apartment, his thin and rangy frame looming in the doorway, laden with an assortment of treats that he'd offer generously—there were rarely any takers—and a half-rack of beer, for which there were always takers, to see what we had goin', which was usually the television.

Arti had started out at a community college then transferred to the university, taking an unprecedented leisure approach to his education. He would start the quarter with a full fifteen to eighteen credits and finish with five. He didn't drop classes because of any intellectual shortcomings, he just didn't want graduating from college to interfere with his lifestyle.

An entire wall of his apartment was dedicated to an entertainment center, a huge black monument to Japanese electronics. He'd kick back on the couch for hours at a time, a stack of neglected books and five different remote controls littering the coffee table in front of him. Outside of his apartment he was game for damn near anything, but once inside, reclined before the entertainment center with a remote in each hand, he became reptilian and transfixed, entertaining himself into a coma.

At some point during late college, preemployment life, I found myself in the basement bar of a late-nighter off the University of Washington Avenue, pouring stout, or what I called solid food, down my esophagus, caught up in an anger binge of lost origin from which there would be no graceful return or retreat.

I had recently finished reading a book about the inevitable demise of our dwindling resources and the burnout of planet earth, her surface, guts, and atmosphere devoured by the people of the globe. I struggled to make a point about this with my damaged thought process and diminished verbal motor skills but found that I just couldn't get the two in sync. The alcohol had reduced my vocabulary by about 50 percent, and that which remained was becoming difficult to pronounce. Offensively uncharismatic, I screamed into the faces of my table mates, Arti and Don among them, who under different circumstances would most certainly have been on my side. I was trying to spill the facts of entropy with convincing, passionate eloquence, and simultaneously admonishing myself of any guilt through my possession of Indian blood—caretakers of the planet and all that. The actual result was a vomiting of disjointed fragments from a badly crippled memory.

What makes me remember this episode as something significant was my shouting, "I want to fight the losing battle!"—a slurred harbinger of more suffering and substance abuse. Eventually I staggered off to the toilet and fell asleep, slumped in one of the stalls. It was Arti who got me out of there safely, offering flimsy explanations to the waitress for the mirror I had broken with my forehead, as she hovered about us ensuring that we move directly to the exit and go away forever.

There was tolerance between me and Arti—an element of our friendship that would gain unhealthier strength over time. Similar transgressions marked the passage of the next few years, and then in the absence of plans, at the age of twenty-five, I stumbled into the field of social work. I had earned a degree in sociology from the university, the job sounded interesting and important, and I was broke with student loan debts closing in. And hell, I was an Indian, after all.

The Friday that Nicki had come to see me, I left a half hour early with the rest of the staff and called Arti. It was time to make a run, far away from the forty-hour week and all of the faces and events that could not be confined within it. This trip was to be farther than one of Don's midnight searches for bleakness, down the Washington and Oregon coasts, drifting and bobbing like wasted vagrants along expansive panoramas of ocean and surf. The plan was to be moving by dawn on Saturday, be deep in southern Oregon by that afternoon, then head home Sunday morning and get back with enough time to set our alarms before crawling into bed. Destination wasn't as important as the drive itself, defying gravity and escaping from the demands of home and debilitating accountability.

Arti volunteered his car for the drive, a badly banged-up white Peugeot that overheated when it wasn't going freeway speed. And after some coaxing we were able to convince Don to forfeit two days of potential work at the office to come along.

We aimed for a 7:00 A.M. departure but actually pulled from the curb at noon, and by 12:15 P.M., Seattle's skyscrapers were falling behind us. Don was sitting in the center of the backseat so he could get a good view out the windshield. In his mouth he had a soggy, wounded cigar held together at the broken center with a band of electrician's tape. Arti was finishing off a dose of whiskey that was cleverly disguised as a single-serving bottle of apple juice, with bits of ice cubes that he had smashed up with a hammer to fit through the narrow opening.

Somewhere just before the Oregon-Washington border, we pulled over, and Don purchased a case of Schmidt and plastic coffee mugs, while Arti bought Funions, Cheese Puffs, jelly donuts, and a sack of old licorice that was half-price because of its age. The whole drive was a blur of little or no expectations. Once beyond the realm of my city, I stopped paying attention to where we were and warmed with the satisfaction of moving farther and farther away. Along the coast, Arti pulled over at every possible stop to get pictures that would never do justice to the reality of the ocean. Don ran to the waves like that same hyperactive kid of years ago, playing with the breakers and tempting the spray of blinding white water that exploded against the worn resistance of rock. For these moments we were all free.

At 12:30 A.M., we pulled into Florence, Oregon, and went from motel to motel, finding that each one was full. Moving on, another half hour south we found an unsanitary dump with an opening. It was a choice of desperation when, after five minutes of contemplation in the parking lot, we finally said, "Hell, there's nothin' else" and sought out the manager's office.

I unlocked the door of our room and pushed it open tentatively, a palpable wall of dust and mildew rushing past us like the opening of a tomb. I flipped on the light expecting a scatter of roaches.

"Jesus Christ," said Don, filing in behind me. "Forty-five bucks for this."

The curtains were a dingy pink chiffon. Pink plywood gingerbread-house fringe ran along the seams between the walls and the ceiling, framing the room. Pictures of cats with pink collars, bows, and balls of pink yarn were all over the walls. Pink doilies were draped on the two recliners, and on the small table between them were several booklets on Oregon tourism and a bowl of plastic fruit so ancient that the ends of the banana were worn off.

"It's a good thing I got half a load on, or I couldn't stay here," Don said, taking a brief but disapproving look at the nicotine cast of the bedspread and pillowcases. He dropped into one of the recliners, raising a plume of dust, and reached into the grocery bag that held the last four beers.

We flipped coins to see who got a bed alone and who had to share the queen-sized one with someone else. Arti flipped the coin—he won.

"C'mon," said Don, beckoning us to center around the bowl of fruit. "Let's do in these last four beers and call it a night."

Arti was lying on his bed, unresponsive. I motioned toward his prostrate form.

"Hell with him!" Don muttered and threw me a beer. I almost finished it before falling asleep in one of the armchairs.

I woke after dreaming that I had wet the bed, and discovered to my relief that I had actually spilled the remaining half of my beer on my crotch and thighs. I blinked a few times in the dim light of the room, a weak, yellow illumination coming through the dingy shade of a small table lamp. Don was still up. He had the little portable stereo playing "Take the Skinheads Bowling," and he was engaged in a hybrid of drunken stumbling and Chubby Checkers' twist.

"Jesus," I croaked. "What are you doing?"

"Issa las' swun," said Don, indicating the last beer that he clutched in a death grip. "On yer feet, and I'll give you the lass warm ssswallows."

I pushed myself up out of the chair. "No thanks," I said.

Don waved the partially crushed can and spilled some beer on the carpet. "Les' sstrangle Arti innissleep." Don had become a slurring, rancorous shit. He grabbed a drinking glass off the kitchen counter and poured about an inch of beer into it. Then he thrust the offering into my hand. "A toast!" he emoted. "Thas all I'm asken." He raised his beer. I raised my glass. "The only two lef' sstandin'—the bastard and the half-breed." Don was referring to his adoption, as he did from time to time when he was drinking.

"Three-eighths-breed," I corrected.

"To the half-breed and the basstard," he continued, moved nearly to tears at the announcement of our similarly disadvantaged lots, both growing up poor and fatherless, proving that Indians and whites can suck competitively.

"The three-eighths-breed and the bastard," I repeated.

"So what if I'mm…member of the massser race and you're not, we're brothers and that's all there's to it." He giggled, gurgling like a baby, his face lit up like a Christmas tree.

I swallowed the warm, flat beer and dragged myself into the bedroom, where I changed into some shorts then returned to unconsciousness.

At 9:00 A.M. Sunday morning, we rose to the sound of crows squawking in the parking lot. Arti rolled over, hugging his pillow. His left arm was severely sunburned from the day before, and it radiated painful color. "What a spacious night's sleep," he said quietly, eyes still closed. "Oh, I just remembered…I cheated. Levi, you actually won the toss. You should have looked at the coin. But seein' how Don's not in bed with you, I guess it turned out okay anyway."

We found Don still in the living room, immobile on the couch, limp with apathy, his eyes heavy-lidded and half open. "Coffee," he moaned, all the fight knocked out of him. "Coffee, now!"

Being home sounded better as I realized the beer was gone, and our clothes were dirty and slept-in. At this juncture, I wondered what I had expected to get out of the trip in the first place. We drove back to Florence, and by afternoon had moved out of the sun and into the shadows to shoot pool and drink again. I was still far from home and not yet ready to start caring again. By 3:00 we were driving away from the coast and up to Eugene to jump I-5 for a quicker way home. In Eugene, we stopped to grab a quick bite in a café. We had all fallen silent, shoulders sagging like gamblers who'd lost their wads, the tinkling of ice the only constant sound as water glasses moved from tabletop to mouths in the rehydration process.

"You ever been here before?" Don asked me and Arti.

"Nope."

"I've never seen so many hippies."

Arti snapped a couple of pictures of Don complaining about hippies, then asked him, "Yeah? So what?"

Don scowled. "I don't know. Peace, Peace, Peace. I guess I prefer violent meateaters who bathe." Don turned his attention to his plate. "Dessication seems to be the theme," he said, holding up a brittle piece of bacon. "This shit's been under a lamp for about a day and a half. And look at this toast—sawdust!"

"You're hungover," I said.

"Bullshit! I'm still tanked."

Arti was listlessly rotating a cheekful of Denver omelet, facing forward but discreetly looking through the window out of the corner of his eye.

I followed his gaze and saw a bum on the corner begging, or pleading actually, more desperate than the norm. Not rooted to a spot, thrusting out a palm to passersby he was prancing from one person to the next, staggering into pedestrians, reeling from one rejection to the next, imploring and reaching out with offensive persistence, like an amateur on a unicycle with the hollowness of a tumbleweed riding invisible currents. His hands were long with swollen knuckled fingers extended tightly together like wings stapled to his shirt sleeves; they stroked the air with fluid absence and a grace mockingly feminine. His lips moved with the same effort, mute against the glass between us, exaggerated syllables rolling off slack lips, his blind eyes searching for faceless forms and white shadows that approached from every direction. He was Indian.

Don's eyes played over Arti's then mine. Then Don looked, too, glancing with brief attention, registering the scene then looking away, back to my eyes, his head giving a very subtle shake of disappointment and understanding.

I didn't see Arti's eyes, but his discomfort palpitated for a few moments with the sound of him readjusting in his chair and sipping at his water to create peripheral distraction, as though he were somehow embarrassed for me, as though it might be my father or a cousin out there on the street. Indian bums always trigger the same unspoken discomfort among white friends—no words, only silence and an ambient respect for the embarrassment they are certain that I am being subjected to. And I am feeling it—always will I imagine. But whether it's caused by the bum or the white friends, I don't know. In some way the heads that hang with a sort of empathetic shame for my people and their unfortunate intoxicated demise tell me that I should be embarrassed. They tell me that everyone notices what I am, and that I can't possibly be separate from an Indian man on the other side of the window, holding himself up against a stop sign, eyes open and unconscious.

It was time to go home. The waitress was taking the remains of Don's breakfast.

"We'll take a round of Buds when you get a chance," I said.

Don balked. "The fuck we will."

"He's just kiddin'." I smiled at the waitress. "We'll take the round. He'll be fine."

When the beer came, I drank mine and Don's, and Arti finished his with no complaints.

Somewhere between Portland and Seattle I dozed off, then woke to the shadowed profile of Arti at the wheel. The sun was setting fiery orange beyond his head like a dramatic aura, and he was advancing the frame on his camera. His window was down, and he was smoking one of Don's cigars. He raised the camera, directed it at the horizon, and snapped a picture, steadying it with one hand. The breeze grabbed the smoke from his cigar, and the thin cloud raced out the window like a ghost fleeing into the night.

Arti set the camera on the dash and picked a beer up from where it was wedged between his legs. "Get 'em while they're hot," he said, and pointed to the three remaining members of a six-pack on the floor at my feet.

I glanced in the backseat. Don was awake and looking at the sunset. "Goddamnit, We aren't going to be home 'til midnight, and I gotta get up in the morning. Life sucks!"

"Go to sleep," I offered.

Don slouched down in his seat, getting more comfortable. "I can't sleep with that light on."

"What light?"

He tapped his finger against the window, pointing at the setting sun, and closed his eyes.

6

Nicki came to visit me on a suffocating day when the air conditioner was busted, and Wilma had informed me that my reports were very good and that I deserved a larger burden of work. She also promised to take me out into the field and show me how to do home study evaluations. I was looking over the home study questionnaire when Nicki appeared in the doorway, smiling and pointing her finger at me like a pistol—her version of waving. She was growing her hair out and had it pushed behind her ears, with the straight locks falling down around her shoulders. The July sun had tanned her face an even copper color, making the whites of her eyes stand out like porcelain. Eating an Almond Joy that was melting in her fingers, she had magenta polish on the nails of one hand and purple on the other.

I almost laughed but then I noticed the healed pattern of shallow cuts on her arm made with a razor blade.

"Howdy," she said, and sat down in the chair by my desk, first dumping the papers I had placed there on the floor. "Are you busy?"

"Not too busy. How's it goin'?" I said, hesitantly.

"Pretty good. Just gettin' ready to see Becky. I'm a little early." She nodded with affirmation. "Yup, and it's quite an accomplishment, 'cause I'm busin' it here. Damn they're slow! I mean, dang they're slow!"

"Have you been getting any writing done lately?" I asked, hoping to open an avenue of communication about her home life.

She feigned surprise, raising her eyebrows. "Funny you should ask. I got a poem here I thought you might want to take a look at."

"Yeah, let's have a look," I answered, glad that she seemed to trust me. She licked the chocolate from her fingers, then reached into her back pocket and produced a piece of notebook paper folded down to the size of a credit card and began peeling it open like the petals of a closed flower. Handing the poem to me, she looked earnestly into my eyes as though she were telling me that the next minute or so was not to be taken lightly.

The printed letters started out small and rigidly square then got more spacious and circular as she neared the end of the poem, as if she had lost her self-conscious focus on penmanship, and the movements of her hand matched her rush of feelings:

I am a child
It's my world
Too bad it's yours, too

I am a child
Counting down the seconds to the fight
In the dark, staring at the ceiling
Clutching blankets like a brother or sister
The morning proves it's not a dream
The mirror says: a new you, black and blue

I am a child
Inside out and shattered into fragments
Each piece with crouching and fearful reflections
What will you tell me this time?
What will you say?
The mirror tells me the truth: A new you, black and blue

I am a child, fighting
I can refuse to listen
I can make you hate me
Pulled by the hair, kicking and screaming,
I found my name in a book
It wasn't given by you
I am Athena the warchild
It's my world, too bad it's yours, too
It's too bad.

I looked at her for a few moments, wondering if she'd open up a little more by saying something about the poem, but she was silent.

"This is very good," I finally said, while waiting for her to provide direction.

"You like it?"

I nodded. "Do you ever show Becky your poems or talk to her about the things in them?" I asked her, still trying to get her to reveal more.

"Nope, I haven't shown her any poems, but some of the stuff I write about are things we discuss, too. It's like, when I feel pain I start thinking in poems. You know what I mean? They just start comin' into my head, almost like I can hear my own voice in there."

I looked again at the creased paper, seeing Nicki's pain in the jumbled sentences. Still trying to draw her out about her feelings reflected in the poem, I asked, "What's the Athena thing—I mean, why'd you choose her name?"

"Well, I was reading this Greek mythology book and...." Her response was cut short as Becky called to her from outside the office. Nicki reached out and snatched the poem from my hand and slipped it into the back pocket of her jeans.

"I like reading your work, keep it up," I said. I wanted to ask her what she was scratching into her arm with the razor blade. I could see the letters A and T, but she hadn't finished.

"Nicki, who are you talking to in the poem?"

She looked at me and frowned. "How do you mean?"

"When you say, 'It's my world, too bad it's yours, too,' who are you talking to?"

"Anybody who knows what I feel. Well, gotta' go," she said, and bounced up out of her chair to go see Becky. "I'll be back."

"And I'll be here."

When she left, I closed the door partway so that no one could see in. I stared out the window for a while, feeling an inner heaviness expanding beyond the capacity of my chest to hold it captive. But I held it in, and an hour later I went home.

The next day I talked to Becky Davies, who worked mostly with kids. She was Makah and Quinalt with high, wide cheekbones, and she had such green eyes that we used to tease her that she was wearing colored contact lenses. She drove a three-quarter-ton pickup that announced her arrival every morning with its rasping mechanical emphysema, sounding as if it was grabbing its last breath as it shook to a stop when she switched off the ignition.

I told her about Nicki's poem, then asked if Nicki revealed to her what she was cutting into her arm. Becky, who had not noticed the razor blade cuts, seemed concerned but assured me that the poem at least was a good sign that Nicki was communicating her anger and fear about her abusive and chaotic family situation. Becky also confessed to me that she could understand Nicki's anger because after she had had her own children at age sixteen and seventeen she had neglected her son and daughter on some occasions when she was young and wild, and her kids, who were now in their twenties, hadn't entirely forgiven her. She said that even if things got resolved with Nicki's parents someday, Nicki would always carry some anger about what they had done, and that was perfectly alright.

"Well, I know it's okay. I just thought you should hear about it," I responded.

Becky nodded thoughtfully, then continued, "Is there something else bothering you?"

I told her no. It was an involuntary lie, as effortless as swallowing a hunk of food. Although I hadn't fully realized it yet as I stood there in Becky's office, Nicki was unearthing something from my own past, a shovelful at a time. Nicki was making me remember, and it bothered me. But I had to grasp it myself before I could reveal it to anyone else. So I just thanked Becky for her time.

"Anytime, kid. Be brave," she said, knowing that I was struggling with something else.

"Hey, Levi, you got a minute?" Luke called to me at work the next Monday.

I took a few steps backward in the middle of my trip to the coffeepot and leaned into Luke's office. "Yeah, sure. You mind if I get some coffee first?"

"No, go ahead."

I filled up my cup with the last burnt two inches and went back to Luke's office. He was on the phone, anxiously tapping his index finger against his desk calendar and bobbing his head up and down. Finally he hung up the phone then punched a few buttons to keep calls from coming through.

"How ya doing?" he asked, checking out my state of mind. His glasses had slid so far down his nose he looked like he'd just been slapped.

"Fine," I said. "So far."

"I got some news for you. Something went down over the weekend that I just found out about this morning. You're close to the Sanders girl, Nicki, enit?"

"Yeah, what happened?"

"Well, her aunt called. There was a blowout at the home again. The auntie says that Nicki's mom and dad got drunk, and Charles started knocking Liddy around. So Liddy took Nicki and went to the aunt's house. They were there all Saturday, and according to the aunt, Nicki's mom was drinking there the whole time, too. But I'll tell you what, it wouldn't surprise me at all if the aunt was boozin' with her. We asked her if maybe she could take Nicki the first time all this shit happened, but she was hittin' the bottle a little too much to be eligible; she didn't exactly beg to take Nicki anyway. So then Sunday morning, Nicki's mom jumped a bus to Yakima and left Nicki behind with her aunt. Pretty ugly, enit?"

I thought about Nicki's poem, with the lines running through my head, visions of her face and the hard glare of refusal in her eyes, fighting the temptation to cry like the little girl that she could not be.

"I've been searching for a foster home all day, and I finally got one that'll take her temporarily until we figure something out. They're real good people," Luke confirmed.

"Why Yakima?" I asked, wondering why Liddy could only go halfway in protecting her child.

"Her mom's got some friend there, I guess." Luke took a deep breath and exhaled heavily through his nose, then continued. "I called Nicki's father, and that man ain't an option. Aside from the fact that he's too dangerous for me to send her back home to, he actually told me to leave her at her auntie's 'cause he doesn't want to look at either one of 'em—Nicki or Liddy."

"What a fuckhead," I blurted out.

"We don't use words like that around here. We use bum, loser, deadbeat," Luke said, forcing a smile.

Vicki had stopped what she was doing to listen. "Well, the fuckin' bum shouldn't get her whether he wants her or not," I continued, staring down at the carpet, where an unidentifiable black liquid had left stains.

Luke shook his head. "There's going to have to be some serious change before either one of them can get her back now."

I nodded. Luke and I fell silent. An understanding passed fleetingly between us. I knew we could both feel the tugging and the snapping of connections thinner than a spider's thread, strung from the centers of our bodies to a significant but fragile living being out there that we had put a part of ourselves into, and that was now a part of us. For three or four seconds we watched in the reflections of each others' faces, something very valuable and delicate being chipped apart and floating away in pieces.

"I talked to Nicki, too," said Luke. "I let her know that I had found a good foster home for her, but she didn't want to go. I told her it was the best alternative, but that didn't make no difference. Finally, she agreed to it, but she insisted on you taking her there. So you go get her, Levi."

"I will," I said. I took a sip from my coffee, which left a residue of leached grounds on my tongue.

"You need to get her at her auntie's, then take her to the foster home. I can get her tomorrow for an appointment with Becky," Luke said, as he looked for the phone number then scribbled it onto a blue post-it.

"Give her auntie a call and get directions. Her name's Frieda. I'll write down the directions to the foster home."

I took the post-it and stared at the number for several seconds as if it were going to tell me something more. "Should I get her right away?"

"Yeah, as soon as you can. I'll take care of everything else. I really appreciate this, Levi. I'm afraid she's going to be a real mess. Are you ready for it?"

"No. Never," I smiled, weakly.

"She trusts you," Luke said. "She knows you're safe."

Although Luke's observation was something I already knew, somehow hearing it said out loud made it seem like more of a responsibility. And I wondered if there was such a thing as a safe place for someone like Nicki. By giving me her story, Nicki had accepted my help. She had allowed me into her life, not to show me something foreign like an explanation to an outsider, but willingly and without thought as the natural progression between two people from the same world, born of a common circumstance. Now we were friends, seeking strength and comfort in numbers.

Nicki didn't greet me with words. She just stared at me with the hurt and defiant expression I had expected. Her face was frozen in the glare of betrayal. Her glassy eyes burned with a bitterness that would not allow the shine of tears to grow heavy enough to fall down her cheeks. She was gritting her teeth, fighting to kill the sadness with anger. Her hair hung down around her face like a thick black shroud. Her aunt was behind her mumbling about Nicki's bags.

"I'm sorry this happened, Nicki," I said.

She had a gym bag, a backpack, and a brown Safeway grocery sack with the top rolled down. Frieda pointed to the bags and said, "These are her things. It's all they brought. The rest is still at her house."

Frieda was perhaps as much as ten years older than her sister, Lydia. She was wearing a faded paisley summer dress. She was shorter and more slender than Lydia, but had an appearance of physical strength, with the muscles in her bare arms well defined and the veins standing out. Her hair was dark brown and streaked with gray, its length hidden in a hasty knot behind her head.

I picked up all the bags. But then Nicki reached out and took the Safeway sack from me. "I'll take this," she said in a barely audible voice. It was as if the words created an opening for emotion, cracking the hardness of her face. "You see? You see how it works?" she said, as if to tell me that all my attempts to be positive were delusional. Not that she thought I had been untruthful. I just didn't see the reality of things, and she wanted me to catch on. Then she turned and hugged her aunt so quickly the woman had barely raised her own arms before Nicki slid past me and out to the car.

"Good-bye, Nicki. I want you to call me, eh?"

Nicki was putting her things into the back seat.

"Her mother just left her here, she was drinkin' you know?" Frieda explained as she looked back and forth between me and Nicki, who had gotten into the car and shut the door.

"Did she say anything before she left?" I asked.

"Nicki was in bed, and Lydia decided to just go to Yakima. She's got friends there. I told her, 'Look, I can't keep her here forever, you know, and she said she'd send for her later. There was nothin' I could do, really. She was drinkin' and all. She got mad at me 'cause I wouldn't drink with her. We used to, all the time while growin' up together. But I told her those times are over, and it's gotta stop. She got really mad at me."

"She said she'd send for her?"

"That's what she said." She looked at Nicki sadly. "Look, maybe I can take her for a while if Liddy doesn't come through. It's just that me and my husband are working a lot, and it makes it tough."

I thought about what Luke had said about the drinking. "That's a possibility, but I better take her to the foster home for now. I'll let her caseworker know you're willing."

"Okay. It's a good home you're takin' her to?"

"Yeah, it's only temporary, though. Well, we'd better get going," I said. "I'll tell Nicki to give you a call, okay?"

"Yes, please tell her to call. And have that caseworker call, too."

I walked to the car, looking back once to see Frieda slowly closing the door, watching through the diminishing space until the door was shut.

When we arrived at the foster home, Nicki gave only the tips of her fingers to the hands offered by the man and woman, dropping her arm limply to her side when they let go of her hand. The man and woman both frowned sympathetically. Finally, the man stepped forward and took Nicki's things from my arms, and the woman put her hand on Nicki's shoulder. "Let me show you your room, honey," she whispered and moved in closely to Nicki's side.

Nicki stepped quickly over and hugged me while keeping her eyes on the few square feet of floor at her feet. Her hair pressed against my neck, and I wanted to hold onto her longer, but I gently eased her back with my hands against her shoulders. "I'll talk to you soon," I said. "You'll be alright."

The woman guided her off, then, looking over her shoulder, asked if I would be calling tomorrow.

"Yes. We will," I said. "Someone will. Me or Luke or…someone."

They thanked me and watched me see myself out.

It had been almost a full week since Nicki had been placed in foster care, and I still hadn't retrieved her belongings. She came in to see me when Luke brought her in for her session, but she looked exhausted and didn't say much. When she found out that I was going to get her stuff, she stressed the importance of her radio, which I promised to get. According to Luke, the foster parents said she was staying up late into the night watching TV, staring into space, smoking cigarettes out her bedroom window, and not eating. He also told me that she had been put on antidepressants.

"At twelve years old?" I asked.

"Yeah," Luke said, "they come in the shape of Flintstones." I didn't laugh. Then Luke exhaled with exasperation and said, "She got in a fight at school, too. So she's got a shiner. Didn't think another little girl could hit hard enough to give a shiner did ya? Well, times are a changin'. On top of that she almost got kicked out of school for a few days. But I talked to the principal about what's goin' on. And I gave our little friend a talkin' to 'bout how I saved her bacon."

"What'd she say?" I asked.

"She said, 'so what?'" Luke laughed and shook his head.

Nicki had been living out of the three bags she had brought with her, and it was time to rendezvous with Charles Sanders. I cut out early to make the drive to the Sanders home, now the residence of Charles only. Charles said that he would not be available but that he had a lady friend called Ellen willing to do the favor of unloading Nicki's stuff on me. When I asked Nicki about her, she said she'd never heard of anyone named Ellen.

I had spoken with Ellen on the phone to make the pick-up arrangements, and she had volunteered "so that the job could be finished." She made a particular point of letting me know that since she did not live there she would have to come over to let me in.

After Nicki scrawled a crude map to the house to refresh my memory, I set out. It was getting cold with the transition into October, but it was sunny and clear so I turned up the heat and opened the sun roof. Following Nicki's map, I found myself on a rural road passing through a spacious neighborhood of mostly older homes, some kept up nicely and others fairly dilapidated. I turned up the Sanders' driveway and parked in front of their small house.

The door was open, but the screen was shut. After I rapped on it a couple of times and said "hello," a woman appeared.

"You must be Ellen," I said. "I'm here for Nicki's belongings."

A tall, willowy white woman with a generous and severe application of makeup, anxiously peered at me through the screen. Wearing a blue quilted parka over a denim skirt, too short for the weather, and a clingy black rayon shirt, she looked like a hooker trying to keep warm.

"Yeah, I'm Ellen. Everything's ready for you. Come in," she said.

I stepped across the threshold, glancing over to the couch that faced the television, where Charles had been sitting the time before. It was empty, and the television was on. I followed her inside as she made her way through the living room and started up a narrow staircase to Nicki's room in the attic. Her belongings were crammed into four boxes and two garbage bags as if her father had stuffed all of it into the boxes and bags with extreme haste. Probably everything she had worn since birth was jammed in unfolded in an overflow of wadded clothing that pushed up past the rims. The boxes were sealed with finalizing straps of duct tape that offered just enough restraint to keep the cardboard from flopping open, while the mouths of the garbage bags were tied into knots.

"This is all of it," Ellen said, gesturing at the pile with a flick of her wrist. "I'll help you carry it down."

"Nicki wanted me to make sure I got her radio," I said, hoisting up one of the bags. "She's really looking forward to getting it back. Do you know if it's packed in one of these boxes?"

"Radio?" said Ellen rubbing her chin. "No, this is just clothes; there was no radio."

"It's a little portable stereo," I said, "you know, the ones with two speakers and a tape deck? Maybe it's somewhere else in the house."

"This is a small place," Ellen said, making her move to the staircase with the other garbage bag. "If there was a radio here, we'd probably see it."

"Why don't we take a quick look around, for Nicki's sake?" I said. "Maybe you just never noticed it here."

Ellen looked up towards the ceiling, her eyes affecting a subtle hint of vague recollection. "Oh, I know what she's talking about. But that radio belongs to her father. He takes it to work with him."

"Oh, I see," I said, stepping past her and starting down the stairs with the first load. "Do you think we could set this stuff just outside the door?" Ellen called sweetly from behind me. "Then you could load it into your car after I leave? I've got to be somewhere in fifteen minutes."

"Sure. That'd be fine."

After three trips, Nicki's life with Mom and Dad was piled up on the front lawn. Ellen locked the door behind her and tucked the keys into a blue plastic purse that was probably Nicki's. Then she zipped up her coat and began moving down the walkway. "Thanks for gettin' her stuff," she added briskly, leaving.

I nodded and watched for a few moments as she turned onto the sidewalk, wondering for the first time about why her father wasn't there.

Somewhere in his heart, in some deep recess of his conscience, wasn't there a faint tug of loyalty or attachment to the life that he had created, on this day when every tangible link with his daughter would be taken away by some stranger knocking at the door? Was he somewhere in a bar or walking a country road, looking at his watch and wringing his hands, choking down regret, the bitter taste of his life, wondering why everything was so fucked up? Or was he just waiting for the day to end so that he could wake to a clean and stringless start? Then he would be free to move on, trudging grudgingly into the future, forgetting a little more each day, until her room at the top of the stairs had no more significance than the dusty, unpleasant storage space that it had become, with junk stacked nearly to the ceiling, blocking out any window light; trudging far into the future, where she would be no longer the child that clung to his shirtsleeves making everything so difficult but a woman walking far away in space and memory. In any case, wherever he was it seemed clear he didn't give a shit.

I rolled down my windows and fired up the stereo real loud, flying past scenes of pastoral America with my disruption of contradicting noise overpowering the peaceful images outside of the car knowing they would never be the same again, as I roared down the highway with a carload of rejection in a land where fathers forsake their little girls.

At the foster home only Nicki was there, and she ran down the steps when I pulled to the curb. The skin around the corner of her left eye was reddish and a little swollen. There was a tiny pressure cut in the center of the ruddy oval of bruising.

"So you got in a fight," I said.

"Yup, you should see the other chic. Actually she looks just fine." Nicki tore open the tops of the two garbage bags, disregarding the knots, and pushed around at the contents, frowning.

"Half this stuff is old; this shit doesn't fit me." She grabbed the torn plastic necks and hoisted the two bags out of the trunk and onto the street.

"Was he there?" she said, opening up one of the boxes.

"No, he wasn't. Just the woman."

"Asshole." Nicki was going quickly from box to box.

"I guess he was at work," I added.

"Shithead," she muttered with fading strength. "Who the hell was the bitch?"

"I don't know."

After the last box, she turned and faced me with her hands on her hips. "Did you get my stereo?"

"It wasn't there," I said. "The woman said that it was your father's and that he takes it to work with him."

Nicki slowly shook her head, poison flowing into her eyes. "Did your parents ever fuck you over like this?"

I felt a ball of blackness grow and consume the space within my upper torso. "My dad left me forever, Nicki. So yeah, I guess so." I was startled by my voice and felt that the moment had some kind of power to it, as though my confession was a gift to both of us—a sentence unraveling to show everything hidden within the coils. Nicki was silent. I went on. "I was younger than you. Quite a bit younger."

"Then you know all about this shit," she said.

There was a substantial difference. Nicki had lost both parents in one ugly drunken split. One had taken a bus over the mountains, and one wouldn't show his face. Right now Nicki had just about nothing.

"Do you talk to him?" she asked, her voice softening with sympathy, or maybe hopes that I might say it all worked out great.

"No, Nicki. He's really gone, like I have no idea where he is. Never heard a word from him after he left."

Nicki was absently clutching a ridiculous baby blue nightshirt with teddy bears on it—something that would have fit her when she was five. Then she abruptly threw it back into the bag. "Well, maybe mine will do me the same favor!" she snapped. "Any news from my mom?"

"Not so far. Nicki, you might have to wait awhile for her to come around, she's fairly screwed up right now."

Nicki's words jumped out of her mouth like striking snakes. "He drove her away by beating the shit out of her! They aren't the same.

She's coming back."

Nicki turned and picked up the two bags, dragging and bouncing them along the ground.

"I wasn't putting your mom down, Nicki," I called after her. "I didn't mean for it to sound that way."

"It's okay," she said without looking back. "I'm not mad at you."

I took a box and followed her.

The next day winter came rushing through the trees in front of my window, sweeping and scattering gold leaves with its breath.

"Let's get the fuck outa here," said Arti, swishing the last swallow of his beer around to wash out the lingering flavor of whiskey from the shots he and I had just taken. We were in the bar down the street from our apartment building. I had gone there, obeying the message on my answering machine, and found him sitting in the most dimly lit corner in the place, partially obscured behind a support pillar with three or four empty tables between him and the closest customers.

He had recently upped his hours in a part-time retail job that was getting him through his seventh year of school, which meant that his dislike for the public had intensified, explaining his position in the corner. We shared our bad vibes nonverbally by slumping in our chairs and glaring at the other patrons while we split a pizza, three pitchers of beer, and the several shots of whiskey that tasted like perfume. Arti had been in Canada the past weekend, and he bestowed upon me the gift of two hundred and fifty tablets of codeine phosphate for nagging aches and pains and difficulties with reality. I'd taken three or four, and the alcohol was speeding them right along.

By the time we left, we'd swallowed about a pint each for every sentence spoken, and I was significantly drunk and vague. It was now late October, cold and rainy. The gray, misty chill and dim streetlights were depressing and made the summer seem long ago. On the way home we crossed the street, and Arti kicked something to me. "Merry Christmas," he said as the thing bounced along the asphalt and came to rest a few feet from where I stood. It was a small teddy bear, four inches high with a loop of string at the top of its head—a Christmas ornament, cream-colored originally, now black and soaked with rain, street dirt, and oil. I picked it up and put it in my jacket pocket.

At home I threw the teddy bear in my dirty clothes basket and brushed my teeth. In the mirror the whites of my eyes were reddish around the edges, and even the skin beneath them had the flushed translucence of exhaustion. "You're drunk, boy," I said, looking at the face that seemed to belong to a stranger. "What a mess you're in." My face pouted back at me from the mirror, looking punished and afraid but fighting to appear strong. Suddenly I looked like a very young boy.

When I was eleven, about Nicki's age, a thirty-year-old man in the neighborhood brought out his dick when my sister was walking past his house. It really scared the hell out of her, and she came running to me. The man had a strange face that looked like shiny plastic, as if his skin were too tight, round gleaming cheeks like a doll's face, and squinting, smiling eyes. He was always out sitting on the porch or in his big rusted-out car, leering like an unwholesome cherub, as if he weren't right in the head. Since my friends and I were too young to take him physically, under Don Boyd's plan for revenge we waited until nightfall, then slashed the tires on his car and broke every window in the car and the house. We pulled it off without a hitch, and I felt better thinking he had paid for his actions.

That same year at school I was in the principal's office several times a month for disrupting class, which boiled down to never shutting up when I should have. Eventually my teacher, who hated me enough to try and prove that there was something wrong with me, ordered a psychological evaluation, which, much to her dismay, indicated no measurable antisocial tendencies or defects. Then only a few days after the evaluation had determined that no special steps were warranted, I was told by Don that the windows had been replaced in the pervert's house. So we mustered a group of four or five little monsters and hit the house again. This time in the fevered pitch of the moment, Don and I lingered too long hurling fist-sized stones, and both of us were caught by the police. My mother and Don's parents paid for the damage, and we were put on a repayment schedule with our paper route money. But I believed that I had been right since my sister had been threatened. As a result, I stopped talking for several months and vowed not to bring so much shame upon my mother again.

With my unsatisfactory academic record and the horrendous property damage, I was at risk of being expelled permanently from school and transferred to an alternative one. I later learned that my mother made an urgent plea involving the fact that I was having a tough time ever since my father had abandoned us. I started talking again and went to a counselor, something that was a condition of remaining at school. The counselor said he was part Indian, although he didn't look it at all, and once, when I insisted that Don and I had acted alone in the vandalism, he asked me if I spoke with a forked tongue. Even at my age I thought this was silly, in part because my mother had always gotten irate over all the broken English, heapum-big-wampum shit that she feared would embarrass me and Tia. Since the whole event scared little Tia, and she didn't want to be dragged into explaining any of it, I told everyone that I was flashed by the pervert. They didn't seem to believe me. They didn't seem to care. Their only concern was my behavior.

As the memory faded, I focused again on my image in the mirror. It was me alright, being born and ruined. I touched my fingertips to my face and began moving them along the line of my jaw, over my cheekbones and temples, pressing lightly. I pulled the rubber band that held my hair in a short ponytail I had been growing and released the locks, pushing my hand through the black hair that had grown down my neck nearly to my shoulders. I watched my fingers extended and rigid. Then I watched them curl inward toward my exposed pale palm, collapsing into themselves like five independent creatures hiding their faces. In an unpredicted blur, the mirror smashed, a triangular shard of glass collapsed across the back of my hand, opening it up like meat under a filleting knife. My image became an ugly collage of disjointed slivers, the blood from my injury running free between the cracks of my face, as my hand stayed resolutely in the glitter of powdered glass, reaching into an illusion, into nothing.

After rinsing my hand in cold water and bandaging it with gauze and athletic tape, I took three more codeine and went to bed. As I slept, I dreamed that there was music so clear and real it was as if I had fallen asleep with headphones on. I was with Don at a bar, in a hot southern place where I had never actually been. The walls were chicken wire, and the darkness was the darkness of a warm summer night, staved off by lamps. In the center of the enclosure, people danced wildly with themselves, their bodies bending like uncontrolled hoses channeling a tremendous pressure of water and sweating narcotic heat.

Don and I were moving through the crowd around the perimeter, bouncing off strangers and the wire of the enclosure, rebounding, limp but held upright by bodies. We had glasses in our hands—ridiculous long-stemmed champagne glasses with flat shallow reservoirs, and from all directions hands holding bottles would fill them before we could empty them. "Someday we gotta quit drinkin'!" shouted Don, insincerity flashing wickedly in his eyes. "Someday we're gonna have to straighten up!"

Then we reeled through the crowd again, twisting and spinning. The music was now "Mudhoney": "I don't got what you want and I don't care what you think, you better back off! Back off! Back off, baby! If you don't, into the drink!" As we pushed through the crowd, we knew no one and owed no explanations. We were floating, drunk and weightless.

As we rounded the last corner before the exit, I looked to the dance floor of packed dirt bordered by benches like the ones from picnic tables. Sitting by herself was a young Indian girl I knew. I ran to her, asked what she was doing there, and told her that she should leave. I picked her up and hurried her through the crowd to the door. I set her down outside and asked her where her parents were.

"They're not here," she said.

"I can help you," I assured her. "I've been through it, too."

Then the alarm went off, and I woke up in the dark. My heart felt very heavy.

7

The next morning I walked up the wheelchair ramp of the building to find that slobbering adolescent punks had smashed our program jack-o-lantern to bits. In life the thing had not looked sinister at all, but friendly, smiling idiotically in the face of very bad things—the things that I walked in to face each day. Because of this, I had the urge to put a foot through its face a time or two myself, and while I picked my way around the mushy chunks of squash, I felt a sadistic spark of pleasure that it no longer mocked me.

Wilma was leaning against the wall next to the coffeepot just outside of her office. Jones was next to her pouring himself a cup.

"Shhh, here he comes," she said and laughed.

"Talking about me, were ya?"

"We tried, but we couldn't think of much to say—No, jokes," Wilma teased. Then she looked down at my bandaged hand and frowned. "What did ya do, kid?"

"I was trying to push open one of the windows in my apartment, and you know how they paint 'em shut? Well, my hand slipped off, and I shoved it right through the pane."

"Yeah, okay," Wilma said, shaking her head. "At least you didn't fall out."

She took a quick sip from her coffee. "We got that home study today, you know? You ready for it?"

"Of course," I said, "when do we leave?"

"We're supposed to be there at one, so we'll leave in about an hour. We want the 10:00 ferry to Bremerton. Can you drive?"

"Yeah, sure, just let me get some of that coffee."

Wilma and I left late because she got tied up on the phone, shaking her head and rolling her eyes as I stood in her doorway with my clipboard, waiting. As a result, we missed the boat by a few minutes, so we shot over to another terminal about ten miles away and caught the ferry over to the Olympic Peninsula, then drove to Hoodsport and the Skokomish Reservation where our client waited.

The two-lane highway was as narrow as a residential street, snaking along a broad canal with the shoulder beyond the road's edge shearing off down an embankment that dropped ten feet to the water. The trees along the bank were topped to allow passage of the telephone wires that ran the same route as the road. Blue kingfishers perched at intervals on the black cables, their feathered crowns static and bristled, their sharp beaks pointing out over the water. On the forest side of the road, evergreen boughs, heavy with water, overlapped the slick, naked wood of deciduous branches mottled with moss and lichen. The air was misty, and the cedar shingles of rooftops and the wood of fences were dark with water.

The homes on the water side were either pontooned on the bay or on small jetties of land, all with docks, decks, and satellite dishes. Storefronts selling groceries and fishing tackle, and trailer parks and motels with ceramic seagulls stuck on shafts of wire, dotted the roadside, appearing suddenly around a turn then disappearing just as quickly. A sign that read "Congestion Ahead" popped up off the starboard bow and Wilma scoffed. "Look at that: the only congestion out here is in my sinuses."

Then Wilma continued, on a more somber note. "I haven't really told you much about this home study, have I?"

"No, you haven't."

"It's a young woman we're going to see, twenty-nine years old. I only know the rudiments of her situation, but basically when she and her husband split up he got the kids because she was addicted to drugs and alcohol. For whatever reason, he was seen as the more fit of the pair. Now, her story is that she's addressing her stuff, and she has some claims of violence against him that she says were ignored during the initial proceedings when he got the kids. So she's going to start a court battle and try to get her kids back, twins no less—a boy and a girl. Now, we aren't necessarily siding with her, Levi, so you keep that in mind. Technically we don't get involved in custody battles. We are going to do a study of her home and her situation, and ask her a lot of questions and see what services she's received to address her problems. If she is capable of caring properly for those kids, and if being with her poses no risks to them, then we'll say so. That's our job, so take notes—lots of notes."

I could feel her turn her head slightly and cast her eyes over me. "Your reports are good. Someday you'd like to move on to something with some more extensive involvement—like doing casework and home studies, wouldn't you?"

I pictured a future tied into the things I was doing. I envisioned the increments of change, more shadows leaping into my eyes and falling upon my face like handkerchiefs until I disappeared beneath a consuming blackness.

"Yeah," I said, trying to muster some convincing enthusiasm. "That'd be great."

Wilma tapped her finger against the window. "Look at this," she said. She was pointing out at the water, where a dock had once stood, now only marked by two parallel lines of waterlogged poles poking up above the surface like the jagged ribs of a prehistoric beast. "Look at the sign on the first post," she continued, "it says 'No Trespassing!' There's no dock, but the sign remains." She laughed, underscoring the irony. "They trespassed then put up their signs—their signs to keep out trespassers."

"Pretty pathetic," I said. "Private land, private water. Like someone can own something so much more powerful than themselves. Ate that godamn dock right up. Pretty soon that sign'll be decomposing under water."

Wilma didn't say anything, like maybe at one time she would have agreed but now no longer—like maybe she was thinking the earth could be killed like everything else.

"These types of jobs have a very high burnout rate," she said, suddenly. "A lot of people last only a couple of years. I don't expect you to stay here forever; who knows what you'll be doin' five, ten years from now. But while you're here you gotta protect yourself from the weight of what you see every day. You can't internalize the problems and take 'em home with you. It takes too much energy and wears you down. There's different ways to cleanse yourself or cope, you know, like smudging with sage at the end of the day, singing some songs, talking to someone, or whatever you can do to keep yourself healthy. But most importantly, you gotta accept that you can't save everyone."

I just couldn't envision finding any solace in the suggestions Wilma had made. Burning dried plants and singing songs. I knew she meant Indian songs, but I didn't know any of those. And talking to someone was just that—talking. I scratched at my bandage where the blood had soaked through and dried during the night. The cut ached. I was silent for a few moments to indicate my digestion of Wilma's advice.

"What's the woman's name and what tribe is she from," I asked, partly to change the subject.

"Her name is Reyanne Cultee, and I don't know what tribe she belongs to. She's not Skokomish, though. I think she just moved here to get away. You can ask her, Levi."

Once in Hoodsport we found the small two-bedroom house Reyanne Cultee was renting, which had a fairly big front yard of mostly dirt with the blighted traces of a lawn struggling up from the muddy soil. She answered the door with a big smile. Her hair was wet, and she had a white towel around her neck to keep her shoulder-length locks off her T-shirt. "Come in," she said, retreating into the living room. "Have a seat."

The living room was small and tidy, lit by a lamp and the pale sunlight that radiated through the clouds and the large front window. She had lots of pictures on the walls—pictures of a boy and girl together in nearly every wooden and metal frame, some on large color paper, others simple Polaroids and snapshots.

I sat in a recliner, while Wilma sat in a rocker with a crocheted cushion. There was a small end table in between us, its surface nearly covered by a doily of black-and-white beads. Reyanne retrieved another chair from the kitchen, centered it in front of us, and began combing her hair. She looked at me, then down at my injured hand. I felt uneasy and resisted the urge to slide it beneath my clipboard. I even thought I saw discomfort in her, the way her eyes paused on the bandage then flashed away to Wilma.

"So you found me okay," she said. "I appreciate you comin' all the way out here."

"It's okay," said Wilma, "it's all worth it for the free lunch."

Reyanne smiled nervously, looking back and forth between me and Wilma, searching for something to indicate whether Wilma was serious or not.

Wilma laughed, "I put everyone through this. I'm just giving you a bunch of malony."

"Malarkey," I said.

"What?"

"You're giving her a bunch of malarkey."

"Yeah, that, too."

Reyanne laughed then shifted uncomfortably in her chair. "I can get you something though," she said, "I'm sure I can whip something up."

"No, don't worry; I'm just giving you a hard time."

"I can at least get you some coffee."

Wilma nodded. "That'd be good. Cream and sugar, please."

Reyanne looked at me with her eyebrows raised. "You too?"

"Yes, please, black's fine."

Reyanne came back from the kitchen balancing two very full cups and handed mine carefully to me, the black surface trembling and steaming.

When she sat back down, she folded her hands on her lap. "I'm nervous," she said. "I'm not really sure what to say."

Wilma smiled reassuringly and leaned forward like she was going to share a secret. "Don't worry, you don't need to give any speeches. I'll just ask you some questions so we can hear what you got to say, and learn a little about your past and how you're doing at present. Levi's here to help me take notes so he can assist me in writing up the results." Wilma sipped from her coffee cup, then set it down on the beaded coaster, slowly and gently as though the weight of the cup might shatter the tiny beads.

"Now some questions are gonna seem like I'm prying, Reyanne, and they're gonna be uncomfortable maybe, but I gotta ask 'em, okay? You just need to tell it like it is."

Reyanne unfolded her hands and nodded.

"This is a beautiful area," Wilma said, sliding the pen out from beneath the metal jaw of her clipboard. "I bet it's wonderful during the summer."

Reyanne grinned. "Yeah, it is."

"How long have you been here?"

"Only about four months. It sure beats the city."

"I grew up on the reservation," Wilma said, nodding in agreement, "and it took this ol' huckleberry a decade and a half to get used to the city."

Reyanne seemed to relax a little more as though she'd been holding her breath and finally let go for some air. "I didn't grow up in the city either, I moved there after we separated and I still had the kids."

I began to write.

"We separated almost a year and a half ago, and I wanted to get far away from him, so we moved to Seattle while the divorce was goin' on." Reyanne put her hand up in front of her mouth. "I moved to Seattle and dumped his last name."

"Why did the two of you separate?" Wilma's voice was soft and unintrusive.

Reyanne's hand remained in a loose fist in front of her lips. "He was beating up on me. I had problems with alcohol and drugs, and when I came to Seattle with the twins, I knew I had to stop or he might get them. And I was tryin', I was doing better."

"You were doing better," Wilma said, more as a statement than a question. "Were you receiving treatment or going at it alone?"

"I was handling it alone."

"And how did it go? Any relapses?"

"Yes, I did, but I was trying. I didn't really get out of hand, but I did drink a few times."

"Yes, that happens," said Wilma.

Reyanne nodded. Her hair was drying and was now chestnut colored. She took her hand away from her mouth.

"What was your drug of choice? You said alcohol and drugs."

"It was mostly alcohol, but sometimes I used cocaine, too."

Wilma was writing, and when she finished her last notation, she looked up to make sure that Reyanne was finished. "Okay, when did your husband get the kids?"

"After me and the kids had been in Seattle for about six months, he petitioned the Tribal Court, and at the trial he proved that I had been drinking and using cocaine when we were together. They wanted proof of treatment from me, and I didn't have any, so they decided in his favor. The babies didn't wanna go; they didn't understand, you know?"

"What about the domestic violence? Did they take that into account?" Wilma continued.

"No, they didn't."

"How come?"

"I didn't say nothin' to the court."

"Were there police reports or hospital records?"

"Yes, there were records from the hospital, and lots of people knew. But I was scared of what he might do if I started saying things, especially if the right people didn't believe me. But I went to the hospital a few times because of him. He broke two of my ribs, jerked my shoulder out of the socket, and broke my wrist." Her voice trailed off like the list wasn't over, but she'd gotten her point across and there was no need to go on.

"I'm not afraid of him anymore, though" she said, her eyes moving back to the rug. "I want my kids. I won't let anything like that happen again. If a man were to do that to me now, I'd kill him."

Wilma thumped her pen against the clipboard. "Reyanne, when you go to court over this again, you make sure you have every record that indicates abuse, and have copies for the judge and for yourself, okay? You need to make those allegations, and that might entail a police report. You'll have to check into it."

"Yeah, that's what I plan on doing this time."

"Okay, good. Now, what did you do after you lost the kids?"

"Well, I kinda gave up and drank a lot. I still held down my job, but then I'd go home and drink at night. I thought it was over, I didn't think I'd get my kids so I didn't care. But I kept calling the kids just like it said in the court order. I called when I was sober just like I was entitled to, and my ex or his girlfriend would answer, and whichever one it was would say that the other one was out with the kids, and sometimes I could hear the little ones in the background. So I started writing down the dates and times of my calls and what they said to me. And I saved all my phone bills, too. He didn't allow no visitation neither like he was supposed to—that was outa the question! I also wrote down the stuff he said when I asked for visits."

"That's how you need to prepare," said Wilma. "Sounds like he's already out of compliance with the court order. Now, tell me about the services you've been receiving."

"About the same time I started writing down the phone calls, I started after-care. I attended AA meetings four times a week. I also got into a support group for battered women, and I still meet with a counselor for private sessions once a week."

"How long have you been sober?"

"Nine months." Reyanne looked from Wilma to me then down at the floor. "Yup, nine months. When I started working on things, the landlord raised my rent. That's when I started thinking about moving."

Wilma then asked her to list the services she was presently involved in while I continued to write. She offered us more coffee when our cups were empty. When Reyanne took my cup, she pointed at my hand and asked what had happened. For a brief moment my explanation escaped me. Then remembering, I relayed the same crap about the window, but my hesitation had been just long enough to wound the veracity of my story. She raised her eyebrows and gave a courtesy nod before heading for the kitchen. I could feel the shame rushing into my face, the heat of sudden self-loathing. What if Wilma or Reyanne could have seen me a mere twelve hours ago, red-eyed, miserable, and stinking of booze? I suddenly felt that I didn't belong in that living room, pretending to be able to help while Reyanne spoke of her battles against substance abuse and poor judgment.

"Oh, hey, what tribe are you?" I called after her, moving the focus away from my injured self.

Reyanne stopped in the doorway to the kitchen and said, "Klallam, and some Cowichan and Lummi. I'm enrolled over at Lummi, 'cuz my dad was Cowichan and Lummi, and my mom's parents moved there from Klallam way back."

"Really? I'm Lummi and Klallam, too."

"Oh no, we're probably cousins," said Reyanne. "What's your family name?"

"The Lummi family name is Friday."

"I recognize that name," she said, "but I don't think we're related. We could be, though. Scary ain't it? You might have a wild cousin you didn't know about." She laughed and went into the kitchen.

She filled the cups, answering Wilma's questions freely and with detail that sometimes strayed into small talk and stories from the past. After nearly two hours, Wilma turned slowly through the two or three pages of sparse notes on her clipboard. "Well, I think that just about does it for today," she said, clicking the button on her pen, "unless you have anything to add, Levi."

"No. Looks good."

Reyanne cleared her throat. "Um...when will this thing be ready so I can give it to the court?"

"Oh, in plenty of time for your court date," said Wilma. "Levi's fast, and he's behind the wheel on this one."

I heard Wilma say my name, but her voice was muted and distant. I was thinking instead about the awful hits Reyanne had taken, the fear in Reyanne's eyes. Suddenly I could see my parents standing in the entryway of our house arguing. I saw my dad shove my mother fast and hard, with an open palm against the front of her shoulder just above her breast, a strong, violent extension of the arm with a snap to it. She was knocked hard against a bureau. The candles that stood in pewter holders, passed down to my mother from her mother, toppled over on the bureau as it slammed into the wall. One of the long, white candles broke in half. There was silence. The muscles in my dad's jaw flexed like he wanted to keep moving, like he was braced—standing on the brink, resisting some awesome rush of energy that gushed against his back. He looked terrifying. Then he turned and stormed out the door. Was that the time when he did not come back? No, he came back. But when? Was it that night? Was I asleep? What happened when he came back? My mom told me that he left to cool off. I remember that.

Reyanne was looking at me, waiting.

"Don't look so serious," said Wilma, "just tell her how long it might take."

"When's the court date?" I asked.

"December eighth," she said, thinking for a moment. "Over a month from now."

"I'll finish it in no more than a week," I said.

Reyanne nodded then looked away from me to Wilma. "What if they don't believe me about the abuse stuff?"

Wilma set her clipboard down on the floor and leaned forward, locking her strong, dark hands together in front of her chin in a knot of knuckles and veins. "Get the records from the hospital, and see about making a police report right now. Also get testimony from your counselors that you've suffered from battering, then provide us with that information, and Levi will write a letter presenting those materials to the judge. How's that?"

"Okay," said Reyanne. "That sounds good."

Reyanne walked us to the door and put out her hand. "Thanks for doin' this for us," she said. "I appreciate the help."

After shaking our hands, she gave an awkward laugh, just a quick expulsion of air and a faint smile. "A couple weeks ago I saw some parrots," she said after several seconds of silence. "They must have gotten away from their owner, 'cause I'm sure they were tropical birds." Reyanne bit her lip so that her two front teeth forced the blood from her lower lip. "They were flying really fast," she said, "and they looked excited like they couldn't believe they had escaped and were flying again. But you know, those things can't live out here. They don't belong. If someone doesn't get 'em, they're gonna die. I don't know why, but when I saw them birds I thought of my kids."

Wilma clasped Reyanne's hands in both of hers and cradled them for a moment. "You just keep up the good work," she said. "We'll talk to you soon."

Once we were on the road, Wilma said, "I saw you takin' a lot of notes back there. Now remember, you must be careful when you're writing about her ex-husband. I believe what she told us, but you can't write everything down like it's fact just because she said it. You'll need to document her counseling for battering and compile all the information that indicates she was harmed or may have been harmed by him, alright? Then she'll present all the materials to the court. Your job is to let them know if you'd recommend her kids be placed with her. The information about her ex-husband is just a little extra help, so make that a separate section to the home study."

"I'm sure he did all that stuff," I said. I was already going over my approach in my head, formulating an argument, figuring out a way to make the court recognize what he'd done and judge him unfit, and not let him slide by on a trail of his own shit.

"I think he did it, too, Levi," said Wilma, "but things must be proven. And if she doesn't win on this one, well, you can at least feel good that you did what you could to help her. The families and kids we're helping are our people. We're the underdogs, eh? When it really comes down to it, we are the ones who've got to save ourselves, it ain't gonna come from the white world. People like me and you, we're trying to reverse what's been done to us. All this stuff you're seeing—none of it was an issue a hundred years ago. We're trying to hold together our people now. That's why it may be even harder for you to separate what you're seeing from the rest of your life, you know?"

I nodded, feeling a little transparent and wondering if she was speaking generally or giving an unerring reading of what she saw beneath the skin. "Yeah," I said, "I know. But it's tough," I said.

"Yes, it's tough."

The slow driver in front of us, who had been taking the speed limit way too seriously, finally pulled off at a grocery store, and I punched the accelerator. "Okay," I said, "let's make some time."

Wilma chuckled. "Crazy kid."

On the way home, I thought about what Wilma had said and recalled a story my grandma had repeatedly told my sister and me. It was about a powerful race of people, warlike and strong in numbers but without beautiful things. If they had had them at one time, now they had been lost. So they went out into the world and collected all kinds of beautiful things they wanted, such as flowers and birds. They took them home and displayed them, but the flowers died quickly since they were cut from the earth, and the birds perished because they were caged and could not fly. So these people had to go out frequently and collect more beautiful things to replace those they had already killed. And the other peoples who lived in the world around this mighty race forever struggled to save the beautiful things that had always been in their world, and that always had been theirs. Wilma knew this same story.

When I got home, I shed my clothes and found that the shelf where I piled my jeans was down to a pair of 501s that were too tattered to wear to work, even in the absence of a dress code. So I pulled out a load of dirty clothes from the basket and discovered the muddy teddy bear. I threw him into the machine with some shirts, pants, socks, and underwear, and fell asleep to the sound of the dryer rumbling on the other side of my bedroom wall.

Wednesday morning I got a note from Wilma that read: "Regarding that Nicki kid. Luke's moving her in with her auntie as you read this. Yessir, relative placement—auntie and uncle are coming through. Now put on a smile and get to work." I had gotten a good feeling about Nicki's aunt. I remembered her struggle as Nicki walked out with her bags. "It's gotta stop"—that's what she had said.

I looked at the note I had written reminding myself to fax a letter and Reyanne's release of confidentiality to medical records begging for the immediate faxing of Reyanne's documentation. I fed the fax machine a few sheets of exaggerated truth about needing the records immediately to prepare for court. Three hours later the fax machine was regurgitating some real ugly stuff from the records department, a list of injuries that a bull rider could boast of, but belonging to the body of a twenty-eight-year-old housewife and mother: dislocated shoulder, broken wrist, fractured ribs, facial stitches, and a concussion. Let the record show that this woman was having a real serious problem with falling down the stairs and running into doors, I thought sarcastically.

I then spoke with Reyanne's past and present counselors, and I got what I wanted. Hell yes, they believed that Reyanne's allegations were true.

"Well, we're trying to get her kids back; it looks like we might be able to do it," I said to each one. "Would you be willing to make that statement to the court?" They both said yes.

I spent the rest of the day on the computer, sorting through my notes and banging out a home study report for Reyanne Cultee. Next I informed the court that in our professional eyes, and in the eyes of the qualified many who had worked with her, she had made a turnaround and that she was healthy, ready, and fit. Then I drafted "Attachment A" specifying the current reality of her husband's non-compliance and disregard for the court order that clearly stated that she had telephone and eventual visitation rights with the kids. Several copies of phone bills were included, with each attempt standing out from the lists with green neon highlighter and the word rejected typed next to each failed attempt, with a grand total of thirty thwarted calls.

Then I moved on to the hospital records, labeling the new document "Attachment B." It stated: "Herein, the worker and the program director have listed the allegations stated by Reyanne Cultee during an extensive interview against former husband Stacey Peterson, the dates of which coincide with the medical records (also attached). Cultee's counselors, who have worked with her in regard to the issue of battery, attest that she was indeed physically abused, and that her accounts of the abuse, and the emotional manifestations of physical abuse which they observed, are genuine. It is strongly recommended by this agency that the alleged abuse be investigated in light of the evidence gathered herein." The accounts of battery followed, including the dates and the photocopied hospital documents.

I signed the finished product in tall, angular letters then retracted the point back into the pen like a copper fang. Next I made copies for Reyanne and copies for our records, then packaged the originals for the court in a crisp manila envelope. When I dropped it in the box for postage I stared at it for a few moments to savor the last step in my role before the results of our effort were sent to the court. Possibly for the first time in her life, Reyanne might have recourse for what her ex-husband had done.

Connie caught me between the postage box and the door, saying, "I got one for you."

It was a five-year-old boy named Timmy who'd been dropped off for children's anger management by his father, who was also a client, divorced with custody of his son. The father was in recovery from alcohol and drug abuse. This father came to get the kid at a designated time every Tuesday as Connie informed me, and it would be impossible for it to slip his mind since he also dropped him off for each appointment. But today he hadn't shown up, and the shop was closing.

"I think he must have relapsed, drifted into a bar on his way here. I've called CPS and the police are going to come and get him. They're on their way now. I need you to help me tell the boy that we don't know where his dad is and that he's going to spend the night in a foster home for now."

"Yeah, okay. Do you need me to wait until the cops get here?"

"No, that's okay, as long as he's under control."

We took the boy into one of the counseling rooms, and I got him to sit on the floor by the coffee table. "We have something really important to tell you," said Connie. He didn't listen, instead playing with the toy car he'd been carrying around, streaking the polished surface of the coffee table with its rubber wheels.

"We've gotta tell you something, and you need to listen 'cause it's really important," I repeated. He looked up.

"We can't find your dad," said Connie, "so we're going to let you stay with some nice people tonight."

He cocked his head, and his eyes frowned with a look like something not frightening but unbelievable had just been said.

"They're really nice people," I said as if I knew them. "You'll stay with them until we find your dad."

"My dad's on his way to get me," insisted the boy.

"He would have been here if he was on his way," said Connie, "so you need a place to stay until he comes."

He gave three agreeable nods, but the wash of doubt stayed on him as though he were perplexed by such an unexpected change in the functioning of his day. I could see a question moving somberly across his face. What does it mean when Dad doesn't come and get me?

Since he was so controlled, there was no need for me to stay and wait for the cops. As I pulled out of the garage, I decided to drive around to the front of the building and watch them pull up and take the boy away, but after a couple minutes I changed my mind and left. By the time I got home, I had forgotten the boy's name, but I remembered the question on his face: What does it mean when Dad doesn't come and get me? I think I know what it means, Boy, I thought. And you will, too. They go out to cool off; they go out to get drunk; they go out to get milk; sometimes they forget their way home. Sometimes forever.

I took the bandage off my hand and cleaned the cut. After rinsing away the dried blood, I could see that it was healing well.

Verna, the receptionist, was calling my name over the office partition. "Mr. Levi! A woman's been holding for you for quite awhile now, says it's very important!"

"Just a second," I mumbled to the client I was speaking with, and covered up the mouthpiece of the phone. "I'll be ready in a minute."

I ended the conversation, and shouted that I was ready. Connie was walking by my door and she shook her head, her long auburn braid swinging from shoulder to shoulder. "Indian intercom," I heard her say as she passed by.

"Hello, this is Levi," I said with more enthusiasm than usual. I was still feeling good about my involvement with Reyanne, and Nicki's aunt and uncle coming through.

"Hi." The voice cracked slightly and died in a whisper like a brief breath of wind through a pile of leaves.

"Can I help you?" Distressed voices weren't unusual and no cause for alarm.

"This is Liddy," said the voice. "Nicki's mom." She sounded as though her nose were jammed full of cotton and her words ran together in one long hiss of S's. If she hadn't been drinking, she probably wouldn't have called. But what the hell, I'd found her. Maybe.

"Lydia, what's goin' on? Where are you?"

"Well, I'm still over on the other side of the mountain." Her voice rose up and down like something trying to take flight and failing. "How's Nicki doing? Is she okay?" She stifled a sob and took her voice down an octave to keep from crying.

"She's doing okay, considering," I said. "She's got a roof over her head, and people are watching out for her, if that's what you mean, but she's far from happy. You're lucky in a way. Nicki seems to have dismissed her dad, but she's plenty ready to forgive you."

"I want you to know that I'm going to get Nicki. I didn't leave her there. I'm going to do some thinking and get squared away, and then I'll come get her, or send for her. Okay? I don't want you to be putting her somewhere and not giving her back. Don't be thinkin' I blew my chances—got it? 'Cause I'm her mother, and once I'm squared away she belongs with me."

Her words wobbled out of her mouth in fluctuating emotion, occasionally bordering on tears, sometimes sounding almost like the drawling threats of an Old West gunfighter. I pictured the woman I had met padding softly and uneasily around in her entryway, and couldn't put the words in my ear with the face of that woman.

"I agree with you," I said, "she should be with you. But like you said—when you're squared away. And, no, you didn't blow it, but you gotta work to get Nicki back with you and work to keep her with you."

"How old are you?" she interrupted.

"Well, Lydia, I'm twenty-five, if it matters."

"Well, I ain't old enough to be your mother, but I am older."

"I'm not telling you what to do, Lydia; I'm telling you some stuff that needs to get done if you want things to work out."

There were a few moments of silence except for several heavy, drunken sighs. Then I asked, "So you're still in Yakima?"

"Yeah, here with friends, a couple Yakamas. The government introduced us."

While I was asking her what she meant by that, simultaneously I realized the answer.

"Boarding school," she said.

"Yeah, I got it. My grandma was forced into boarding school, too."

"Well, they weren't exactly forcin' people anymore when I went. But what's the difference, what do I know, what do you know?"

My grandma and her brothers and sisters had been taken away to boarding school and returned home for the summers. I remembered hearing some of their stories. They were sad and ugly stories about the conclusive capper to the victorious policies of dealing with the Indians—a concerted effort by school, church, various agents, and enforcers of government law, to dilute the threat of families living under the same roof. The threat of a unified people, holed up on their reservation nurturing dangerous ideals about tradition, could be solved by taking the children, taking their language, taking their customs, taking their pride, and taking their ability to receive what was waiting to be passed on to them.

"Lydia, maybe you should come back for starters," I said.

"Hmm. Not just yet, I ain't ready just yet," she said. Then her voice floated away. The volume held, but she was whispering. Something had kicked its way to the surface of her thoughts, and she was remembering it out loud. It was as if the phone were not there at all, and I were hearing the vision in her head.

"The girl has no fear I think. Several years back she and a friend went out onto one of them bridges that goes up for ships. They went out on it just as it was goin' up, and they lay down and held onto the grating with their fingers."

She paused for a moment, and I could hear her taking time to visualize it, and I could see it vividly, too.

"She rode it all the way up, just hangin' way up there. People waiting in their cars got out pointin' and screamin', 'Hang on, hang on!' She went all the way up and all the way down. She did lots of things like that. I swear that girl's fearless."

"No, she's afraid of things," I said. "She's afraid of all that she stands to lose. She's afraid of not getting back everything that's already been taken away from her at the age of twelve."

"Do you know her better than me?" Lydia tried to sound indignant, but the bite of her question was toothless.

"Of course I don't." My whisper almost matched hers. "Listen, why don't you just come back—get out of the scene you're in right now and start gettin' squared away?"

She ignored my request. "Is Nicki with Frieda still?"

"She will be at any minute now, I imagine. She was in a foster home for a while; Frieda wasn't up to it at first, but now she is."

Lydia drew out her response in a long, bitter, drunken slur. "Frieda gave her up?"

"Lydia, do you hear what you're saying?" I could hear advice Wilma had once given me about talking in circles with drunks popping off like signal flares in my head. "Lydia, Luke Child is the caseworker for Nicki, I'm just doin' some outreach to help. Luke's the one to answer your questions about placement, the case plan, and all that, okay?"

She ignored me again. "I'll call Nicki at Frieda's to let her know that I'm comin' to get her."

"Don't tell her that," I said, with unintended admonition. "You can't just take her. Not anymore."

"I'm going to get her, and I'm going to raise my daughter," she said, as if pleading for her car keys, trying to convince me she was sober enough to drive. "You write that down; you make a note sayin' that I want my daughter back!"

"Come home," I said. "It's time to get squared away."

She attempted to hang up with drama and defiance, but there were a few awkward seconds of clattering plastic before she got the phone into the cradle. I leaned back on the heavy spring of my chair, wondering if I had said the right things to encourage her to come home. I knew what I had wanted to say: "What the fuck are you thinking? How can you possibly justify leaving your kid?"

There was the sweet smell of burning sage, cedar, and sweet grass in the air. The counselors often used it to smudge clients, themselves, and their offices before and after sessions to purify and eliminate all the bad energy floating around. The practice wasn't used by the Indians here on the coast, but with the mix of Indians coming through our door, clients and employees alike, anything positive was used.

I went to Becky's office to tell her about the call from Lydia. Her door was ajar, and smoke was coming from within. I knocked a couple times then eased the door open, poking my head inside. Becky was just setting down a large abalone shell that held gray smoldering ashes and placing an eagle feather next to it.

"Hey," she said with a tired smile, "c'mon in."

I shut the door behind me and sat in a chair in front of her desk.

"Oh, that was a rugged one," she said, dropping her pen on her notepad. "You know the little Jacobson girls, right—Raven and Keisha? You've brought them in here before, haven't you?"

"Oh yeah, the Tlingits," I said. "They look almost like twins. I delivered their Christmas presents to them last year, and brought 'em in here a couple times for groups."

Becky gave a pained smile. "They both provided full disclosures of sexual abuse. I don't know who the perpetrator is yet, but these kids have been sexually abused, and it looks like it was in the home."

Overwrought with disappointment, I shook my head but made a point of not asking anything else about them.

"Wilma was able to get them scheduled for psychological evaluations based on their behavioral problems, but that was before I saw 'em today. They're scheduled for this Monday at 9:30. I'll be talkin' to Wilma about this, and if she says to go ahead with the eval' as planned, I'm wonderin' if you can take them in?"

Enough goddamnit? I'd rather not see them at this time, I thought to myself but wished I could say, feeling the urge to flee the whole scene rising like bile. Instead, my voice floated out with an amiable barbiturate dullness. "Sure I can."

"Good," Becky said. "After I talk to Wilma, I'll let you know if it's still on. If it is, you need to keep an eye out when you're with them."

I nodded, then blinked at Becky a few times, trying to focus out the smear she had wiped across my thoughts. "You're still working with Nicki, right?" I said. Becky slouched forward onto her desk attentively, her miniature dream catcher earrings swinging back and forth from her earlobes.

"Well, do you guys talk about her mother much? I mean, does Nicki talk a lot—wondering where she is and all that?"

"She knows where she is. She's in Yakima, right?"

"Yeah, I just got off the phone with her. She's still in Yakima and she's drunker than a lord. She kept saying stuff about getting Nicki but when she was ready."

"Give me a copy of the narrative for my file, and I'll be talking to Nicki about this during our next session," said Becky, throwing open her black vinyl appointment calendar and scanning the pages. "She needs to know about the call."

"Yeah, I think so, too."

"What'd she say?"

"Just said she was going to get Nicki when she was ready, and not to try and take her away. When I told her to come home and get down to business, she hung up on me."

"Oh, by the way," Becky said, her eyes wandering over the ceiling, "why'd she call you instead of Luke?"

"I don't know, maybe my name was the only one she remembered."

Becky nodded. "Are you taking care of yourself alright?" she asked, sounding concerned.

"I think so," I answered, wanting to acknowledge her concern without discussing it.

She smiled and asked, "Would you like to smudge before you go back to work?" I followed the wave of her hand to where Becky had spread a cloth for the eagle feather and the shell to rest. I nodded sheepishly.

Becky crushed the bluish gray sage leaves into a small ball in the palm of her hand then nestled it in next to the expired ashes. She struck a match and sent several glowing points of fire creeping around the fibers of the ball like tiny fuses. Then she fanned it with the eagle feather and they glowed fiercely and accelerated through the tangle, the living smoke rising forth like spider's silk.

Then Becky got down on one knee, holding the bowl before me and fanning it occasionally with the feather. I put each hand into the smoke, the way I had seen it done many times, cupping it and guiding it over my feet and legs like splashing water from a basin, working my way up my torso and over my face and hair.

"There you are," Becky said when I was finished. "You can go back to work now."

Next I stopped by Luke's office to also tell him about Lydia's call. He had his notebook and clipboard under his arm and appeared to be trying to make a hurried exit. Jones was in the chair by his desk telling a story about social work in Alaska and a client who attacked the foundation of the building with a chain saw while the program director heaved bottles at him through the windows. Luke's face reflected his urgency in trying to depart.

"This'll be quick Luke—sorry Jones; Lydia Sanders called from Yakima, drunk," I reported.

"Is she comin' back?"

"No immediate plans."

"Has she talked to Nicki?"

"I don't think so."

"Leave your documentation of the call on my desk, we'll talk later."

"Got it," I said.

8

Friday afternoon a lesson came disguised as a coup de grâce in my inflamed crusade against the wrongdoers. Having sided with Reyanne against her husband, knowing that Nicki was at least staying with family, and after having three cups of coffee, the pendulum of my mood was for the moment on the upswing. Then I got a crisis call transferred to me from Verna, after the caller apparently confused her with vague babble charged with despair about her missing children, court orders, and child custody. First-time callers rarely asked for specific departments or individuals, so Verna had grown accustomed to assigning new clients. Any indecipherable calls usually went to me.

It was a young woman named Trudy, calling from out of state. She claimed that her ex-boyfriend was in possession of their two children, and that since she had the most current court order awarding her custody, he was holding the kids in Seattle illegally, and she had found out where.

"You say you got the court order awarding you custody?" I said, trying to get a feel of things.

"Yes, I got the order signed by the judge here. I'm at the Tribal Court right now."

"What exactly do you want us to do—I mean, if you have custody why aren't they with you?"

"Well, he had custody at one time, but I got this order now; the appellate court decided in my favor. He was supposed to be at the hearing, too, but he ignored it. He was also expected to have a home study ready for the court date, because I had allegations against him for drinkin', and he didn't do it. So what I'm asking is if you could go help me get the kids. I got his address, but I don't know the area." There were several seconds of silence. "And I'm afraid of him," she added. "He's a violent man—that's why I got away from him."

I wondered why that was always a factor in every goddamned case—a seemingly isolated perversion of family life that in reality thrived behind closed doors with a pervasiveness that cast a leaden gloom over the very foundation of man's integrity and worth. Well let's get the bastard! I thought to myself.

"Where's he have 'em?" I asked.

"I got the address." She read it off. I knew where it was.

"Oh yeah, that's real close, but I'm not sure what we can do for you," I said, wanting to help her make the grab though aware of our limitations. "I mean, we can't actually go take kids, even if you have custody," I continued. "It's probably something that the police have to do or the courts have to ask the police to do—I'm not really sure."

"You can't get them even with the legal order?" she asked, as if the thought were outrageous.

"I can check into it for you if you got a minute," I said. My gut was telling me that this was a decision for someone else.

"What I was thinking," she said, as if she wanted an answer from me and no one else, "was that we could go in tomorrow morning when I know the kids will be there, and you could show him the order and he'd have to give the kids over."

"I'll tell you what, I'll go talk with my supervisor," I said. "I'll tell her the situation, and then I'll call you back, okay? What's your number down there?"

She gave me the number, and asked how long it would take me to call her back.

"Within a half hour," I said.

She thanked me and hung up.

Wilma was frowning as I worked my way through Trudy's story, serving it up as a sequence of unjust facts that demanded our involvement to make things right. When I finished, Wilma's frown turned into a cautious smile and a subtle shake of the head. "Well, you're right about one thing, that you can't go take her kids. If she's got something in her hand from the court saying she's got custody of the kids, she needs to get the police to go get 'em. But maybe it would help if you took her to the precinct out there to help explain her situation. A lot of times our people aren't comfortable with cops. A talker like you could help get things moving—just let the cops get a word in lengthwise, eh?"

"Edgewise," I corrected.

"Ah, get outa here! I was just seeing if you were listening. Now, call the Tribal Court, speak with the judge, and confirm that Trudy was awarded custody most recently. Then meet her at the precinct tomorrow—if you are willing to work on a Saturday—present the order to the cops, and explain what's going on. And be real specific about your role—you are simply there to present the order to the dad and explain it to him; you cannot take the kids if he refuses to give them up. You ask him if he will give them to Trudy since she has legal custody, and if he says no then you wish him a good day and go home. Tell the police you only want them to observe so that no dastardly deeds go down. You got that?"

"Yeah, sounds good."

"Now if the police will not escort you on this little venture then you are to wish her luck and go home. You don't know anything about her husband, and we're not in the business of gettin' hurt. Got it? Remember, you're not a cowboy, you're an Indian."

"Good one," I said.

"What'll probably happen is this guy'll see the police, see the order, and think he's up against more than he actually is, even though the police aren't there to take any physical action. See, what they need in order to take the kids by force is a pick-up order not a custody order."

I got up to make the call, and Wilma followed me to the doorway. Vicki and Becky were out of their offices getting coffee and stretching their legs. "The kid here is working Saturday," Wilma announced. "He's going out with the police to grab some kids. Yup, I remember when I was young."

Vicki and Becky both smiled at me.

"No social life, huh?" Vicki teased.

"Come to think of it, no," I said, slipping into my office to avoid any further abuse.

I dialed the number for Tribal Court, and a woman picked it up on the second ring.

"Hi, can I speak to Trudy, please?"

"Oh yeah, she's right here."

"Hi, Trudy. Okay—what I'll need to do is talk to the judge to confirm the order. Can you have the court clerk transfer me to her extension?"

"Well, the judge is gone home for the day, and the court's closed. My friend is the clerk here, and I'm using her phone."

I looked at the wall clock. It was 4:40 P.M.

"Here's what I can do," I said, explaining what Wilma had told me. "If he closes the door in our faces, then we have to leave, and you'll have to go back to court and get a pick-up order. Do you understand?"

"Yeah, that sounds alright," she said.

I gave her directions to the precinct closest to her kids. We chose 10:00 A.M. for the meeting time.

"Hey, one other thing," I said, worried about not having talked to the judge. "Hang on and I'll be right back."

I stuck my head in Wilma's office.

"Wilma, the judge isn't available to confirm the order, but since we're not taking the kids—since he'll be handing them over of his own free will and the police will be there, it's still alright, isn't it?"

Wilma looked at me for a moment, processing what I'd just said. "Yeah, leave it up to the police."

I went back into my office and picked up the phone. "Okay, it's set. I'll meet you at the precinct."

"Fuckin' lightweights!" I slipped into a long drifting pause and took a gulp of beer. Arti and I were now alone in the bar. Two classmates of his had joined us for a drink, and I couldn't wait for them to leave. After a couple of hours of watching me grow exponentially uglier, they had done just that. I don't think Arti really gave a shit about my treatment of them; I hadn't treated them poorly, exactly, I just hadn't made much of an effort at being friendly or tactful.

Don, who had been with us, too, had also left, about twenty minutes after the two students. He had put his hand over the mouth of his glass, claiming he was full and had to get up early, which was undoubtedly true because Don would simply tell me to fuck off before making an excuse.

"I think everyone leaving had something to do with your negativity," Arti said. "Just maybe."

"Let's go stomp someone," I responded, glaring at each person in the bar and pondering why I'd probably hate him if I knew him.

"Who do ya wanna get?" asked Arti, agreeable person that he was.

"Some deserving bastard! There's plenty of 'em!"

"Suppose you get someone who doesn't deserve it?" Arti cautioned. "You're opposed to that and you'd regret it."

"Naw, I'm talkin' about some fuck who deserves to be kicked into a bleeding heap of jelly! Someone we know's got it comin'. Let's find that someone and stomp his goddamned guts out!"

My voice grew louder. I felt eyes on the perimeter shooting glances, the white flash of faces suspended and turning like plates on wires, quickly there, then gone again.

"Shit, I can't think of anybody," said Arti.

"Someone who's got it comin'. Think! Has anyone fucked with you or your family lately?"

Arti was thinking, not trying to pacify me but making a genuine effort at thinking. "Umm, not that I've noticed."

"Okay, let's go find some real asshole," I hissed, leaning forward over the table.

"Someone worse than you?" Arti said, beaming, his eyes as cloudy as the scuffed glass of a gumball machine.

"What are ya talkin' about? Someone much worse! Some piece of shit!" I shouted. "What are you lookin' at?"

There was a guy at the next table looking at me for too long. He turned away pretending not to have heard. I stared at the back of his head, hating him.

I poured two more glasses of beer, emptying the pitcher. One of the tables next to ours had a half-full one that someone had left so I leaned over to grab it but almost fell out of my chair. I retrieved the pitcher and slammed it to the table, the beer sloshing against the sides slowly and heavily like molten copper.

"Hey, my cousin broke up with her boyfriend 'cause he punched her out. How's that?" Arti offered, nodding his head up and down with sudden recollection, in time with the rise and fall of the beer. It made me momentarily seasick so I reached across the table and palmed his forehead to hold him still. His slender face and weighted down eyelids made him look kind of seedy, with the corner of his mouth cranked up into a stupid and threatening smile.

"Let's go!" I settled back into my seat instead of rising accordingly to my feet.

"Wait a minute," he said. "What are you plannin' to do, go fight him? Here's an idea. He drives this car, it's his life—you've seen the type. Works on the fuckin' thing all the time—big muscle car. It's got these big ol' racing tires, big ol' fuckin' engine, polished to a shine, the envy of all prepubescent fuckers with no driver's license."

I slammed my fist against the table. "Let's go trash the fucker!"

"Okay, lemme finish my beer."

"Finish up," I said. "What time is it anyway? I got business bright and early. I have kids to save, goddammit!" Everyone in the place hazarded a glance our way.

Arti brought his wrist up to his face. "It's 12:15."

Arti drove. I stopped at home and got a crowbar, a filleting knife, and a .357 magnum.

"If he comes out, we kill him! He comes out, we fuckin' kill him!" I shouted.

Arti drove straight to the place and crept slowly past, pointing and whispering, then stopped half a block down the street. He reached up and turned the switch on his dome light so that it wouldn't come on when we opened the door. "Do a job on it," he whispered. "His pride and joy, his wet dream, his life—go fuck it up!"

It was all polished up for the showroom, a deep inky blue thing with white streaks of streetlight burning along its buffed edges, undoubtedly a look he'd sweated into it, rubbing with a shammy—

like anybody gave a shit. In the illumination of the distant street-lights, it looked like it had never been driven, with immaculate white lettering curved around the wide, unblemished, tires.

I circled it like a stalking animal, reveling in its probable importance to the asshole who slept in the house forty feet away. Then I punched the thin blade of the filleting knife into the soft rubber and slid it along with a tremendous gush of air, the car sagging awkwardly with the collapse of each tire like a slaughterhouse steer dropping to its knees.

I looked around the neighborhood, which was dark and still. So I wound up the crowbar and smashed out the back window, two feet of safety glass dropping into the backseat of the car with a sound like thousands of beads scattering on a linoleum floor. Then I smashed the side windows and the windshield in several swings, glittering cubes of glass like an explosion of ice spraying off the curve of the crowbar. Then I went around to the front of the car, still looking at the windows—shut like big dull eyes with drugged heavy lids—and took the .357 magnum out from my belt. "Yeah fuck!" Boom! Boom! Boom! Three huge bullets punched through the hood like secondary explosions, the paint around the holes disintegrating in circles of shiny silver. The barrel swung around and up at the windows of the house, the blunt, fat muzzle searching the curtains. I wanted to keep shooting, to empty the thing.

But instead I started to jump into the car, and Arti ripped away from the curb before I was all the way in. "Jesus Christ! What the fuck? What the fuck?" he shouted.

"I got carried away."

Five blocks went by. "I hope that fuckin' gun ain't registered!"

"It's not."

Six more blocks. "Did you see any lights come on?"

"No. Nothin'."

Finally we hit the freeway. A bellow tore spontaneously from Arti's throat—primal, rising to a scream, blazing and feeding on its own energy.

When I got home, I called my mom. She answered with breathy urgency before the second ring, like all mothers fearing calls that come in the dead of night at 2:00 A.M.

"I'm falling apart," I said. "Something's wrong with me."

"What are you saying—what's going on—where are you?" All the lights were out in my apartment, the pistol a black lump on the table in front of me. "You haven't been calling. And now you do, and it's this. What's goin' on?"

"Who gives a shit? Caring doesn't change a thing, and I don't give a shit!"

"Your job. You're having a hard time dealing with it. That's it, isn't it?"

I began raving and slurring about doom and futility. She offered suggestions and tried to give supportive advice, but I shot it all down.

9

I woke up and sat on the edge of the bed with a headache, drinking pints of water in the darkness, some morning light struggling through the dusty blinds. Then I took a shower, some Maalox, some vitamins, and was ready.

On the way out to the police station, I was already running late when the bridge on Eastlake went up for a huge yacht. I sat for five crawling minutes with thirty other motorists, amazed at the rich bastard and his power to stop an entire row of traffic as he sailed out to get his jollies on a floating condo. The mast passed through the gap, gliding before our faces like an enormous middle finger, and the bridge slowly came back together like a settling compound fracture.

I was preparing my spiel to the cops as I worked my way up the hill overlooking Seattle, concentrating on the strength of persuasion and the impact of appearance and presentation—a straight back, a sharp unfaltering gaze, and a verbal whirlwind of bullshit.

Being behind schedule I was moving at a good clip when I suddenly came upon the off-kilter image of a wreck. The jarring picture before my windshield sent my foot to the brake and my mind to the block beyond, as I perceived the immobile battered cars in my path. Both had been flung wildly, only seconds ago, by the hands of uncompromising forces, coming to rest in dangerous contrast with the yellow painted rules of the road. One of the cars was a Honda Civic turned fully sideways so that it completely blocked the oncoming lane, while the other was a mid-sized four-wheel-drive pickup that had apparently not stopped before attempting to cross the street where the Honda had the right of way. The pickup was at an angle in my lane, its front bumper crossing slightly over into the oncoming lane. The Honda was about forty feet beyond, its passenger door completely concave, glass and black rubber blemishing the pavement between the point of impact and the Honda's final resting place. Hardly slowing, I moved into the oncoming lane in a sudden slalom around the truck, and having cleared it—after briefly perceiving a young woman, still clutching the wheel and shaking her head in disbelief, I saw the driver of the Honda, already out of his car, his face near the center of my windshield. He moved toward me with his hands raised palms out—the silent instruction to stop—so that I could go for help, serve as a witness, or perhaps more fundamentally to stop his bleeding. His palms were white and thrust out with command and urgency, and his eyes, whiter yet, bulged out at me through a mask of blood that covered his entire visage. He had obviously shattered the windshield with his forehead. Head injuries bleed like the dickens, but he seems alright, I thought.

I continued my move around the redundant scene of bloodshed that had arisen not from injustice but from idiocy—from mankind pouring into one another's screwy, overcrowded space, impatiently, negligently. I slowed a little and swerved to the right, back into my lane, then, quite accidentally, up onto the curb, the two tires on the right side of my car bumping up onto the stretch of grass on the side of the road. I was still looking at the man with the bloody face as I maneuvered away from any involvement with the scene and plowed into two brown plastic garbage cans on the curb. They exploded off the bumper, their lids popping up like champagne corks, catching air like parachutes then smashing into the windshield and over the top of my car, with refuse confetti fanning out over the hood and blowing forward in an impressive arc—grass, milk cartons, avocado peelings, and other unidentifiable human byproducts. A used tampon rolled toward me in a spinning blur and got caught beneath a wiper blade, while a damp spray of coffee grounds soiled the hood. The plastic cans passed beneath me with the disagreeable scream of eggshells in a garbage disposal, and within a second or two they were gone, and I was off the curb and back into my lane. I shot a quick glance in the rearview mirror, and saw the bleeding man looking after me with his arms hanging limply at his sides in a mundane sort of amazement, the kind devoid of true wonder or excitement, the kind of amazement that comes from witnessing something fatally disappointing. For a moment I was ashamed that the bleeding man had read me wrong. But I had important business to attend to, and he seemed basically okay.

When I walked into the police station, I saw the two Indian women who appeared to be in their late twenties seated in a small waiting area of dark brown sofas centered around a circular glass table. They stared at me, and one of them looked as if she were going to get up but became unsure and settled back down. I walked over and said, "Is one of you Trudy?"

"I'm Trudy." Her eyes were swollen, probably from driving all night. I thought this reflected a real hardcore maternal commitment and how eager she must be to get her children back. She was wearing gray sweat pants and a well-worn, white and green Pendleton coat that was too big for her. The enthusiasm and fire that Trudy had shown over the phone had mysteriously disappeared, completely. But as tired and nervous as Trudy probably was, her wilted demeanor was understandable.

"I'm Levi," I said putting out my hand. She took it for a moment then quickly let go to point at her friend. "This is Elsy," she said. "She drove us." Her eyes hit mine, then bounced over to her partner.

Elsy shook my hand like a white person, a hard squeeze and two firm shakes. She looked tired, too, but she was alert in a strung-out sort of way—bristling a little beneath the surface. She was wearing heavy black eyeliner, with blue shadow painted right to the tops of her eyelids and out past the corners of her eyes, where the mascara ended in two black tails, pointing slightly up. Her brown bangs were sprayed into a stiff sail of hair that fanned about five inches off her forehead. She gave me a challenging look reflecting both seduction and disdain.

"Have you talked to the police yet?"

They both answered. "No."

"Do you have the court order?"

Trudy had been holding it in her hand and gave it to me. I scanned it quickly. I walked to the front desk, where an officer was talking on the phone. He glanced at me then looked up at the ceiling as if the sight of me were muddling his train of thought. I took the last moments of his conversation to read through the order awarding Trudy Williams custody of Luanna and Donny Reeves.

Soon the officer hung up the phone. I introduced myself and the program I represented, not giving my job title but presenting myself as an advocate for Trudy. I showed him the court order and unleashed my explanation of the father's unauthorized detainment of the children, his noncompliance with court attempts to reach him, our plan of paying him a visit, and then threw in our suspicions that he might be dangerous to boot. He held up his hand to stop me, then told me I was going to have to speak to the sergeant.

I walked back to where Trudy and Elsy waited.

"He's checking with the sergeant," I said, annoyed at the thought that he might present our plan without sufficient explanation and doom the whole thing.

Elsy looked out the window and Trudy at the floor. I moved to the couch across from them and set my clipboard down on the coffee table.

"How long's he had the kids?" I asked.

Trudy's eyes widened, and she rolled them up toward the ceiling. "Umm, about a year, I think—we didn't know where he was."

It didn't enter my mind at the time to ask how he had gotten custody in the first place, and why it had taken a full year for her to find them.

"Do you think he might put up a fight, do you feel that he's dangerous?" I asked. She had answered this before, but I wanted to hear it again.

"Oh, yeah," she said.

Elsy was still gazing out the window. "He's an asshole," she muttered.

I looked from her to Trudy. After a moment she looked at me and nodded confirmation of Elsy's statement.

An officer with a full blonde mustache and sergeant stripes came out and asked who I was. I rose quickly to address him, and my hangover washed over me. I could feel myself turning green as I gave my name and the name of the program. Then I produced the order, ready to pass it to him but keeping it just close enough to my body to let him know that he couldn't take it until I had completed my colorful tale of the law that was being broken. He kept his eyes on mine, frowning subtly, without so much as a glance at the paper in my hand. When I was finished, I handed him the order.

He worked his way through the document. "This is a tribal thing," he said, more as a statement than a question. "I'm thinking that a court order may have to be issued in Washington for it to be acted on."

"Actually I don't believe that's true," I offered. "Because it's tribal, it stands in any state. Tribal members fall under the jurisdiction of Tribal Court in Indian child welfare matters." It wasn't a child welfare matter, it was a custody matter, but my head was aching, and I wanted to get this thing underway.

He thought about this while scrutinizing Elsy and Trudy.

"What I mean is," I continued, "Tribal Court orders carry the same weight as state or county court orders. These children are under the jurisdiction of the Tribal Court, and they've been awarded to the mother."

"Wait here," he muttered looking back down at the order. "I'll be right back."

When he returned, he had two more young cops with him. They formed a semicircle around me with their hands resting on their heavy black utility belts that creaked when they shifted their weight. Both men had perfect haircuts, the creases of their bulletproof vests embossing lines through their pressed blue shirts.

Trudy had moved forward, sensing that things were going in her favor. "Are you the mother?" the sergeant asked, gesturing toward her.

"Yes."

"Would you describe your ex-husband as aggressive or potentially violent?"

"He's not my ex-husband; we were never married."

"The man is potentially violent?"

"No, not potentially. He is violent. I got his address," Trudy said, all in the same breath, as if his address somehow correlated with his violent temperament. She pulled a piece of folded yellow notebook paper from her coat pocket and nervously pressed out the crinkles against her palm.

The sergeant looked at the address. "This is just down the road," he said, handing it to the officer to his right.

"Here's what we'll do. Officers Sullivan and Mitchell will accompany you to present the order to the father. Your advocate will need to present the order and see if he'll relinquish the children voluntarily. If he refuses, I would recommend you see if the King County Superior Court will issue a pick-up order in support of this one."

"That would be perfect," I said. "We appreciate it."

"Okay, why don't you just follow the escorting officers to the home."

"That'll work." I looked over to Trudy and Elsy. Elsy had the traces of a smile, like the ones you try to suppress when you've gotten out of a speeding ticket. Trudy looked nervous.

"You two might as well ride with me," I said to her. She nodded.

Trudy was in the passenger's seat, Elsy in the back. I could see Elsy in the rearview looking from side to side, our eyes occasionally meeting for a fraction of a second in the eight inches of mirror.

"Are you two related?" I asked.

"Nope," Trudy said. "Just good friends."

I could see the cops acknowledging other squad cars that we passed on the road with nods and waves. After a few blocks, we entered the project, a shelf of low-income housing that curved like an apron around the base of Capitol Hill in the shadow of several hospitals. It was a small tract of gray, uniform housing with "no trespassing" signs posted about every twenty feet, all defaced with swirling, territorial gang scribble. There were small play areas at intervals, with swing sets, sandboxes, and slides, cordoned off from the streets by high chain-link fences. Some units had clotheslines stretched from back porch awnings, weighted down with sheets and towels, while others used the short picket fences for drying laundry.

The asphalt street was warped and shattered in spots like the mortared tarmac of a landing zone, with holes big enough to hold puddles. We took a right and headed down a gradual decline. A young black kid, wearing a shower cap watched the cops and our car pull up to the curb and decided to take up a spectator's position against a telephone pole. I parked behind the cops, scanning for addresses on the units, each a mirror image of the others. I saw that number 243 was the corner apartment.

The police were already out of their car. I took my clipboard with the order fastened to it and followed. The car parked behind us was a brown station wagon with the front end so mangled it looked like one of the automotive casualties the police haul around to high schools to scare the shit out of potential drunk drivers. I could hear the sound of Harborview Hospital's chopper overhead, its rotors beating the air above the neighborhood, racing to a tragedy somewhere far away.

Then I saw the kids in the front yard, wearing baggy sweats and puffy ski jackets, the girl sitting on the lawn and the boy next to her, a few bright plastic cars scattered around them. They both looked at the police and me. Then their mother got out of the car, whispered loudly, "That's them," and began moving forward. The police had already ambled onto the lawn toward the children, making a few nonchalant semiturns as they advanced.

When the children saw their mother, they froze, both immobile as illustrations without excitement or joy.

We began marching up to the two little statues, their heads tilting back in sync with our approach like they were watching storm clouds rolling overhead. Finally the kids got up, and the boy said, "Mom?" the area around his mouth stained orange with Kool Aid. The police turned to face us and asked, "Are these the kids?"

Trudy was still closing the gap. "Yes," she answered, speeding up. "What should I do?"

Mitchell looked up to unit 243, then back at the children. "Just take them," he said.

Trudy broke into a run and scooped up the boy. Elsy, close behind, grabbed the girl.

"Take 'em to the car," I added and hurried up next to the police. I took one quick look back to see the two women scooting off to the car, the kids lost in their coats, legs swinging from side to side.

We walked up the stairs to the house, and I got the court order ready. The door was halfway open, propped in place by a heavy can of commodity lunch meat. A man was sitting inside facing us, elbows on his thighs, slender forearms resting between his knees. He had a broad forehead, and his hair was combed back from it in a sweep of black. The tidy living room immediately struck me as familiar. I saw pictures of his family near the couch where he sat, portraits in stands and frames, or hung on the walls with finish nails and tape: young men wearing crew cuts and dress uniforms of the Army and Marine Corps, elders and children in black-and-white and color. There was an American flag sagging on the wall above the couch, and next to it the flag of the American Indian. A pair of deer antlers stuck out between both flags, with one long wing feather hanging from a horn point, the quill bound in beaded leather. Suddenly the man's eyes moved from the TV to the three figures in the doorway, and he rose up in shock. Then his eyes ignited with alarm, although his face remained composed as he approached the door.

I could feel the police moving up behind me, one on each shoulder, our presence feeling large as we encroached on the small space, knocking the sun's light out of the doorway. Now near the door, the father leaned forward, placing his hand against the doorjamb as if to barricade against any thoughts we might have of entering.

"Are you Jerry Reeves?" I asked.

"Yeah, that's me. What's the problem?" he answered sharply, making quick eye contact with all three of us.

I removed the court order from the clipboard and showed it to him. "Well, this is a recent court order from your tribe."

He craned his head forward with a jerk, his eyebrows diving into a frown like I was showing him a photograph of the devil. "For what?" he barked, his eyes pouncing on different paragraphs of the document too erratically to be reading it.

"I'm with Urban Native Support Services," I said, and took the card that I had previously placed in the inside pocket of my coat. I removed the court order from the clipboard and handed it to him with my card. "It's the most recent order from the Tribal Court, giving your ex-wife custody of the children."

"We were never married," he said defensively. Then quickly realizing there was something much more important at hand, he snapped, "I have custody? When was this decided? They can't decide this without me gettin' to say something!"

"The court doesn't conduct proceedings like this without notifying the parties involved," I said, still holding the order for him to take. His eyes remained locked onto mine with a look of total bewilderment. Finally, he snatched the order out of my hand. Trying to calm down enough to read it, he was more frightened than angry. Suddenly, the gathering tension dropped from his face, and he said, "Is she here?" sticking his head out the door. He could see that the kids were gone, but he couldn't see the car from his vantage point. Officer Sullivan took a step forward, physically blocking him from passing me.

"Now wait a minute," Jerry implored, retreating into the house. "Let me show you my court papers givin' me custody."

"Just take a look at this latest date," Sullivan said in an attempt to de-escalate the situation. "That order was signed by the judge yesterday, and obviously that makes it the most current. You missed this hearing, but you have the option of getting another day in court by contacting your tribe and requesting it—I'd imagine—and that's when you'll have your opportunity to present your case. We're just here to inform you of the order."

Jerry thought about this for a minute, his whole body edgy, fighting the urge to push his way outside and confirm his suspicion. "They didn't contact me! I heard nothin' about a hearing!"

"You're going to have to take that up with the court," I said from the doorway. "Apparently they made efforts to contact you."

He focused back on me. His hand that held the order dropped to his side. "Do you work for the tribe?" he asked.

"No, but I'm presenting this order on behalf of the tribe."

"How can you do this—comin' here with the police and takin' my kids?"

The question caught me off guard and angered me. "What do you mean by that?" I said after a moment of blankness, feeling my eyes narrow bitterly and hearing the deliberate loathing in my voice.

"A system Indian, huh?" he muttered, shaking his head. "Don't even know what you're doin'."

I let out a sarcastic laugh and said, "What's that supposed to mean?"

System Indian, I thought to myself. "Don't pull that red apple shit on me, like you're some kinda victim. Fuck you, piece a shit! You don't know the first thing about me." A red apple is someone who is red on the outside, white on the inside. I had heard that one before.

"She took them, didn't she?" Jerry finally said, directly to me.

"Yes, she did," I said, "and your opportunity to get them back is through the court system—just as she did."

We began moving down the steps.

"Something's wrong!" Jerry blurted. "Just let me talk to her." He moved around me, his back rubbing against the side of the house with a sound like fingers against a chalk board. Jumping down the cement staircase, he could now see the car with his children in it.

Sullivan and Mitchell stopped and stood shoulder to shoulder blocking his path. Sullivan had begun repeating our position. Mitchell turned to me and whispered, "Take them out of here."

I nodded and turned to go. Halfway to the car I looked back to see Officer Sullivan holding his left hand against Jerry's chest, his other hand resting on his belt by his nightstick. Jerry was leaning slightly against the hand, looking from the cops to me and speaking rapidly, his eyes trapped and desperate.

I marched up to the car with confident steps, the adrenaline ebbing, enjoying the ensuing catharsis of doing right. I got into the car with the mother and her saved children. The kids were sobbing hard, not tears of joy but of fright and anguish. Each woman held a child tightly as if to squeeze their shaking to a stop.

"What's wrong with them?" I asked. "Are they okay?"

"Oh, they're just scared," she said, turning her daughter's face away from me. "We'll go get some ice cream," she whispered into the soft brown hair, but the words had no effect.

I suddenly felt strange, like people weren't acting the way they should be—mainly the kids. On the side of the road some cardboard boxes that had probably been stacked at the corner for the Salvation Army had been upset and were lying at a haphazard angle with spilled clothing and bags. Lying on her face was a doll about as big as a one-year-old child, her artificial hair sprayed forward and spread around the head as if from the impact of falling, with arms outstretched, palms flat down on the sidewalk in an effective mimic of unconsciousness.

I dropped the family that I had just reunited off in the parking lot of the police station and got out of the car. The children had quieted to soft whimpers, wiping at their eyes and cheeks as the women loaded them into their battered blue Plymouth.

"Drive safely," I said.

Trudy looked over at me like she'd forgotten I was there, then waved and said, "Okay."

Their car rattled to life, and they pulled away with no semblance of a thank you. I stood in the parking lot for a moment like a jilted lover, trying to make sense of the events of the last twenty minutes. I couldn't and drove home confused, sensing that something was wrong, and that this was not over.

Monday morning when my alarm went off I woke with a start, emitted a short strange gasp, and nearly leaped out of bed, feeling like an aberrant Chicken Little with doom descending. I looked up, expecting tons of garbage to come down on me like an avalanche, but the crush was from within. I was sick with angst, knowing that something born of the Saturday child grab would come for me at work: a phone call, a memo, or perhaps the father himself. A scolding voice began to babble: You acted too quickly. You assumed the woman was truthful. Somehow I knew that today I would begin to find an answer to my question of why the whole episode had left me feeling like the gavel had been dropped before all the evidence had been reviewed.

Friday afternoon there had been a memo in my mailbox from Becky stating that the Monday evaluation for the Jacobson girls was on. The appointment was at 9:30 A.M., early enough to prevent me from checking in at the office first and sufficiently time-consuming to keep me away from it until about noon.

Consequently, I went and got the girls, Raven and Keisha, and thought about Becky's warning to keep an eye out for any sexual behavior. This was a very strange thing to think about with girls only seven and eight years old. While Raven played with the radio stations and abused my speakers with excessive volume, I began thinking about Saturday's child grab. Mentally I dissected the circumstances, considering my role, trying to ascertain how much of my resolve had been based on legalities and how much had been based on wanting to believe that Jerry Reeves deserved punishment and vilification. What mattered now, however, was keeping the program and myself in the clear. Worried, I remembered what Wilma had said about the need for a pick-up order. I wondered if Trudy had needed a pick-up order to legally take the kids from his care, regardless of the fact that he wasn't standing in the yard to stop her. If so, then she shouldn't have taken the kids. If so, then I had helped her. Finally, I concluded, the kids were hers, plain and simple—to hell with it.

I escorted the little girls into their appointment with the mental health worker, then grabbed a bite to eat at a nearby diner. I thought about calling work for my messages, then decided against it. After the appointment, I dropped the girls off at their school and headed for work.

I walked in, ready, looking to the black memo caddie on Verna's desk. I greeted Verna, waiting for her to say something about an angry father who'd been calling all morning. "You got a few calls," she said smiling and returned to thumbing through the Sears Catalogue.

I had four phone memos: one from Josie Tall Fighter, one from Nicki, one from Jerry Reeves, and one from the judge at the Tribal Court, as well as a note from Wilma saying, "Come see me."

Wilma's door was open a crack so I walked into her office and took a seat, clipboard across my knees.

Wilma initiated the exchange, saying, "Well, you got the kids." It wasn't a question but a statement.

"Yup, we did." I made sure I pulled the other parties in with me.

Wilma frowned and chewed the inside of her lip. "We have some sorting out to do. First, you can tell by your memos that this is a little more complicated than it might have seemed."

"Yeah, I know," I said.

"The dad called looking for you, really pissed off. He said you came with cops, scared the hell out of him, and took his kids without giving him any kind of chance to show you that he had custody. He said that he called the Tribal Court and demanded to know what was going on, that he was never notified of any court date or told to have a home study done. He also claims that the drinking allegations made against him in court were not only untrue but that Trudy couldn't possibly have known anything about what's going on with him because they haven't seen or spoken to each other in over a year. Finally, he said that the court clerk claimed she sent instructions by certified mail, return receipt requested, telling him to have the home study conducted, and that she then called him to follow up, informing him that he needed to be present at the hearing. But he swears that he never spoke with her, never got any mail, and that this particular clerk is friends with Trudy." Wilma sighed and rattled on in monotone. "I told him that I would talk with the judge down there, then I phoned her. She told me that she had called for you and that you weren't here. She had already talked with Jerry. As you know, on the reservation everybody knows everybody, and after checkin' into things a little, she found out that the court clerk, whose name is Elsy something, came to Seattle with Trudy to get the kids."

"Oh, shit," I muttered, preparing to defend myself.

"Did she?" Wilma asked, knowing the answer.

"Yeah, she was there."

Wilma's voice assumed the grave tone of discovery. "Well, this is the same clerk who supposedly sent the summons and instructions to the dad, and supposedly made phone contact to inform him verbally of the court date and to let him know that he was to have his home study completed and filed with the court before the review. The clerk also said that he was in a drunken rage when she called—

a little bit of added color. Real conflict of interest here."

"Yeah, she seemed to be the driving force behind the whole thing," I said.

"Well, the judge is real concerned about it, and she's looking into the situation right now. Oh, yeah, another thing is that Trudy isn't a member of the tribe; she belongs to a Canadian band. But she said to the court that she'd be getting tribal housing on the reservation with her kids, since the kids are enrolled there. The judge is checking around to see if she's returned with the kids yet."

It was sounding pretty ugly, but Wilma hadn't addressed the most important item. "No one's blaming us are they?" I asked with trepidation.

"Jerry is. He thinks you were totally unreasonable and rude." Wilma smiled despite the virulence of the situation.

"But the order was real!" I said. "We had no way of knowing!"

"Right," Wilma said, shaking her index finger at me with conviction. "The order was a valid Tribal Court order, and the judge said that she appreciated us honoring it. No one knew about the court clerk crap yet."

"Right," I said, concentrating on firmly establishing my innocence and proper conduct, not yet thinking about the children. "We had no way of knowing."

"I'm waiting to hear back from the court to see what they found out about the mother's whereabouts. If Trudy's still in the state, they might need our help."

I sat in silence, idly fingering the memos.

"Don't worry about those," Wilma said. "I've pacified the dad for now. He's waiting to hear from you, though, after you've gotten more info."

"Okay. Do you want me to do anything?"

Wilma put her palms together and rested her chin on the tips of her fingers. "You've done enough." Then she laughed. "Jokes, we'll wait and see, but I'll tell you one thing, don't work on Saturdays anymore, eh?"

I decided not to ask about the details of taking the kids without a pick-up order and whether or not Trudy's taking them from the yard made any difference. There was enough to think about.

"What's really too bad," said Wilma, "is that this type of crap reflects badly on the court, you know? This one woman pulls a stunt and puts a bad light on the Tribal Court system."

"Yeah," I said. "Is the court gonna call for you or for me?"

"I left your name, too, though she'll probably ask for me. But don't worry, if there's any work to be done I'll let you know. You gotta be wary, you know?" continued Wilma. "Some of our people will pull the wool out from under you. Oh, shit, I got that wrong, enit?"

"Yeah."

"It's rug, right?"

"Yeah, pull the rug out."

Wilma closed her eyes and rubbed her temples, rocking back and forth slightly like she were going to sleep in her chair. "Let me ask you something," she said. "I know your dad is Indian. Is your mom?"

"No, just my dad."

"Where is he?"

"I don't know."

"How old were you when he left?"

"I don't know—five, six, eight. I'm not sure."

"Wow," Wilma said, her eyes widening. "You really don't know how old you were? You could have been five, you could have been eight? Did you see him after he left?"

"No."

"I got a story for you. When I was about fourteen, a couple of girls on my res decided they didn't like me so they jumped me, and I got my ass kicked. My mom, Violet, flew into a rage—nothing could go unavenged with her. She hauled me into the car and went around asking questions based on the descriptions she'd pried out of me. It was really embarrassing, sitting there, all sulky with my fat lip sticking out. My mom was able to figure out who the girls were, even though I volunteered as little as possible. She called the Tribal Police, and they picked 'em up. The first time my mom saw the girls was when they were brought before the judge. They were smaller than me, and they were wearing moccasins. My mom's eyes narrowed when she saw 'em both standin' there lookin' just cute. Then she scolded me in front of the judge and everyone else in the courtroom because she thought I should've been able to take those little girls. As a result, she dropped the charges and dragged me out of there in disgust. I died right there on the spot. I didn't care if those girls got in trouble, but my mom managed to show me how worthless I was in front of the whole damned world." Wilma laughed loudly, shaking her head. "Oh, those two little toughies in their moccasins," she said, gasping for air. "I hated my mom for that, but damn it, it's kinda funny now, dontcha think? My mom's not much different now, just older. But I forgive her for all her shit, and we get along alright."

"That is pretty funny," I said. "My dad was a little like that, I mean he had a chip on his shoulder like yer mom. He wouldn't give me a ride home from school once until I punched an older kid who kicked my books out of my hand while I was waiting for my ride. But that was nothin' really compared with other things he did. He was pretty angry."

"How old were you when he left?" Wilma asked me again. The look on her face was determined, insisting I admit to myself what she was certain of—that I knew more than I acknowledged.

"I was eight," I said.

Wilma nodded with a frown that was somehow a resigned smile. "Yer situation was different than mine in that your dad left. My dad was absent in the sense that he worked and watched TV. My mom ruled the household on a lifetime supply of fury stored up from boarding school. She lit into my dad with her fists and fingernails on many occasions and had complete disregard for her own safety. I looked just like her, people would see me comin' and say, 'There's Little Violet. She's half the size and half as mean.' As an adult I needed to forgive her, at least to some degree, for my own sake. If a person's parents did something so bad you just can't forgive 'em, then maybe it's best to try and understand what made 'em that way. You ain't gonna get even with 'em."

"That's what I told Nicki a little while ago, when I told her not to hurt herself," I said.

"Think real hard about what you said to her," added Wilma. "When one of my workers starts showin' up with bandaged hands and looking like he hasn't slept in a week, I take it as a sign of bad things goin' on in here." She placed her index finger on her heart.

I held her gaze then looked down at the floor. "You really had it in for Jerry Reeves, didn't you?" she said. "I could feel it. You wanted him to be wrong. You're a smart kid, you're a good kid, and I'm not jumpin' on you about this. Just don't think people don't know yer havin' a hard time. You can't just ignore it. You gotta pay attention to it."

"Whether I like or not," I said.

"Yeah, whether you like it or not."

Despite Wilma's empathy and support, I was embarrassed and kept my eyes on the floor. Then Wilma announced suddenly, "The Jacobson girls. You drove 'em to that eval' today."

"Yeah, I did."

"Becky talked to me Thursday about their disclosure. She reported to CPS immediately, and now the state's got the case. Becky's going to keep working with them after she gets a disclosure about the perpetrator, and they'll use the psychological evaluation in conjunction with Becky's findings. Apparently the physical exam found the oldest girl to have some tissue damage from penetration. The worker's already filed a shelter care order."

"So what happens?"

"They stay in foster care pending all the findings. But here's the thing, I don't want to put you at risk by driving them anymore. The foster parents and their worker can do that. You don't know what abused kids will say, you know?"

Codeine and a six-pack, goddamnit! I screamed within the confines of my skull. "Yeah, okay," I said, "they play their music too loud anyway."

Wilma didn't ask what I meant but just said, "They're such cute kids. It's just pitiful."

10

I did not go straight home for codeine and beer. Instead I decided to run out and check up on Nicki at her aunt's place, justifying my decision by telling myself I would bring her a Walkman that I never used to somehow make up for the radio that her dad wouldn't give up and to tell her about the phone call from her mother. Maybe I just wanted to make sure she was okay. Luke would have cocked his head and asked, "Why are you going? You shouldn't be giving her presents. I'll tell her about her mother." Any of our counselors would have raised an inquisitive eyebrow and given me some advice about healthy boundaries. But it didn't matter. Whatever my reasons, I was adamant about going out there.

Her aunt answered the phone, and I told her that I would be in the area, which was true—we were all in the Pacific Northwest—that I had the Walkman to give Nicki, and that I had to discuss the matter of Nicki's mother with her. Her aunt said that it would be fine.

When I pulled up, Nicki came skipping down the driveway with a lit cigarette dangling from her lips as if she had been watching for me. "You got a present for me, huh?" She took the cigarette out of her mouth and exhaled a cloud of smoke.

"I guess I do," I said, taking the Walkman off the seat next to me and handing it to her. "I never use it, and I figured you would."

"You know it," she said. "So watcha been up to?"

"I've been out punishing the evil fathers of the world."

She laughed. "Did you get mine?"

"Sorry," I said. "I'm jokin'. There's another reason I came, Nicki. Your mom called the other day. She said that she loves you and that she wants to be together, but she's still in Yakima and still drinking. I explained to her that she's gotta make some changes if she's gonna get you back. I told her to come home."

"Well, is she?"

"I don't know. She hung up on me."

Nicki shook her head, shivering. "Oh well," she said, "I gotta couple of real winners, huh?"

She reached into her jacket pocket and pulled out a cassette tape. A plastic baggie twisted into a knot came out with it and drifted silently to the street. Nicki froze with the fear of being discovered, her eyes going wide with alarm and guilt. I also froze—but with the more undefinable fear of suddenly having the responsibility of confronting the guilty.

We moved at the same time. In a flurry of parental resolve, I went for the baggie. She made a quick grab for it as well, but it had landed closer to me, and I was able to snatch it first. It had about five or six little blue pills in it with the number ten stamped on each one. "Talk to me," I said.

"Aw, shit."

"That's not enough. More detail."

"What do ya wanna know?"

"What is it?"

"Vitamins."

"Talk to me."

"If I tell you, will you give it back?"

"What are they?"

Nicki turned and looked up at the house. "It's Valium. Okay? You happy?"

"I'm overjoyed. Where'd you get 'em?"

"In the youth home."

"Goddamn den of dope peddlers," I mumbled.

"Watch yer mouth," Nicki said.

"Have you been taking these? How many have you had?"

Nicki leaned in toward me. "My life sucks shit," she hissed, gritting her teeth. "I've taken two of them so that I can sleep, so that I don't have to think, so that everything goes away for a while, got it? That's what it all seems to boil down to, don't ya think? Whatever it takes to hack it." She put her hand out with the palm open, and her fingers splayed like she was going to drive it through my chest.

"I'm not giving these back, Nicki. Jesus Christ, think about it!" I barked, staring at her open hand incredulously. I thought you can't use substances to escape your problems, and started to say it but couldn't. The sentence formed in my head as the next logical point to deliver, but I didn't have the physical strength to spit out such a heavy portion of bullshit, and it died on my tongue.

Nicki moved closer. "What's your deal anyway?" she said. "Why are you so concerned about me? Is it because you're paid to, is it because of your job?"

"Hell no," I said. "I wanna help you." Whatever it was that had been happening between us could not die yet; and I could not let it be injured. It wasn't only that I wanted to help. It was much worse. I needed to help. It was as though there might be a sort of salvation in keeping her out of harm's way. I had to preserve the link between us.

"I can take care of myself," she said. "Those little kids that you work with, save them from their parents." She was completely still, leaning toward me and speaking as if the cold had made her immobile. Only her mouth moved, her words coming at me in silver clouds: "Save yourself."

Then I could feel her relax and shrink back a little. Maybe she had seen something in my face. Maybe she had the answers to her questions of me, the ones I could not fully answer myself. She changed. "Go ahead and take them," she said, "but don't tell anybody, please. I only took a couple, I promise."

"I won't say anything," I said.

I had promised not to tell. What was I? I couldn't say I was a social worker. I was a lie, a mass of unavailing good intentions set afire by the things I had witnessed and the inability to answer my own questions. I felt that I had to get out soon, but I knew that I would not. I knew that I could not step away from this thing that would be with me no matter what I did, no matter where I slept or crouched or hid; it would be as impossible as stepping out of my own skin.

"It's cold," Nicki said. "I'm gonna go back inside."

"Yeah, I better get going, too."

I could tell she felt bad. "Thanks for the Walkman," she said. "You're alright." She flicked her cigarette out into the street.

"No problem," I said. "Take care of yourself."

From the car I watched her go inside, then I drove away. A few blocks down the street I pulled to the curb and undid the knot in the plastic baggie. In a laughable but effective effort at rationalization, I told myself that I wanted to know what Nicki had felt, and I popped two of the pills into my mouth and swallowed them. "Hell with this," I muttered. "Fuck it all."

When I got home, I went straight up to Arti's apartment and banged on the door. The drug had taken full control of my bloodstream on the way home, and while I listened to the reassuring beat of Arti's footsteps approaching the door, I became acutely aware that I was smiling stupidly at what a shit-head I was for taking a drug that I had just confiscated to protect a child.

"Bummer of a day," I said pushing past Arti. "Do you have any beer?" I sat down on the couch.

"This job's doin' you in. I think it's time to start checking the classifieds."

"This is a respectable service I'm performing here, Buddy."

"Look at the dive yer taking, though. What the hell's goin' on with the Indians that's so depressing, anyway?"

"Well, it all started when your ancestors couldn't stand living with each other in Europe anymore," I said. Then I told him briefly about Nicki.

"Yeah, that's sad alright," he said. He trailed off, focusing his attention again on the TV. I'd never really told Arti the details of what I did, an omission reinforced by his lack of interest.

I ended up watching TV and drinking beer with Arti for an hour or so, but he kept making reference to some woman that he had recently dated, and I began to get depressed. After he informed me that he and this woman were thinking about catching some theater that upcoming weekend, it got too sickening, and, after thanking him for the beer, I glided out of the apartment.

Alcohol, exhaustion, tranquilizers, and dread—they make the

dreams a little weirder, a little darker. I shambled down to my apartment and went to bed in my clothes. I fell asleep to find myself driving the old roads one last time. It was night, and the areas where the streetlights were on threw the bluish, uncertain light of their faint perimeters into places no longer illuminated in the dying city of random light and expanding darkness.

Along the water where the exhausted Puget Sound slapped listlessly against battered bulkheads and jagged remains of docks and pilings, I drove. It was here where the seagulls that once reeled and scavenged and picked the fish bones clean of their red flesh, now stood like ceramic casts staring out over the water, mourning the extinction of the salmon. Here the shocks of the car trotted horse-like along the fractured street and I saw an Indian woman walking to nowhere, walking because she sensed that her knees were nearing the end of their longevity, afraid that if she rested she might wake to find them locked, unable to move.

I pulled to the side, and the car rolled along with her pace. Her face turned fully to mine, and we recognized each other from another time when, like instinct, pain had purpose, and the ends of struggle were not wholly illusions.

"Ride with me," I said. "I'm going nowhere, too. We'll get there a lot quicker in the car."

She thought about this for a minute, and seeing that my point made sense, nodded her head and got in.

"You're sober aren't you?" I said, seeing the beaten nature of her shoulders, knowing she had nothing in her system to buoy up the weight a little.

"There ain't no more alcohol in the stores," she said. "All bought and looted. I been sober for weeks."

"I'm sober, too," I said.

Then she looked at me funny, and I confessed, "Oh, hell yes, I'm a drunk like you. Never even suspected it back then did ya, ayee?" I saw her teeth in the dimness of the car, white and a little predatory, her long, black hair spreading over her shoulder and the upper portion of her arm in limp strands.

"Well, that's somethin'!" she said. "You always looked so important."

"Well, goddamnit!" I said, maybe a little stung. "I was important."

"Yeah," she said, "I guess you were, huh?"

"Have you seen yer kids lately?" I asked, like it still mattered a little.

"No, it's been a long time. They died of old age."

"Oh, of course," I said. "Man, you were a pain in the ass back then. I'd think you were ready to get them back, and you weren't. I'd think you were gonna show up for the visit, and ya wouldn't. Back and forth, back and forth."

"Oh, yes, I remember those days. I was really tryin' at times," she said. Then she snapped her fingers and announced, "Hey, you know, I think I may even have one of your cards." She reached into her back pocket. "Wouldn't that be something?"

After a moment she fished out a square of yellowed paper, toilet-paper-soft like the cracks of a map folded and unfolded thousands of times. It was torn about the edges, the print barely visible. "Hah!" she laughed, "I do have one." Then she rolled it around some lint off the floor and smoked it.

"But, hell," I said, as the acrid smell of my burning card filled the car, "let's not talk about those rough times. I have something here in my pocket, and to hell with the disappearance of alcohol." I pulled out the bottle of pills, a scuffed brown prescription bottle, which in another period held something with ephemeral salvation like opiates or Valium. Now it held only two pills, each with the potency for a lifetime—one for her and one for me.

I spilled them into my palm, where they rolled into each other—so deep and shiny black that they appeared to be circles of liquid defying gravity, so black they sucked the color from my hand so that it supported them cold and white like a fish belly.

"What are they?" she asked, with curiosity.

I made up some names. "Peacefire, Implosion. One for you and one for me."

She understood, somehow—reading the vibration in my voice and watching the movement in my eyes, the dancing light of human pupils, grow sluggish like the oil sitting upon the Puget Sound. She tossed her pill into her mouth, swallowing it right out of the air like a porpoise snapping a herring as it falls from the trainer's hand.

I watched the lines wash from her face, which became liquid smooth, as though an invisible artist's brush were gently stroking it back to the unstressed skin of birth.

Before I took my pill, she stopped me by pointing with a finger that penetrated into the tissue of my heart. Then she pointed at my hair, which was a hand's length past my shoulders. From the fire of the pill, she forged her finger into a straight razor and with this cut off her hair then mine. Out the window we threw our hair, which scattered in wisps of blood and memory.

The pill went to work like a scalpel cutting out what was not needed, and in moments I had gone muddy, far beneath sensation and the yearning for sensation. "The name of the drug," I said with fleeting clarity, "is resolve, no, resignation."

Then I was in an unfamiliar region, where it looked like trees once were. I noticed the needle had dropped to the bottom of the gas gauge, a punch-drunk fighter unconscious on the canvas. And there was a wall that had been built across the road, an anomaly that registered without time for contemplation. I thought of words of defiance to shout at the last second in case someone might hear them, but I didn't have enough profundity left to muster and instead uttered something unmemorable, profane. And the drug butted heads with adrenaline, and shock, and an ember of fortitude not completely snuffed out—that stuff that makes you want to stick around to see what might happen next; they collided with conflicting polarities, knocking the vision from my eyes, so that I didn't see the wall to the finish. I just felt the emptiness of the woman next to me, and the needles of all the gauges dropping. And the name of the drug came to me too late to write it down.

11

At 2:00 on a cold, bright afternoon, the Tall Fighters charged the car before I could turn off the ignition, racing for the front seat. They were each allowed to carry their own lunch bag now, and the bags were swinging and bulging like socks full of marbles. I knew it was Amelia's turn and was ready for the scramble. I'd taken to carrying the teddy bear that Arti had found in the street in the glove compartment in case the impulse to give it away overcame me, and now I was considering throwing it into the midst of the screaming faces and elbows jockeying for position in hopes that it might slow them down. Stevie was carrying a nerf football tucked up under his arm, his lunch bag was in the other hand banging against his knees. He was wearing green sweat pants and a Seahawks sweatshirt. His quilted winter jacket looked too big, and unzipped it flapped around his narrow torso like a cape.

I got out and went around to the other door, which I'd taken the precaution of locking. "Okay, guys, now listen and remember. Think back, way back when you were mere children. Stevie rode in the front on the way down and Rosie on the way back, and that can only mean one thing..."

"Meeee!" Amelia screamed and fumbled at the door handle.

"Yes, it's you. Now hang on a minute, it's locked."

I unlocked the door, and Amelia shot in and hunkered down as I collapsed the seat forward for the other two to get in back. They hung their heads in acceptance and climbed in.

I pulled a U-turn and sped away with their mangy dog biting at the tires.

"Guess where you're going today?" I asked, thinking that I had a surprise for them.

"The aquarium!" they chimed in unison.

"Oh, how'd you know?"

"Our other mom told us."

"Well, now that the surprise is ruined, have you been there before?"

"Yup," said Amelia, grabbing the knob on the stick shift, "and you know what?"

"Oops, take yer hand off that Amelia, that could cause a major tragedy." I eased her little fingers off the shift.

"Umm do you know what," she said pounding her fists on her knees. "We like the aquarium."

"That's good," I said. "I like it, too." Amelia's face was constantly undergoing change, her eyebrows jumping around expressively. She stuck her jaw out with a bulldog underbite and grinned broadly, looking like a little old lady.

We got a parking space just a block down from the front entrance of the aquarium, close enough to see the subtle gray wave of a flounder moving like a tremor over the silty bottom of the wall tank that ran along the walkway to the front entrance.

"Do you see her?" Rosie yelled from the backseat. I scanned the front of the building then down along the sidewalks and the salty bleached wood of the pier to our right. I didn't see Josie. I looked at the clock on the dashboard. We were five minutes early. "Ah, look, we're early," I said.

"Watch both directions of the sidewalk," I said. "She could come from anywhere."

Five minutes passed.

"How's school going, you guys?" I asked.

"Pretty good," they all agreed.

"Do you like your teachers?"

Amelia shook her head so her bangs bounced erratically. "Yeah, mine's the best."

"Not mine," said Stevie, "I want to take him to Yellowstone and feed him to the bears."

"That sounds pretty serious, Stevie," I said. "He can't be that bad."

"Let's shave off his hair," said Amelia.

"Yeah," Stevie chimed in, "we'll shave off his hair and put it down the back of his underwear."

"Man, you guys are tough," I said, waiting for Rosie to raise the stakes. I turned to look in the back; she was sitting on her knees facing out the rear window. "Look!" she yelled.

I thought it must be Josie, and I breathed out a few pounds of relief.

"Look, a volcano!" she shouted, pointing.

Off on the horizon, a smokestack, invisible except for the gray expulsion billowing up into the sky, had created a picture very similar to an erupting volcano.

"No, that's just pollution, Rosie," I said, disappointed, "nothing to get excited about."

"Then we'll make him into a mummy," Stevie said, still thinking about his teacher and ignoring the volcano. "We'll take out his liver and we'll wrap him in bandages. Then we'll bury him, and when we dig him up, his face'll be all fat and round."

"Okay, that's enough, Stevie. It's getting a little too graphic."

"What's graphic?"

"It means it's gettin' to be a bit much."

I looked around the waterfront, sorting my way through the faces and bodies walking along the street and hanging out in the shadowed storefronts. No Josie.

"How long are you gonna be our caseworker?" Rosie said out of the blue.

"I don't know," I said. "Well, actually I'm not really your caseworker, Luke is—you know Luke. I guess I'm your outreach worker."

"Do you take other kids to see their real moms?" Rosie continued, her voice soft and eager.

"Yeah, sometimes."

"Where's our mom?" Amelia demanded suddenly, pressing her hands against the window and squirming up onto her knees.

"Maybe she had bus trouble," I offered. "Buses are a reliable explanation for tardy mothers."

Stevie had taken an interest in the seafood bar near where we were parked. "Can we have some hot chocolate?"

"I don't know where we'd get something like that, Stevie," I said, on the off chance that it might work.

"Right there." He pointed at Ivars.

I tried again. "I don't think they have it."

"Let's go see," said Rosie.

"Hot chocolate!" screamed Amelia.

Once out of the car, they mobbed the seafood bar, grabbing the countertop and chinning themselves up.

"C'mon everybody, calm down or you can't have any sugar." The waitress smiled and looked at me, then at the kids. "Can I take your order?" she asked, her pale blue eyes involuntarily darting back to the disembodied heads of the three Indian children, as though they might suddenly scramble over the counter and dive into the deep fryers.

They did have hot chocolate so I ordered three.

"Well, now that we're here, do you guys want anything to eat?" They all started talking at once.

"Rosie, what do you want?"

"Chips! The orange ones." She pointed at the Doritos hanging on the metal rack.

"We'll take a bag of the orange ones. Okay Stevie, what are you havin'?"

"Oysters!"

"And a small basket of oysters."

Amelia was fine with the hot chocolate. The waitress lined up the cups with dangerous-looking heaps of whipped cream sagging over the edges. "I'll bring the oysters out to you," she said.

"Go sit at the table over there. I'll carry the hot chocolate," I ordered, pointing to the nearest table.

They ran over and took their seats.

They all ate their way through the whipped cream, hazarding a tentative sip now and again, testing the heat. As the cocoa cooled down, they began to slurp and fidget, and I began to realize the magnitude of my mistake.

"Did you see the movie about the guy who wore the mask and killed people?"

"You didn't see it, did you, Stevie?"

"Yeah, and there was this part where...." Stevie began rambling about gruesome scenes from the movie, getting more excited with each babbled word.

"Stevie, who took you to that movie?" I asked, as I realized that he had actually seen it.

"I saw it on TV, on a VCR."

"Who rented it?" I pressed, "your foster mom and dad?"

"No, I saw it at a friend's house."

"That's a relief," I said. "Don't go there anymore."

Amelia rose up in her chair, commanding attention. "Did you see Dances with Wuff?"

Before I could answer, Stevie's oysters came and were accosted violently by two more unwelcome sets of fingers, grabbing handfuls of hot, greasy fries. He screamed in protest.

"Okay!" I shouted getting my arm between the two girls and Stevie's food. "Now you two should have ordered something when I asked. For the sake of fairness, though, Stevie will share the fries with you, but the oysters are his 'cause he ordered them. Now relax, and don't let that sugar get the better of you."

They seemed to be satisfied with the squashed handful of fries they'd each taken on the first assault. Rosie devoured hers, then tore into her bag of chips and began rationing out handfuls to her sister and brother, showing me that she could be fair.

"You know what I like to do?" she said to me suddenly, her round face beaming and displaying her teeth, widely spaced across her broad mouth, stained and dusted with salt and orange food coloring.

"What do you like to do, Rosie?

She thought for a moment then blurted out, "The monkey bars! And skipping rope!" She laughed. "And petting doggies!" She was nearly vibrating out of her seat as she navigated the straw into her mouth and sucked down the last inch of chocolate milk.

To her immediate left, Stevie was trying to do the Chinese torture on Amelia. She recoiled, howling with laughter, and leveled her cup with her elbow. It splattered over the table and onto her lap, the chair, and the pavement. Stevie, who saw this as a successful execution of the Chinese torture, blew a mouthful of hot chocolate on the sleeve of my jacket.

They all roared with laughter, choking on whatever they had crammed into their mouths.

The sugar had distracted them from thoughts of their mother. I scanned the streets as best I could from within the recessed cove beneath the awning. The wall of the restaurant to our left, and the weeny vendor on the sidewalk to our right, limited my field of vision to the road and shops directly in front of our table.

"Now listen, you guys," I said, standing up to appear more firm and imposing, "I'm going to step out onto the sidewalk and take a look around, and I don't want anyone to move from this table."

I walked out from beneath the awning, glancing back to see if they were obeying me. They'd forgotten all about me and were making spit wads and firing them at each other point blank through their straws.

I looked up and down the street, waiting in vain for the casual, aimless walk of the kids' mother. She was now more than half an hour late.

When I returned to the table, the kids appeared to be winding down from a seizure or gearing up for one. The table was covered with crumbs, fries, soggy napkins, and pools of chocolate milk. All three were chewing their straws in desperation as if trying to suck the residual sugar from the mangled plastic tubes. Getting them in the car would take some strategy.

"Here's what we need to do. We can't see your mom from in here, so we're going to sit in the car for a while and watch for her. She's very late so I'm afraid that she may have had bus trouble or something else, but we're going to watch for a few more minutes. Now let's get in there and work together." They scrambled out to the car, with me walking quickly in front of them to keep them out of the street. It was Stevie's turn in the passenger's seat, and strangely they seemed to remember this. We watched together, up and down the street, but without seeing Josie.

After several minutes, Stevie curled up on the seat and sighed loudly several times. I put my hand on his head and palmed the soft straight hair. He looked at me to see what I wanted, and we gazed at each other. I wondered if he ever thought about our odd relationship and why it existed. I thought about Nicki telling me to save those little kids I worked with. I thought about her telling me to save myself.

"I'll tell you what, guys," I said, "we're going to have to head home, but I'll do my best to set up another visit, okay?"

"No!" They wailed in unison.

"A little while longer," Stevie pleaded, putting his hand on my leg to strengthen his entreaty.

"Stevie, we can't. We have time limits."

"You're a bad parent!" he cursed. "You're just a stupid parent!"

"Hey!" I interrupted with the superior volume of adulthood. "I'm no parent."

He looked away from me, frowning. I stared through the windshield. "Goddamn you!" I whispered.

I started up the engine.

"Your mom couldn't make it. You know this happens sometimes, so all we can do is try again, okay?"

With dried whipped cream plastered around her mouth, Amelia shouted, "Let's go look for her!"

"We can't do that," I said, my voice trailing to a whisper. "We can only try again next time."

"Are you gonna come and get us?" Rosie asked, wedging herself in between the seats.

"Yes, I am."

"You promise?" asked Stevie, preparing to forgive me, no matter how bad and stupid I was.

"Yes, I promise," I said, knowing that I shouldn't make promises. Then I reached into the glove compartment and took out the teddy bear. "Since Rosie's the oldest, I want her to hang this bear somewhere in the house, and it will remind you that I will be coming back." I handed it to Rosie, who snatched it from my hand with a big grin. The sentimentality of the scene ended abruptly as I pulled from the curb while Amelia and Rosie fought over the teddy bear.

I pulled Josie's file from Luke's cabinet. It was after 5:00 P.M., and he had gone home. Reading the file, I discovered that she had gotten some services here and there for many years, but she rarely saw anything through. There were a few evaluations done by shrinks and counselors, done to get her started in programs. The file was a beast—about five inches thick, one folder for each Tall Fighter child, all three cross-referenced so that anything that applied to all of the kids was in each tattered brown folder. The file was divided into sections, including correspondence, medical records, court documents, and narratives. The narratives were in the back—handwritten notations of anything that the caseworker in charge at the time had done that minute, hour, or day in regard to the children, the mother, or both. Written by Luke and the state worker who had the case before him, they included occasional notations by others in contact with the case, such as myself.

I thumbed through, waiting for telling words and titles to jump out at me, scanning intently as though somewhere within was information my life depended on, as though in a matter of minutes the building would self-destruct.

I started with the narratives—"Took the kids to the zoo to meet their mother. Gave them tickets. They seemed happy. The visit went well." "Josie didn't show up today. Called the shelter, hadn't seen her." "Called Children's Orthopedic for immunization recs—RN Johanson is sending release." Towards the top was one of my reports about the children and one of the visits I'd taken them to, including my important note about Josie entering treatment.

In the correspondence section, I found some brief, sterile references to Josie's history, fragmented descriptions, weightless in comparison to the nauseating veracity of the reality. Josie was late-stage alcoholic. She had grown up in Missoula, Montana, until high school when she was shipped off to a school for Indians. She dropped out when she had Rosie, moved back to Missoula, had Amelia and Stevie, and drank. Amelia and Stevie had a different father than Rosie. Amelia and Stevie's father dropped off the map after Stevie's birth, and never resurfaced. Josie had been raped by some white men, who snatched her off the street one night when she was staggering to God knows where with her kids camped out at her mother's. She identified the men, and apparently they were brought in. What followed was her humiliation as they walked, walked because she was a drunk Indian with worthless testimony against a couple of white good 'ol boys. The file said that "pressing charges was unsuccessful." I knew that scene all too well without reading the court transcription.

After this, Josie had run to Seattle with three kids and twenty some years of pain that she dulled to a smoky haze of haunting memories with liquor in whatever form she could get it. The price was enormous and tragic. When I met her I thought she was about forty, but according to the file she was twenty-eight. And I blamed her for her situation. Blame is the element to put a finger on so that sense can be made of events, and good and evil can be defined. But what happens is you think you've narrowed it down to the space covered by your fingertip, so you point and find yourself scowling with malice at the wrong person because someone before them set the course.

I saw Josie pulled into a car, drunk and reeling beyond the concepts of responsibility, and shown what the world thought of her—a glob of spit in her face, a desecrating scream tearing through her body, confirming the accounts of history and stories of malevolence carried in the voices of her elders when they spoke of the past, when they gritted their teeth and fought for their pride, and lived with the incomprehensible crush of horror and hatred vented on their parents and grandparents. She was guilty of her own crimes, but fault was an entirely different issue.

I saw Josie's grandmother, small and alone, one of thousands of young curiosities from the savage New World, now tamed and out of place, standing under the guidance of the white obligation to save the descendants of those who were left alive, standing in a row with their hair chopped off, as uniform as lab rats.

I saw Indian children with their young, red tongues on the frozen pipes of boarding schools in winter, the tissue and saliva stuck like epoxy, because the children spoke Indian, because the children were wrong. I saw the children under the stooped figures of adults, of educators, of holy people, told that the blood from which they were made was bad. I saw the faces that could tell them this—the faces that believed it, because without belief such horror could not exist, without belief the faces that watched could not feel such purpose, without belief the faces that fought so hard to destroy a people could not feel so fucking right.

And further, I saw Josie's great-grandmother, and her great-great-grandmother, and the guns and the missionaries brimming over with the purpose, bringing the belief to save the savages from themselves; missionaries bloated with the pride of self-sacrifice, swinging Bibles, too full of themselves to know their actual design of inflicting slow death, of wasting an invaluable history, of wasting families, of wasting hearts and tearing out voices, and fashioning an invisible people in the shadow of the white world's generations, holding tightly to the belief. Until one day the belief slips a little, and its luster pales. Embarrassment slithers in, and systems are created to deal with the living reminders, to pacify the victims of the belief—the survivors, the descendants. Then the belief changes its shape, shifts its color, and conjures up safe images of drunk lazy Indians; it severs the connections—the causal qualities of history—and paints innocuous pictures: In 1492, Columbus sailed the ocean blue. It must do this because the truth is always too painful.

And I could see it moving like a storybook, pages turning, from the great Spanish ships to the treaties and the reservations, and the voices telling a free people that they each have a plot of land with plenty of room to grow vegetables. I could see it moving and closing in: the promises and the lies, the deceit and the betrayal. And the alcohol and the cycle. And Josie.

It had been two weeks since I had helped sweep Jerry Reeves's kids away. The call finally came in from the Tribal Court, shedding a little more light and a little more disappointment. Elsy, the conspirator, had faked sending the document to Jerry by certified mail, forging his signature on the return receipt. The document was supposed to inform him that a study of his home was required prior to his appearance at the next hearing, of which he was also not informed.

The purpose of the home study was to either clear him or condemn him in regard to the allegations of drunkenness that Elsy and Trudy supposedly had been privy to via telephone conversations with him during the past few months. Apparently Elsy's composure hadn't held up well when the heat came down, and Wilma was told that she had been "let go" immediately.

After filling me in on all of this, Wilma again ended her narrative by telling me not to work on Saturdays anymore, then gave me the phone numbers of various agencies in Canada where Trudy had supposedly fled with the children. The tribe was almost certain of this, and we speculated that Elsy had told them to thwart a little of the animosity and punishment that was being heaped upon her.

"So what do we do?" I asked, staring at the phone numbers.

Wilma was eating microwaved soup from a tiny Styrofoam cup, and the thin brown spoonful she held poised before her face trembled with her laughter. "Well, the court issued the most recent order granting the father full custody with a pick-up order. They're sending copies of the stuff to us right now. We do our damndest to locate the kids, then he'll go get 'em. You need to call those numbers and tell them the situation. Let them know that the mom is holding the kids illegally. They are American Indians enrolled in a tribe down here, and we want 'em back. The tribe would still like a home study for Jerry, if we'd be willing to do it. Maybe you can do that when the time comes, eh—a chance to make amends."

"Sure, why not?" I said without pause. "They're probably on the reservation up there, huh?"

"Hopefully," said Wilma.

I called Jerry, who picked up the phone on the first ring. He asked if I had found the kids yet. The question was far too unrealistic. I stammered for a few seconds, opting not to tell him that we were nowhere near. Instead, I told him that I'd been making calls and that we had some connections. I asked him to tell me where he thought she might go and about her citizenship. He went into a fervent liturgy of defamations, losing himself in the history of his deceitful ex. Since I felt I owed him an ear to vent, I listened silently.

"Okay, this information helps quite a bit," I said during his first pause. "I'll call Canada again and see what I can find out."

There was silence on the other end. He wasn't goin' to let it end on such a businesslike note. I felt it coming. "You know, if you would have let me explain the other day we wouldn't be goin' through all this now." His voice stayed very calm and matter-of-fact.

"Jerry," I said, hoping I could express regrets while telling him he was wrong at the same time. "Jerry, it's not my position to listen to each party's story and decide who's right and who's wrong. That's the court's job. We had a legal document from your tribe's court giving Trudy custody. Since we had no way of knowing what she'd done to get that order, we respected it just like we would if it were from the state court here. Now that we know what's up, we'll offer you our services to get them back." I was right about respecting the court order. It was my integrity that was a little fucked up at the time.

I could hear him thinking on the other end. Finally, he said, "They were doin' real good here. They had plenty of clothes and food; they were goin' to school. Their mother wants them 'cause she found out that she could get more money from welfare by havin' 'em with her. She won't use the money on them neither."

"I know," I said, interrupting. "We're going to try to get them back. The recent court order giving you custody is on its way from the Tribal Court to both of us."

"Yeah, I know. Call me right away when you find the kids. I'll be lookin' too."

"I will," I said. "Talk to you soon."

He was pretty damn civil about the whole thing. I had hated Jerry when I went to his home with the police. I couldn't wait to see him get what I thought he deserved. But I had been wrong.

I called my most recent Canadian connection, a worker with the Ministries for the Province and gave her the information. She said she'd check into it and call me back.

From one of our offices I could hear the distinct Indian laugh. It sounded like Luke, Vicky, and Becky, their voices rising in unison, swelling to a crescendo and ending in Becky's characteristic wheeze, followed by Verna telling them to keep it down. I remembered

Jones's awful story about the violated dog. It seemed like a thousand years ago, back at the beginning of a journey into overwhelming feelings, and old memories pulled out like rotten teeth.

I decided to think about the last thousand years at 10:30 A.M. Saturday in a tavern that reeked of bleach. There were four people in the bar, including the bartender, who was a wavy-haired blonde in her early forties, hanging on to a good figure, clad in black stretch pants and a white blouse just high enough over her breasts to dissuade the rude goons who frequented the dive from losing control. She was very energetic, snapping her fingers to the rock 'n roll that she was playing, strutting up and down behind the counter, occasionally throwing a leg up onto the bar to do a quick hamstring stretch, sweeping her rag over spots already clean.

Sitting several chairs down from me were an old man drinking beer who spontaneously announced that he was eighty-three and a young woman with a crew cut, drinking coffee and smoking cigarettes. All three knew each other, calling one another by name. Since I had the look on my face of a person contemplating the last thousand years none of them engaged me in conversation.

I was about to leave when a funny thing happened inside my head. I had a beer in my left hand and my right hand was idly flipping a coaster between my fingers. With a twitch of my body the coaster fell, bouncing off the counter and down onto the floor.

Then I saw it. There was a man and a woman fighting, and at first I thought I was picturing one of the beatings that Nicki's dad had dished out to Liddy over the years. But it wasn't them in this picture. The man had a fistful of her hair, half the hair on her head springing out between his fingers as he wielded her like a feather duster, her body following the direction of the force, like if it didn't keep close behind, her head might come off like a Barbie doll. Her arms and legs moved in awkward, panicky spasms, flailing like a marionette being beaten to pieces, trying to steer with and against the jarring force that sent her about the room, up against furniture, walls, and the floor, her face disappearing in the flash of light brown hair, then coming into view again, her eyes appearing as two circles of nothingness, pupils sucking like two punctures in a dam, blackness gushing out then in, with incredible energy to their blank expression but with no vitality—life devoid of the fire that dictates fight or flight.

Her forehead hit the corner of a coffee table, busting open, blood running down her white skin and into her hair. Like an obscene dance the Indian man pulled his partner back from the table, the motion like the lash of a whip, jerking her back and releasing the hair, so that her body was allowed to gather completely behind the direction of her head. She collapsed to the floor and began crawling along the length of the couch up against the base. He walked up and kicked her hard in the back of the leg, high up on her hamstring. Her entire body seemed to close around the point of impact like a time lapse of a blooming flower in reverse, her hands moving involuntarily from her head to the most recent injury, her entire upper body curling up unnaturally tight over her legs. Then, just as quickly, the immediate instinct of her movement was overridden by a stronger impulse, and she again covered her head with her hands. There were streaks of blood on the carpet, painted by the brush of her hair. She was still. The man turned and looked at me. And then it started over from the beginning, ending again with the meeting of our eyes, and the nauseating recognition of family that crackled and flashed like an electrical fire. It was my father. It was my mother. It was the memory of a beating that I had witnessed as a boy; of the many that had occurred, it was the only one I had actually seen, at least the only one that had come back to me thus far.

I was sweating. My eyes glared back at me from the mirror behind the bar like two bulging chicken eggs. "Holy shit!" I hissed out loud. The other three people stopped what they were doing and looked at me. For the moment I felt truly delusional and insane. But I was sane and it was real. Flushed with shock, I finished my beer in one long swallow and went home. When I got there, I took Nicki's baggie of Valium out and dumbly stared at it like it was some mysterious object of power. Then I swallowed one and put the baggie back in my sock drawer.

12

Christmas was coming. Expeditious Christmas tree lots sprung up in the parking lot of every grocery store for those who'd finished their turkey sandwiches from Thanksgiving and were in need of the next ritual. Lights were strung up on the naked trees of downtown Seattle, in the windows of shops, and far out into suburbia. The Christmas boats were cruising the lake in front of my apartment, and occasionally watery snow would fall then turn to slush and be washed away by the rain that always followed.

One crisp night Arti and I went to a hill overlooking Lake Union, after leaving a social gathering we could no longer stomach. Arti was wearing a Santa hat he'd taken from the party and was trying to reach the lake with empty beer bottles, heaving them into the night with a grunt. I joined Arti in the bottle throwing, screaming out the song, "Jesus loves the little children!" Minutes later I passed out face down on the lawn.

Anything contrary to reality had become a craving that rolled over and showed its stomach around 5:00 P.M. every day. My apartment was becoming my world after work, the most suitable place to slump and sip and engage in my ongoing battle of attrition against my supply of codeine from the Great White North. It generated a warm fuzz around my head and a slightly screwed-up but acceptable view on the drabness of my apartment and my life, my eyes dragging around the room as if shot full of Novocain, almost groping like the blind but sensitive nose of an aardvark, regarding the dirty dishes piling up around the sink with comprehension but without concern. I'd gawk dumbly at the cans and bottles and bags with groceries that hadn't been put on the shelves—my vision fading like the blur of binocular lenses held too closely to the subject, perception deadened into vagueness so that I could reflect a little without going bat-shit, and dabble loosely with possibilities and attempted explanations for the state of things. Anything contrary to reality had become a craving, and objectivity was fucked. I knew why I had hated Jerry. I knew why I hated Charles and Reyanne's ex-husband. I knew why I hated and hated and hated. They were symbols of my father—each one of them a piece of the past and the unavoidable present, together rebuilding a comprehensive memory shut out long ago like an unwelcome pariah—a memory now rude and violent, banging on the door, refusing to go away.

Disturbing dreams had been occurring more frequently. One night I had a dream about my sister, Tia. She had somehow gotten her hand cut off at the wrist. When I first saw the emptiness beyond the straight border of her injury, I wailed loud as a child, as if pleading with someone very far away, an intense anguish that I've never felt in waking life and that may happen only in dreams so that it can be survived by waking. In the dream, Tia's hand was found and sewed back on. I stared at her hand as we walked together toward an unknown destination on a path somewhere unvisited by me in real life, through a sprawling woody landscape of hilly greens and browns. The hand was curled like stiff, heavy rubber, and she kept her elbow bent, cradling it to her as if to protect it within the shelter of her body like something breakable. I prayed that the hand would take to her once again, and every so often I would resume sobbing. She didn't utter a sound, and a weighty silence was upon her face. I could feel the loss that she dragged invisibly, a hole created by the past and affecting all her future years, a burden infinitely larger than the physical loss of this one part. We kept walking, waiting for the blood to bloom within the grayness of her flesh, and watching for any movement in the fingers, walking together and looking for something.

The next day I called her. She was going to New York University and sharing an apartment with two other women. I didn't call to say anything about the dream. In fact, the feeling it left was so horrible that vocalizing it would have been too overwhelming, and confining it within the realm of dreams seemed more possible with silence.

Instead, I called to tell her about something also very difficult—my recent memory jog. Initially, I had stuffed the memory back down, hoping that it would suffocate and die an illusion, though I knew that it would come back, invited or not. I began with small talk, deciding to see if it would come.

When I asked her how things were going in New York, she told me she wondered what she was doing there. "I think the only people who can really cope with this place were born here and know nothing different," she said. "I was walking down the street after class today, and this tiny whirlwind like those dust devils in eastern Washington came swirling down the street picking up garbage on its way. I moved to get away from it but it followed me, blowing right up around me. And I walked in this whirlwind of leaves, candy wrappers, newspaper, and other sidewalk shit, and it all stuck to my clothes. I started crying and knew that I wanted to come home."

"Are you thinking about it?"

"We'll see," she said. "Maybe I'll transfer to UW."

"If it sucks that bad, then maybe you should. Otherwise it's two more years there."

She made a resigned humming noise but didn't answer. Then she asked me how work was going. "How's it goin' with all them Indians?" she said, laughing.

"It's kinda like the whirlwind of garbage," I answered.

Then after a few moments of silence, I asked, "Tia, have you ever seen an image of something that wasn't in your memory? You know, like seeing something as though it's a scene in a movie, but it's you or your family?"

"You mean like a dream?"

"No, not a dream. When you're awake. You see it as if it's happening, and then it becomes a memory. But it's so out of the blue that you begin to doubt whether or not it's true."

There was silence, silence with all the motion and quiet of a big fish moving beneath the surface. Finally Tia spoke. "What did you see?"

"A fight between Mom and...Dad. He was beating her, actually."

Tia sighed. "Levi, is this the first time you've remembered that?"

I suddenly felt very weak. I could tell by the stifled surprise in her voice that she had the memory. I had to block the memory out, but she had remembered.

"Levi, do you remember when I would come into your room when we were really little and crawl into bed with you, when they were fighting?"

"They weren't fighting," I said, the image flashing into my mind. "He was beating her."

"Do you remember me coming into your room, scared and crying?" she repeated, her voice diminishing to a grave whisper.

"You were only in preschool," I said, still wondering at her memory. "How can you remember?"

"You remember my age," she said. "You remember, too."

I thought about this. That memory was accessible. It took no effort to see Tia padding through the small crack of light as she silently opened my door and slipped inside, closing the door behind her, trying to shut everything out.

"Tia?"

"Yeah?"

"Are you proud of being Indian?"

"Of course," she said. But there was a pause, as though the tiniest ugly doubt had tripped her up, as though her subconscious had quickly calculated Dad's influence out of the conclusion. "Of course I am," she said again with emphasis. It was like her hand in the dream. It was there with her, and she cared for it deeply, but it was wounded and she was at risk of losing it.

"But it's hard sometimes," I said, the phrase sounding like a question, which it was. I knew it was hard. But was it for her? Already she seemed stronger than me.

"I guess I haven't thought about it much," she said. "That's probably not good, huh?"

"No, you have to think about it. I'm seein' that now. There's no way out of it. It's one of the few things that's permanent, which makes it a good thing. It won't go away, and it can't be taken away."

"Yeah," Tia agreed, "that's a good way of putting it."

"When are you coming home to visit?" I asked.

"I can't come home 'til summer. I have to work through Christmas to keep my job."

There was silence again, then Tia added, "Levi. Thinking about being Indian means thinking about Dad. That's what makes it hard."

"Come home as soon as you can," I implored, feeling lonely but not alone.

"Summer's the soonest, Levi. But while I'm gone, you work harder to take care of Mom. Okay? You've been upsetting her lately. She called me a few weeks ago."

This was the first time I had been confronted by the fallout of my dysfunctional behavior with such embarrassing clarity. "Shit, I know," I said, my integrity muted with shame.

"If you're going to call someone drunk, then call me, okay?"

"I just get that way, it's been really tough lately."

"I know, but that's not good enough. Take care of yourself or you're hurting her. You're hurting me. Got it?"

I was looking out the window at the frozen weeds and shrubs on the other side of the glass. The cold moved through me like an icy wind. You're hurting her, you're hurting me. Hurting my family—my mother, my sister, I thought with agonizing honesty.

"Oh shit, I'm sorry," I said.

"Call me more," Tia answered, her voice sounding very young and small, as if she had suddenly become frightened, the way she had been frightened a long time ago.

"I will," I promised. I looked out the window for a long time and imagined her doing the same—looking out the window of her apartment in a huge city, in an even colder place.

"When I come home in a few months I'll have to come check out yer office and hear more about the Seattle Reservation," she joked finally.

I smiled. "Yeah, you will," I responded. "You need to check this stuff out with me."

"Okay big brother. We'll check it out."

13

It was late December and very bleak. The chill cut right through my jacket and sweatshirt as I went down the concrete steps to the parking lot below the building. The inside of my car was like a meat locker, just warm enough to keep the moisture that soaked the floor carpeting from freezing over.

I picked Nicki up at her school. We were going to visit the grave of her grandfather on the Suquamish Reservation, the very place where Chief Sealth was buried, an undertaking that I thought would make her very sad and thoughtful. Yet she was happy and as spirited as the day when I first saw her, possibly with the thrill of getting pulled out of school early.

"So how's school been going?" I asked, my voice ringing in the stairwell.

"It's alright," Nicki said, working her arms into her green winter coat. "I'm a little behind right now—I don't really understand some of the stuff we're doing 'cause I got behind when I was in the home. I was in an alternative school in the group home, but I didn't do shit."

Wilma had consented to the trip enthusiastically, to my surprise. It was a trip that would take the better part of the day, but there really wasn't anything urgent to be done at work. More importantly, though, Wilma had understood the need for Nicki to visit the grave. She saw what was necessary, and if it took a day's work for an alienated little girl to stand at the grave of her grandfather, then so be it.

"Hey, do you mind if I run to the store across the street real quick?" Nicki stopped outside the building and pointed to a corner mini market just off the school grounds. "I wanna get something to drink."

"Yeah, okay, but hurry; you got two minutes."

"Two minutes," she said. "You got any money? Just kidding."

She took off across the street, then pushed through the glass doors and disappeared. Soon she came out transferring a large paper cup with a stir stick back and forth from hand to hand. Wisps of steam rose from the lid into the chill air.

"What'd you get?" I asked.

She sat down grinning and pulled her seatbelt on, the smell of coffee filling the car. Then she reached into the deep pocket of her coat and pulled out a small purple flower with a long stem in a sheath of clear plastic. "I got a flower for the grave," she said, and set it on the dashboard.

"Cool. What's in the cup?" I pressed, "hot Pepsi?"

"Coffee," she said. "C'mon, let's go."

"You're drinking coffee now? Do your auntie and uncle know you drink coffee? How long have you been drinking it?"

"Just this past year, and, no, my auntie and uncle don't like me drinking coffee."

"But they let you smoke."

"Yeah, they let me smoke."

"Well, I'll let you drink that coffee, but you can't smoke. How's that?"

She pursed her lips and blew air through the small hole in the lid, then took a sip. "Okay," she said.

She leaned back coolly, her body turned at an angle so that her arm rested along the window ledge of the door. "A twelve-year-old coffee drinkin' smoker," I muttered. "You only get one cup."

"That's okay," she said. "It's a double Americano."

"God, I can't win. It's gonna stunt your growth."

"I'm tall enough," she laughed. "Such a parental figure—how long have you been workin' this job anyway?"

"It's closin' in on a year now."

I had made good on my errant promise not to tell anyone about the Valium, a decision made in no one's best interest. By comparison her coffee consumption was hardly a concern.

On the ferry it started to snow light watery flakes that became dryer and larger with each minute. We sat by the window and watched the snow come down.

"So why'd you pick this week to go to the cemetery, Nicki? Is it the anniversary of somethin'?"

"No, I was just sitting on the porch the other day—the day I called you to see if you could take me—and the wind was blowing, rustling papers on the table and the pages of an open book that I'd been reading. The sound made me think of water on the shore, like when the tide's comin' in. It reminded me of my grandparents' place and the beach, taking the ferry to see them."

By the time we drove off the ferry dock on the other side, the world had turned white. Lazy, fluffy snowflakes rushed at our windshield like enormous dandelion seeds.

"Nicki, this doesn't look good," I said, noticing that there were already a few inches of snow accumulating on the roofs of houses along the road. "We're going to have to be quick, alright? If we stay too long we're gonna get stuck out here."

"Yeah, okay."

When we got to Suquamish, it looked so much different than when I had come in the beginning of spring to get Nicki, since winter now covered it like a picture on a Christmas card. I looked at the flower where it rolled back and forth on the dash. "Were you pretty close to your grandfather?" I asked.

"Very close," she said. "My grandma, too. I used to stay with them a lot on the weekends. My parents would send me over on the ferry. Sometimes we'd all come over, but my dad usually stayed home. He didn't like comin' out for some reason. Even after my grandma died, I'd go there and stay. Grandpa always told me stories about how it was out here when he was young. It was really neat, imagining things the way he described them. Other people and relatives on the reservation would bring him things they'd hunted, and he'd always make stew or soup with whatever it was—fish, ducks, or deer. He used to tell stories, too, and never forgot how they went. My grandma was like that, too, but she died of cancer when I was really little."

"Do you remember the stories now?"

"Yeah, most of 'em."

"My grandma was like that," I said, remembering. "She was a storyteller."

"What kinda Indian are you, anyway?" Nicki asked.

"Lummi, Klallam, Flathead. Lummi's where I'm most connected, I guess you'd say."

"Did you grow up there?"

"Naw. But we went there a lot before my grandparents died. Before my dad left. I remember we used to get our teeth cleaned by a dentist up there because it was free. He worked out of a trailer in the parking lot of the tribal center. He was a white guy—must've owed some kind of community service for college grants or somethin'."

"So you don't know where your dad went, huh?"

"No, Nicki, I don't. Just away."

"Ran like a coward, huh?"

"Yeah, I guess so."

We parked in front of the graveyard, and Nicki gently eased the flower out of its sheath. Then she led me in through the wide opening in the gray fence of rough-hewn wood. The snow was nearly up to our ankles and still falling heavily. There was no sound, only the motion of infinite falling snowflakes in every direction, like thousands of tiny angels or fairies descending earthward.

I followed Nicki to a section of the cemetery where there were no headstones. The markers underfoot were already covered under a powdery blanket. "It's right in this area," Nicki said, pushing the snow off one of the grave markers with a sweeping motion of her leather sneaker, revealing that this section of the cemetery had rows of copper and gray stone plaques, flush with the frozen grass and hard earth. She began stooping to read the names of them. Then she pointed to a tree bordering the field. "It's not further up than that tree," she said, jogging ahead.

"What was his name?"

"Clifford James."

The graveyard was completely empty except for us, off in a far corner beneath the bows of cedar trees growing heavy with snow. At the middle I could see the posts and the canoes over the grave of

Chief Sealth, and all around were the graves of Indians who came after him in the snow-covered ground beneath our feet.

Nicki was hurrying along, her hands withdrawn into the long sleeves of her parka, sweeping snow off the names of possible ancestors, her young eyes squinting in the cold, searching faster and faster, as though she had but one chance.

"It's getting deeper, Nicki. Are you sure it's in this area?"

"Yes, I'm sure." Nicki had pulled the hood up out of the collar of her jacket, and wisps of hair were pushed out along the edges of her face.

I looked beyond to where the car was parked and saw that the snow was a quarter of the way up the tires.

"Nicki, we're going to have to head back pretty soon or we're not gonna make it. You know that he's right in this area, so if we don't find it, then at least you'll know you were right by him."

"Just a few more," she said, now zigzagging this way and that, dragging her foot along the markers, the rubber of her shoe stuttering against the raised lettering.

I began to do the same, wandering randomly from grave to grave, noticing that there were sections where the markers bore Indian names—long, multiple-syllabic, Coast Salish gifts from elders and naming ceremonies, carried proudly by their owners in life and left proudly behind in death.

Nicki began to notice them, too. "Oh! I remember looking at these and trying to pronounce all the Indian names," she said. Then she turned to me and asked, "Do you have an Indian name?"

"No, I don't."

"Indian names sometimes are like descriptions of things, or things that a person did. You know how they are."

"Do you have one?" I asked.

"Yeah, I do, but I can't remember it. I'll have to ask my mom when I go meet her."

I looked up and caught the mischievous smile that bloomed on her face, the look of the cat still choking on the canary.

"What do you mean by that?" I asked, stopping my search momentarily.

"She called me at my auntie's. She's going to call again and send me a bus ticket out there."

"How long ago did she call?"

"A couple days ago." Nicki started looking even more frantically.

"Nicki, don't be taking off anywhere by yourself. We'll try to get your mother back here. You have school to worry about."

"Excuse me," she said, exasperated. "This is my life we're talking about."

"Yes, exactly," I returned. "So, don't go running off; stay where you're safe until we get things worked out. We can talk to Luke about the possibility of you going out there, but don't count on it happening right away."

She shrugged and then dropped her shoulders heavily. "Whatever," she said, and resumed searching. Then she called out, her face still intent on the ground, "Describe yourself."

"What?"

"Say something that describes you."

I spoke the first adjective that came to mind. "Angry."

"What's something you do a lot or what do you do when you're angry?"

You don't want to know, I thought to myself, and I don't want you to know. She was waiting for an answer.

"Well, in a sense I run; I go away. I don't deal with anger right, I suppose."

She looked up at the opalescent sky in an exaggerated gesture of thinking. "Madchild Running," she announced sternly. "That's your Indian name."

I smiled and shook my head. "Not bad," I said. "Not bad at all—except the child part, I'm more than twice your age."

"You're a child," she mumbled. Then she raised her voice as though she were addressing an audience. "You know, the Indian boys from this part of the world had to go off by themselves, really far away, way off into the woods or the mountains for at least a year or two to search for their spirit guides. Then when they got 'em they'd return to their village with their powers. They would be totally different, and they had to be careful when they interacted with other people because their guides were so protective that they might hurt someone they thought was a threat to them. Kinda cool, huh? I know the Lummi boys did that, so you better put in for some vacation and get out there with a blanket and a knife."

"Okay, I'll get right on it," I said, laughing. "How do you know all that stuff, anyway?"

"From Grandpa mostly. But I know the Lummi tribe did it 'cause I read it in a book."

"Damn you're sharp!" I said. "Hey, Nicki. Speaking of names, what were you cutting into your arm awhile back?"

She looked at me, and the corners of her mouth revealed embarrassment that was quickly replaced by a questioning frown, as though she might pretend not to know what I was talking about. "Athena, right?"

A smile moved over her face. "Smart," she said. "You remembered the poem."

"That ain't no Indian name," I joked. Scratching those letters into her arm didn't seem like a serious issue anymore like it had been back then. It didn't reflect suicidal thoughts, I realized, so much as the power and strength that went with the name.

"I bet my Indian name is something cooler," she pondered. "I better check it out, huh?"

"Definitely," I said. "And imprint it on your brain, not your arm."

I moved away from her and stopped about ten feet down from the Chief Sealth grave, facing southeast. Over the green-shingled roof of the church where snow was piling at the pinnacle, past the steeple and across the water, Seattle's buildings stood on the horizon as tiny as a postcard. The path was so clear between the two that an executive atop the Columbia Tower, looking through a telescope, could surely make out the white walls of the church and the canoes resting high on four log posts, and maybe even know the race of people buried there.

Suddenly Nicki yelled, "I found it!" Then she bent down, and wiped the marker with her slender fingers until its copper surface was clear of snow. New snowflakes landed on the ridges of his name and melted as if the metal were warm. Nicki took a few steps back and stood in repose. She looked away from the grave marker that bore her grandfather's name and down at the pure, glistening sparkles of snow that had fallen at her feet. She held onto the flower for a minute or so, then knelt down and laid it at an angle, its color lush against the white background. She got back up and pushed her hands deep into her pockets. As I stood by her side there, she was no longer a child in Luke's caseload, and I was no longer a social worker assigned to drive her around. We were something more, something that transcended the world and its systems, as well as the contrived state of people and their roles and jobs. For that moment we were part of the way it once was and the way it was meant to be. And something else became apparent to me as we stood closely together at the grave. We were walking down the same road, with me thirteen years in the lead. But she was coming up fast behind, twisting her ankles in many of the same holes gouged by the passage of some of those before us. Even the others—the other children whom my soul flapped about, wounded and ineffective, even my coworkers walked the same road, their footprints before me and behind.

"Okay, we better go," Nicki said. She was eager and ready to move again. She knew the way it was supposed to be, the way her grandfather had lived, and she wanted to reach that place again for a moment or two. I also knew the place. I thought of my grandparents. I remembered my grandmother and the old stories she had told in a slow, deliberate voice. And my grandfather, a silent, good natured Flathead Indian who had relocated to the coast, and had worked hard as a fisherman all the way into his mid-sixties when a stroke left his right arm and leg numb. At that moment, I missed them terribly. I missed the answers they could have given.

On the way back to the car, Nicki started pelting me with snowballs. I remained composed and mature for the first two hits, letting them explode against my back and the side of my head. Then I started throwing back. She finally stopped when her fingers could no longer tolerate the cold, jumping into the car and fiddling with the heater.

As the car pulled forward, I could feel it grind over the deep snow that had piled up around the wheels. It was growing dimmer outside so I turned on the headlights, illuminating the snowflakes still falling in front of the beams like shiny pieces of abalone shell.

"Let's play yer tape," said Nicki, and she pushed the cassette in as we drove slowly in low gear back to the ferry dock.

"I didn't know caseworkers listened to loud music," she said, as if it were something refreshing. "Pretty cool."

The Pixies song on the tape roared with the barking of Black Francis, then skidded abruptly to a halt. There was a short spot of static, then the Cowboy Junkie's cover of "Sweet Jane" started up.

"Well, that was too quick," I said. "Maybe we can come back again and stay longer, alright?"

"Yeah! That'd be great. Do you think we can?"

"I don't see why not. Are you hungry?"

"Uh huh—a little."

"We'll get something on the ferry; we don't wanna risk stopping."

"No problem," Nicki said, kicking the empty paper cup on the floor with her toe. "They have good coffee, and I'm comin' down."

14

Christmas came and went. I gave out food vouchers and helped Luke deliver presents to all his foster kids. Most of them got what they had written on their wish lists from their sponsors in the community. I drove the Tall Fighters to the Christmas Carousel in downtown Seattle to meet Josie, and she showed up. Jones and Luke flipped coins to see who would be the Indian Santa at our Christmas dinner for the clients. Luke lost, but for all his reluctance he played a decent black-haired, white-bearded Santa in prescription shades.

Unfortunately, Tia's job didn't allow her to come home for the two weeks between quarters. But during the days leading up to Christmas, my mother came out to my apartment on two occasions. The first time she called to say that she was coming, giving me time to sweep things under the rug. The visit lasted for about an hour. We drank coffee with melted vanilla ice cream in it. I reclined in my black Naugahyde easy chair that Arti and I had swiped from the lobby of an apartment building a couple years earlier. She did most of the talking, while I listened, feeling like a kid in the principal's office, expected to give a voluntary confession of involvement in the food fight. I answered questions curtly, mostly with a yes or a no, reminding myself of some of the clients—the ones who answered questions with such stark reluctance that awkward silence became the most memorable thing about the interactions.

Over the past six months, I had noticed that it took quite a bit to get my mother to come out and ask what was going on in my life, or rather, what was going wrong with it. During her first visit, she did her best to make up for my lack of verbal participation, glancing about the room, raising trivialities, her concern about the reality of my present state showing only in the subtle strain lines around her eyes and in the agitation of the eyes themselves, as the brief interims of telling silence unnerved her. It was her way of stepping back from something that frightened or threatened her. But she was not a weak person, and she would only step back a pace or two, waiting to see if the threat would pass. During the second visit, she did not step back. She now worked in the medical records division at one of the hospitals downtown, and she had come over directly from work, dressed neatly, color coordinated, and wrinkle free. She sat on the bar stool at the kitchen counter, which gave her a perch several feet higher than my position. And with her back straight and her palms on her knees, she came right out and asked what was going on with me. It appeared as if she were balancing on the only clean space in the room above the other surfaces of the apartment, which were cluttered with clothing, cans, bottles, dead plants that had been housewarming gifts from her, dirty dishes, unpaid bills, and unopened junk mail.

When she asked what was wrong, I said, "the usual." She asked how this could be so, and pointed out that I was not like this before the job. Next she told me that when I had called her with a mind and tongue freed yet crippled by alcohol, I had said plenty, and that if I wanted any help then I had better talk now. I told her I didn't want any help.

Then she asked me if I had any ideas about why I was being affected so much by the things that I was seeing and learning, and if I thought that maybe I should quit my job. I told her that it didn't work that way, that it was too late and that I already knew too much.

"What do you know?" she said, with pressing unrest and curiosity darkening her face, like something elemental was missing from the picture.

When I shrugged and didn't answer, she opened her mouth to speak but stopped, her eyes averted to a pair of jeans on the floor, turned inside out with the socks still sticking out of the ankles. Then she exhaled and blurted out, "Do you remember much about the reservation—about your relatives? Do you remember going there as a kid?"

"Sure," I said. I followed her gaze to the pair of jeans on the floor and waited. She then told me that I had known things already, before my job. Looking hard at me, she asked if I remembered the funerals. The topic was heavy, but she was working up to something else.

I remembered that my dad had bought me a new football on the way to a funeral up at Lummi. I had a medium-sized plastic one, and he thought I should transition to the real thing—official-sized, top-grain cowhide. In the parking lot, he tore it out of the cardboard box, and handed it to me with a manly shove to the chest. "Don't let those boys up there take this from you," he said. I couldn't get a comfortable grip on the vast, bumpy surface of the football, and was only able to send it tumbling fifteen or twenty feet off to one side or the other.

We were going to the funeral of a cousin, who must have been in her late teens. She had been gang-raped and murdered there on the reservation. I had either been told this directly or picked it up from my parents' conversations. I knew that it was something terrible, but I don't remember feeling anything.

At the funeral an uncle beat a hand drum and sang songs. Then the church choir followed with a few hymns. The five members of the choir were sisters—an attractive family in pumps and dresses, all with their hair still long, but curled and brushed into blossoms of style like a group of middle-aged white women. The circle of family and friends gazed at the grave and its damp pile of rich upturned earth heaped next to the hole like finely ground coffee, many eyes shimmering and holding their tears, for to cry by the grave can hold back the departing spirit since it becomes concerned for your sadness and lingers to comfort you.

When the singers reached for a high note, a wail rose from the back of the circle, something like the howl of a wolf or the bellow of an elk in almost cliche melancholy harmony. Every head in the place turned, including mine, to see the face of a teenaged boy standing at the back, just as his breath carried the last of his forlorn cry into the air. Then scarcely before it had cleared the hollow of his mouth, he became abruptly self-conscious of what he had apparently done entirely spontaneously. He gave a darting glance over the wall of attention that his heartfelt release had brought upon him, then bowing his head so that his shaggy bangs dropped down into his eyes, he moved quickly off into obscurity. The distraction was only momentary, and before the boy had relocated somewhere in the crowd, everyone had reclaimed their attention. I glanced back, though, half expecting to see the teenager turn into an animal, jump the low sagging fence that bordered the graveyard, and disappear into the brambles with a flash of white tail and black hooves. Later, I found out that the boy was the younger brother of the cousin being buried. He had had no power to save his sister, and not knowing what else to do at her funeral, he had opened his mouth and out came the sound of anguish. For him, it was probably just the beginning of years of helpless noise.

I think my first visual contact with this deceased cousin was her framed high school photograph that smiled from a shelf in her parents' home, where we went to eat after the funeral. It was a gathering of very grim faces, seated around a long dinner table, chewing methodically. I remember there was fry bread and boiled potatoes—yellow and skinned like smooth stones; there was hot stew and coffee; and there was a metallic plaque on the wall with a picture of the Virgin Mary and a thermometer down its side.

Outside, the kids played on into the dark, eating desserts that we'd taken from inside the house. Some of the adults said that if you ate outside after dark the spirits ate with you. As a kid that didn't seem so scary, and I thought that if it were true then they didn't eat that much. The other kids and I tossed my new football around in the dark for hours. I was prepared to stand my ground if another kid had tried to take the ball from me, only believing that one of them might because my dad had said it with such forewarning. If it were to be taken from me, it would be difficult to face him. I wanted to please him. My dad wasn't strict just stern. He didn't punish me, that was my mom's job, and she wasn't much of a disciplinarian. But to disappoint him was a frightening prospect. He was the figure that I was supposed to live up to, an expectation made more mandatory by the grim power that would come and go in his eyes.

"Maybe this job is making you really remember for the first

time," my mom said. "Perhaps it's not that you're getting so upset about what's happening to all those kids for their sake alone. Maybe they're reminding you of things."

This angered me a little, and I became defensive. "Sure I remember," I sniveled like a petulant martyr, "but I didn't have it so bad."

I hadn't said anything about the flashback I'd had in the tavern, but I could imagine the bruises on her face. Then she looked me firmly in the eye and said, "Don't call me drunk anymore. Don't call in the middle of the night, ranting and raving about all these things that are hurting your soul. If you want to talk, which you do, then call me sober."

When she finished, she held my eyes, but I looked back to the pants on the floor. I thought of Tia and what she had said, and I thought of what I had said. Shit, I know, I just get that way, I thought. As weak as it sounded, at the time it was as genuine as the struggles of the drowning.

My mother went on. "Your father drank, too, when we met—but not all the time. Sometimes, when we were young especially, he would just drink for fun, like everyone else around us. Then he could have just a couple and stop with no problem, though if there wasn't a reason to stop, like at a party with our friends, he might get drunk. But he'd stay in a good mood. Later on, he started drinking when he was depressed, frustrated, or angry. And then he became very sad, right to the core. But his sadness, as real as it was, couldn't buy any sympathy once he started hurting us."

Bam! I felt a rubber stopper in my throat, a pound of crystal desiccant in my mouth. All the blood was sucked from my brain pulled from the top of my head, down through my body by a monstrous syringe. I could almost hear the noise it made as it rushed down and away like the throaty suck of a toilet, leaving an empty roar in my ears as I stared into the lovely tortured face of my mother. She heaved a heavy sigh, and her eyes effused release from the prison she had lived in for years, attempting to spare me and Tia the memories that had battered her. Finally she was telling me what she had wanted to say.

I gave a slow, pained nod, expressing a kind of repressed awareness of her attempts at communication.

"I know we've never talked about the violence," she said. "It was my responsibility to do that. As long as he wasn't hitting you kids, I could make excuses for staying with him. I could make excuses for why he was like that, doing it so well that I could actually end up feeling sorry for him. Looking back now I realize what a terrible impact it must have had on you kids, though I'm not sure if Tia would even remember."

"She remembers," I said. "I talked to her about it a little while ago. I think she remembered it better than I did."

She considered my subtle, frightened acknowledgment. "So, you do know. Now what are you going to do with it? You have to do something. That's what all this pain is about. It's pain you've had since you were a kid, just waiting to be unleashed. So do something. At least start thinking about it. And you better think hard, and you better reach out. Because if I get an ugly call in the middle of the night, and it isn't you...." Her eyes became glassy with tears. "If you hurt yourself, I won't forgive you. And you won't ever be able to undo that kind of hurt. So think long and hard, and goddamnit reach out to someone."

I nodded again, more adamantly this time.

Her eyes moved over the apartment. "And clean this place up. This would depress anyone."

I mumbled something like "Yeah, good idea."

Then I offered her some coffee. I was out of ice cream to melt in it so she asked if I had any cocoa powder. I didn't, but I went upstairs and got some from Arti. As she was leaving, she stopped in the doorway and said, "I want you to call me when you're hurting. I want you to call me before you pick up a beer bottle. If I don't hear from you, then I'll call. If you don't answer your phone, then I'll come out. I'm your mom, and that's just the way it is. And Levi, I'm so sorry that you're going through all this. I could have protected you guys better. I thought I was then, but I wasn't, and I'm sorry." She started to cry, and I hugged her until she stopped. Then she wiped her eyes and put her hand gently on the top of my head.

Christmas came and went. My mom got me some new clothes and a book by a Native American author about a mixed-blood embarking on a life-threatening search into himself. Inside the jacket it said, "Merry Christmas. I hope this will help you on your own journey, my son. Love, Mom."

I got her an espresso maker and a dream catcher to block out the bad ones, if there were any. Two days before Christmas I received a card from my sister, Tia, and a little plastic cicada key chain. It had a button on its chest that made it buzz when you pressed it. But the first time I pressed it, it stuck down, and the thing buzzed itself to death. Though I buried it beneath pillows to make it less annoying, its death took two hours.

I mailed my sister a couple of CDs and a card with someone else's Merry Christmas and best wishes for the New Year printed inside. I also wrote that I'd gotten the card and cicada, and that I couldn't stop thinking about her for the following two hours. That Christmas had been a few moments of unexpected reconnections with my family, even if mostly through memory.

Despite the sting of memory and the increasingly inevitable but burdensome task of walking through the ever-widening doorway of reality, I could not immediately defeat the urge to struggle against the torment of clarity and the responsibilities that came with it. But there was no turning back, and I was learning how to welcome the ugliness that had been growing outward from the same origins as my compassion, providing a weak protection, somewhat like the pain of a hangover that temporarily dulls concerns about the behavior of a previous evening. I felt compassion transmogrifying into something more bearable, radiating from within to meet the ugliness from without, the ugliness that was sinking down into my bones and making a home for itself, swimming in my blood. The night after the talk with my mom I dreamed of a new job—in vivid, shocking colors and with ephemeral catharsis.

In the dream there was a rapist on trial—the tenth one that had been tried that day. And after I'd patiently watched turgid, educated faces referring to article this and scrutinizing revised code that, I still had not yet seen a loophole big enough for a rat to squeeze through. I got bored with waiting, so I slipped into my outfit, knowing that this case would not end in the opportunity for the pursuit of Boy Scout merits for good behavior.

And I was right. Before I had finished donning my gear, the rapist was already standing in the center of the small room with his hands cuffed in front of him—in front so that he could feel free to raise them above his head, the way they always do, in a gesture that begs for sympathy, a gesture that futilely attempts to close out the horror of what's to come, to draw death out for a little longer.

The room was empty because it had only one purpose. The floor was smooth concrete with a slight slope toward the drain in the center. From the single door I entered, wearing a rubber suit and a mask. The mask was to keep the blood off my face, clear plastic like the ones worn while operating a propane torch, clear so he could see my eyes. In my hands I had a Louisville slugger.

He knew that he was going to die. Without his options—his catalogue of pleas and appeals—he had only his own innate wish to live, and it set his whole body shuddering beneath the shadow of impossibility.

His cuffed hands squeezed around his head, and wailing with infantile indignation, he made a loathsome and blubbering appeal to humanity as he felt the first swing of the bat crash against his body. "Cruel and unusual!" he screamed. But his front teeth had been knocked out, and they dribbled down the front of his shirt in a thick mixture of blood and saliva. His jaw had been shattered, and one side was torn from the socket, so his words were retarded by broken bone and pulverized tissue. At this I couldn't help laughing a little, swinging with precision, my suit spattered like a butcher's apron. He fell to his knees with my mocking laughter exploding against the softening boundary of his skull, begging right down to the coldness of the floor, his cheek pressed against the place of his funeral, searching for refuge against the implacable hardness of stone. His hands suddenly scrambled along the floor towards my feet as if to embrace them, as if to try and hug himself to my legs with passion and repentance. And I stomped on his fingers repeatedly until his hands were broken and curled like dead and desiccated spiders. And he looked up from the sticky, crimson mask of his face, and though one eye had been ruptured down the center of the retina, he perceived the final downward swing, arcing and descending from high above, the hatred of his own construction giving him a bloody and splintered send-off into the world of harmless organic matter.

15

A woman in her twenties who was raising her little nine-year-old brother called asking for someone to counsel him because he wouldn't listen to her. They were from the Speaks To All family of Montana, Crow or Blackfeet. After the intake, Connie decided to put Jeffrey Speaks To All through the children's anger management group, then pass him on to Becky for some one-on-ones if it seemed necessary. When the twelve-week program was over, his sister called again, asking if something more could be done. They still weren't getting along, and she felt he was slipping rapidly out of her control. He had cut open his hand punching out a window and had kicked a few holes in the walls of their apartment. Jones, the facilitator for the children's anger management group, thought that the kid could use a positive male role model. Consequently, it was decided that I should get together with Jeffrey a few times and see if he would bare some real heart, soul, and demons in a more relaxed, low-pressure environment with a stable Indian role model like myself. We had lots of tickets to the aquarium donated to us for client use so if all else failed we could look at the fish.

Since I wasn't really a counselor, I battered Jones with questions, trying to get a feel for exactly what it was that I might accomplish.

"You're a role model," Jones said in response to my questions.

Goddamnit! Quit saying that, I thought to myself.

Jones smiled like he thought I was nervous. "Just be yourself."

"I just wanna know if I should be talking to him about his fights with his sister and that type of thing?"

"Well, if it seems appropriate to you, then yes. It's okay to ask him how he's feeling about things. You could ask him how it's going at home and just see if he opens up to you a little. Maybe he'll tell you things he didn't say in group, and we can figure out how to help him better." Jones smiled again, pressing his palms together and pointing all ten fingertips at me. "You sat in on the anger management training, you know what to do."

During the first twelve weeks of my employment, I had gone through the anger management course as part of my training but, ironically, my own anger was hardly managed. Despite this, I wanted to help Jeffrey if I could.

I picked Jeffrey up at his school. I had forgotten the general size of a nine-year-old boy, expecting him to be much bigger. He had thin arms and legs, and a straight torso as even from waist to neck as a bag of rice, with no broadening at the chest or shoulders. His face was handsome and serious with light hazel eyes that seemed translucent in contrast to his full black eyebrows and dark brown hair, which was cut short, revealing that his ears stuck out a little. His small, straight nose contrasted with a broad mouth that he sucked in until his lips almost disappeared, turning up the corners just a little as I walked into the office—more of an acknowledgment of my arrival than a smile.

In the car on the way to the aquarium, I asked him questions about school, hobbies, and sports, each question offset by a good stretch of silence. He didn't seem shy, and sometimes his voice would become animated and loud as he talked about something funny that happened at school or an exciting scene from a movie. The quiet was a result of caution, like he knew that his recent bad behavior had summoned me from a place other than friendship or family to give him yet another talking to—and as life had taught him so far he needed to keep his defenses up.

The aquarium was nearly empty, and the lingering awkwardness abated as we moved through the dimly lit corridors, standing for several seconds in front of the rows of illuminated tanks, staring at the unblinking, saucer-eyed creatures on the other side of the glass. The octopus was glued to the front left corner of its rectangular domain by hundreds of white suction cups.

Jeffrey tapped on the glass. "I want this thing to move," he said. He had a look of amazement and anticipation, hoping to see the strange, fleshy animal slide across the space before us. But the thing seemed disinterested, as if it could tell that there was no reason to respond, that moving would be pointless because this child, like the thousands before him, could follow him to nearly every corner.

"You know, that thing sees you almost as clearly as you see it," I said, remembering a piece of appropriate trivia. "The structure of that thing's eye is very similar to that of a human's."

Jeffrey moved around the thick mass of legs and tentacles to get a look at the sagging head, with its swollen passionless eyeball, that bobbed almost undetectably in the current of the tank. "Oh," he said quietly. "I like these things."

Doubting that a significant revelation would come through talk of sea creatures, I decided to go for it.

"Hey, Jeffrey, can I ask you a question?

"Sure."

"Your sister says that you're mad about some things, and I was just thinking that maybe I could help you out a little. You know, we could talk about those things just to get 'em off our chests, and I'll tell you if I got any ideas—ways to keep our anger from gettin' us in trouble."

He just stared into the aquarium.

"What do you say?"

"I don't know," he finally said, his voice subdued.

"What makes you the maddest—when you fight with your sister, for example?"

"She doesn't let me do things, go outside when I want to, stuff like that. And she gets on me about homework."

"Do you think that maybe she makes rules because she needs to watch out for your safety?"

"I don't know."

"What do you do when you get mad?"

"Go to my room."

"Do you yell sometimes or break things?"

He put his hands in his pockets and looked down at the floor, into the shadows beneath the glow of the tank. He knew that I had the answer to that and that his silence was acknowledgment enough.

"Remember when you took that anger management course?" I asked. He nodded his head. "Did that give you some ideas about letting yourself be mad without doing things to get you in trouble, or hurt yourself or other people?"

"I don't know. Maybe a little."

"Do you think that you might like to do some more of that type of thing?"

He twisted up the corner of his mouth into a frustrated grimace, and I noticed for the first time that we were both clearly reflected in the glossy black placard on the wall next to the octopus, where a school of little fish was grouped into the shape of an arrow, pointing the way through the exhibits. Seeing my face, I suddenly felt strange, as though I had been unexpectedly reminded that it was me standing next to the angry boy.

"It doesn't change anything," he said.

So the kid fights with his older sister. What of it? I thought, as if trying to excuse my own behavioral explosions. Yet I had been charged with trying to help Jeffrey so I continued.

"Does your sister get mad sometimes?"

"Yes." His face settled into a frown. I was looking at him in the reflection as if viewing him directly would be too confrontational. I was looking at a picture on a wall of a small boy and me, our faces shadowy in the inky gloss of the reflection, obscured in places by white fish pointing down the hall.

"She's mad a lot," he continued, "so why's she talking about me? Why's she get to tell me what to do? She's not my mom."

"Do the two of you talk together about what makes you mad?" I asked, almost whispering to my own reflection.

"We don't have to talk about what makes us mad," Jeffrey said. "If we're fighting, then that means we're mad."

"But you love her," I said, meaning to complete the sentence by adding, "don't you?" and making it a question. But it came out a statement.

Jeffrey looked up at me and said, "'Course."

I shifted my gaze from the reflection to Jeffrey and said, "She loves you, too."

Jeffrey nodded. "I'm sure she does."

"Are you Blackfeet or Crow?" I asked. "Someone told me, but I forgot."

"Blackfeet."

"You ever live on the res?"

"When I was little," he said. Then, he added, "It's just a place."

"It's an important place, though," I said. "I know there are some bad things about it, but the good things that are there and the people who were there before you are very important. I probably can't even tell you why it matters so much, but you'll just have to trust me now and figure it out later."

For a while, I looked into the silver bubbles that wobbled like beads of mercury up the back of the tank, wondering where my father was and what he was doing at that exact moment, wondering what I was doing, and wondering how my nine-year-old brother next to me would wield his rage in a man's body.

"Hey, why don't we check out the rest of this place?" I said, motioning with my head in the direction that the school of fish pointed. "We can talk some more later."

Jeffrey jumped in step next to me, relieved that, for the moment, he was off the hook. The octopus had glided down the glass like the pouring of thick fluid, and it was moving across the rocky bottom as we walked on.

When I took Jeffrey back to the apartment he shared with his sister, I told him that things can get better, that it's good to talk, and that we could talk again, with his sister, too, maybe. I also told him that when he got angry to think that his sister was also hurting and that they needed to support each other. He held my gaze and nodded. But he didn't ask me if we could get together again. I watched from the car to make sure he got in, thinking that his sister might open the door for him, but he had his own key.

When I got back to the office, Verna had gone home, and all calls were going to Wilma. She shouted from her office that my mother had called.

"What'd she want?" I asked, checking the employee board to see if Jones was in.

"She wanted to know what you were doing at the aquarium during work hours. I told her you were down there lobbying for our percentage of the fish—ayyyeee! She wants you to call her."

I found Jones shuffling a stack of papers at the photocopier. "How's it goin'?" he asked.

"It's goin' okay. Jeffrey's got no parents," I said, plunging right to the heart of the matter. "That's why he's mad. And it's probably the same with his sister."

"Yes," said Jones, "we talked about that some in group."

"Did he and his sister ever come in for sessions together?"

Jones considered the idea thoughtfully. "That's a good idea. In fact, that's usually the way we do it. We'll talk about bringing them in together, or maybe you and I can go out there for a couple home-base sessions. Regardless, I think you should continue seein' him." Then he gave me a pleased smile and shook his finger at me. "See, you didn't need to doubt yourself; you're okay." Ultimately, Jeffrey and his sister did come in together, but I never worked with them or saw him again.

Another dream came, but this one during the day while I was awake—like a vision perhaps. I was able to see through the eyes of my great-great-grandmother, a woman who died before my birth but of whom I had seen a picture. Actually it was more like eavesdropping on someone else's vision, or possibly the result of my subconscious painting me a vivid picture of things lodged in its deepest recesses, presaging a possible future from out of the transpired past. It came on quickly and clearly, presented to my senses like a real scene as opposed to being constructed by imagination.

First I saw her on the porch of a low, square house, and I knew I was viewing her at the turn of the century. The house, made of gray planks, was comfortable and weathered looking, manufactured and milled by saws but faded like beach logs worn by surf, current, and salt. The sun was shining brightly upon the boards so I knew they were warm to the touch. The house blended in with the wild landscape that surrounded it. Blackberry bushes had grown into impenetrable thickets where some of the trees had been cut. Since it was a sunny day, Mount Baker, or Komo Kulshan, "the white, shining mountain" as she called it, appeared close in detailed clarity of rock and white snowdrifts.

Granny, which is the name my father called her, had rolled a cigarette. She didn't smoke all the time like people do now but only once in a while, at times like these, sunny days when there was no more work to be done, and she was compelled to sit on the porch with Komo Kulshan seemingly just a few fields away. She was wearing a long skirt of thin, faded, dark blue material and a shirt buttoned up to the neck, the soft, loose-looking cotton not restraining even though it was fastened across her throat, its color subdued like the plumage of a seagull's breast.

The wooden chair she sat in had been constructed haphazardly from scrap wood, with floral needlepoint cushions, one on the seat and one draped down the back and secured with thin straps. The whole contraption seemed to relax beneath the slight burden of her weight.

I saw how much she belonged, how right her being there was. The image of her figure on the porch of her boxy government-built house, on her land, was as perfectly normal as the trees that towered behind her. Her face was exactly as I had remembered it according to the picture I had seen over and over for years of my life, a portrait of her with a shawl wrapped around her shoulders. In the picture, she was very old, and her eyes appeared entirely black with no white showing. The lines of her face were so defined that I realized I had seen only a few elders in my lifetime with faces so powerfully etched—faces that had lived nearly a century of a lifestyle that is now extinct, bearing the sun's heat, and the full bitterness of winter.

In the vision, her hair was pure white like the mountain snow next to her, even though she looked about twenty years younger now than in the portrait, and like the snow her hair reflected the sun. It was pulled loosely back behind her head, having probably been secured more neatly at the outset of the day before the day's tasks.

She exhaled a cloud of smoke, and in the haze came a transition, a sight that filled the familiar scene before her sharp eyes.

Whereas I had seen her in a world that was not of my time, she now saw something that was not merely anachronistic but alien and alarming, for it was from a time yet to come, of which she had no knowledge through pictures in books or the spoken accounts of others. She saw a small room where the walls were clean and newly painted, but somehow in their newness the unblemished whiteness possessed a force of its own that was exhausted with experience and history; a force that gobbled up the scenes and energy that pulsed within the space, like a starved person or a person being force-fed faster than he can chew and swallow. In this room she saw items with colors that were as bright and shiny as fish scales, small cans that she thought to be a type of commodity—a reservation fixture truer than the promises of any treaty—cans of sustenance from government to Indian. But these new cans were small and busy with blue and red and names that meant nothing to her. And stacked on the shellacked surface of a desk were black boxes of a glossy, foreign material that gave off concentrated points of light—red, yellow, and green—that burned within themselves but shed no light as a candle or a lamp does. Also, there were plants inside the house; plants with fragile spreading leaves like no plant she had ever seen in the forests, living in the stuffiness of this room with brown, desiccated edges.

There was fabric in piles on the floor—clothing it appeared to be, striped and checkered and patterned with colors and lines and shapes, even bolder and brighter than what white people in the city wore. She saw what she knew to be a lamp because of the light that issued from beneath the circular bonnet of metal, but it was skeletal looking, long, jointed and bent like a fleshless arm growing up from the desk and throwing its light in a harsh white splash against one of the walls.

In the center of the room, with the reflected light catching him at an angle and partially illuminating his immobile figure like the subject in a still life painting, was a young man. She recognized him as a descendant she would never see. She could feel her blood in him, though he did not look like the Indians of her time, just as he did not look like the whites. The room was blotchy with shadows—

shadows from the light and shadows emanating from the man. And she felt fear when she saw that the shadows that came from the man were fragments of his spirit. They moved over the mute shapes and machines in the room that were like those of the whites but different, each with an empty presence, fragments of spirit moving over and around them.

The man held one of the shiny cans that he tipped to his mouth at listless intervals, taking a liquid into his body with a motion as passive and automatic as a broken tree limb moving in the wind. She recognized the liquid from the way its ingestion accelerated the detaching shadows—the vague fragments that seeped from the young man to wander about the room. When the can was empty, the young man set it down and picked up a six-shooter from the floor, which was covered to every corner with a yellowing, spongy turf, shaved as close as the fur of the wool dogs that her people once had had decades before her birth. Then the young man pressed the blunt barrel to his forehead, but the room became so dark that my great-great-grandmother could no longer see what was happening. So she began to sing. And soon the vision was gone and she was seeing only the mountain Komo Kulshan again. And she prayed for all her grandchildren.

16

The Lummi Reservation was located about two hours from Seattle. My great-great-grandmother had belonged to the first generation born to live there under the freshly penned mandates of the 1859 Treaty of Point Eliot. With the image of her undaunted spirit still vividly in my mind, I began heading north to the land that she had walked upon. I had told Jeffrey Speaks To All that the reservation was an important place. I would go to the house of my oldest living relative, my Great Aunt Rita, the sister of my father's mother. I was almost there.

When I had asked my mother for my great-aunt's address, she had looked through one of her old address books that she had moved to the bottom of a drawer with the others that held outdated information. She was very silent while she searched, as though something very significant was taking place. I asked only for the number and told her nothing else. She would help me in any way that she could, although she knew there was something she could not find for me or replace with her support. In her silence I could feel her strength with me and I could feel the urgency in her movements, as though quickly acting upon an opening in the blackness.

Before I left, she gave me a firm hug. "Go up there and see her," she said. She had written the number on the back of a grocery receipt. I had been nervous when I had called my great aunt and when she answered began talking quickly to explain who I was. There was a soft laugh at the other end as she said, "I know who you are."

With the sound of Auntie Rita's voice, I could see her face vividly and feel the intangible sensation of a different time, the way a smell from a certain period in your life triggers recollection—not so much the memory of sights and sounds but the exact weight, shape, and feel of your thoughts and perceptions at that past time being brought back to life. I felt ashamed that so much time had elapsed since I had visited the reservation, told her that I wanted to see her, and asked if maybe she could teach me an Indian song or two.

Now I was almost there. There were flood-damaged fields to each side of the road, now plains of hard mud, spotted with the blackened stumps and twisted roots of trees, the earth around them eroded away, leaving them hulking on the surface like fallen big game.

I was thinking about a past visit to my grandmother and grandfather, and an older cousin of mine, who arrived with her sister at the same time as us. We had all taken seats in the living room when my auntie suddenly asked my cousin where the little girl had gone—the one who walked up to the house with her and her sister. "There was no little girl," my cousin answered.

But our auntie was insistent, saying, "Sure there was, she looked just like you."

Somebody pointed out that maybe it was my sister, Tia, who was nearly three at the time. But no, this was an older girl she had seen, four or five years old. As it turned out, my cousin was pregnant but had not told anyone until then when she knew her child had been seen by Aunt Rita. My great aunt saw things like that all the time and didn't consider it a big deal. I wondered if she would see something in me and have a better idea about why I was there than I did—probably.

The surroundings looked the same as they had years ago. The fireworks stands were still sagging at the roadside—shacks of bleached plywood, chipped paint, and splinters. Purse seiners and gillnetters had their nets spread out over huge wooden cable spools and sawhorses, waiting for repairs. Yards were strewn with dismantled cars, their hoods thrown open like beaten dogs exposing their throats. Packs of Indian children stopped during their play to watch me go by, and mangy res dogs charged the road, barking, their chests and paws spattered with mud.

As my memory stirred, uncurled and stretched, I realized that we had come to visit fairly often when my grandmother was alive and my dad was with us. After my grandfather died, which was about five years before my grandmother's death, we would get her and bring her over to Aunt Rita's place if she felt like getting out of the house. With Grandfather gone, she seemed to welcome the opportunity of leaving the house for awhile. Other times we'd just stay at her place. She'd tell stories, we'd eat, and I'd catch snakes in the yard and hold them captive in a big Folgers coffee can. My grandmother always told me that I couldn't take them home with me because they might get killed trying to find their way back. Then she'd laugh.

I pulled into Aunt Rita's sandy driveway. The front yard and the porch were in full sunlight, but the rest of the house was in the cool, pungent shade of several tall cedar trees. It was a small, one-story home with big clusters of scallop shells on fishing line hanging from the porch, making a dry scraping noise in the wind like muted rattles or wind chimes.

I walked up onto the porch purposefully slow, looking around and remembering. There were twisted pieces of driftwood on the porch, white and gray and sanded smooth by the elements. There were piles of bleached sea urchin shells to either side of the door, protected by an awning from the light drizzle coming down. A few more urchin shells with the greenish-black hue of algae were spread about in the sandy garden like strange little skulls.

As soon as I knocked on the door, I could hear the legs of a chair scraping against linoleum, then footsteps. Aunt Rita opened the door and stood there for several seconds smiling broadly, her eyes studying mine as if slowly recalling the image of the little boy that had once played in her yard, and the skinny adolescent that came around a couple times a year with his mother, before disappearing completely after the death of her sister. Auntie Rita's face was now much older and thinner, her dark skin heavily lined with living. Her hair was an even mixture of black and white in many tight wispy curls. Her black eyes gleamed and twinkled like ocean water under the moon's reflection, and she nodded her head up and down with a warm smile on her face.

"It's good to see you, Auntie," I said, feeling like a child who'd come to visit without his parents.

"It's good to see you, too." She embraced me then stepped back to look me over again. "I'm glad you came back." She turned to go in, beckoning me to follow but soon looked back at me out of the corner of her eye and asked, "Where the heck were you anyway? Did you get lost? Ayyyeee!" Then she laughed with the same heartfelt volume as Wilma. I laughed and followed her inside.

Photographs covered half the yellowing wall space, and each picture seemed to be just a little crooked, creating a sort of chaotic collage that was consistent enough to work without giving you the urge to start straightening them. Because I wanted to look at them all closely I began walking slowly around and saw army photos of young men in dress uniforms from World War II to present day; family portraits; recent school pictures of children; and portraits of stern-faced elders, their skin looking alabaster in the overexposed and fading prints. I realized that most, if not all the faces, were my relatives.

My eyes stopped on one of the family portraits where the little boy in front held his lips tightly together with one corner of his mouth cranked up into a smile and the other side not quite making it, as if it was the last shot on a roll, and he was fed up with the whole affair. His hair was cut bowl-style, the straight bangs whacked right across the eyebrows then angling down the temples and over the ears like a helmet. The mother, an attractive white woman in a green pastel dress, was holding a chubby baby that had been stuffed into a polyester dress with a monkey sewn on the breast of it along with white tights and black, silver-buckled shoes. Full and heavy, the baby's cheeks pulled her short, serious mouth into a slight frown. The father had one arm around his wife and the other long-fingered hand on the boy's shoulder. His hair was just longer than a crew cut, black and shining with styling oil. He had a broad smile with large white teeth and prominent smile lines down his full face. It was my family, when I was about six. A thumbtack held a black and white baby picture to the corner of our portrait, the infant's feeble, dimpled hands up under his face, the eyes swollen shut.

Aunt Rita was at the sink cleaning geoducks, working around the flaccid white bodies with a paring knife, then rinsing them off and tossing them into a mason jar. "You seein' that picture of you folks?"

"Yeah."

"That look on your face makes me laugh," she said, chuckling.

"Is that baby picture me, too?"

"Yeah, that one's you. You were really a screamer. Your grandma got so tired of it she'd just ignore you. So eventually you got to changing your own diapers; you'd just sprinkle on a handful of commodity flour and tape yourself up, heh heh heh!" Her shoulders jostled up and down.

I laughed with her and took a seat at the Formica table placed between the living room and the kitchen. Aunt Rita toweled her hands dry and came over to the table. There was a shallow, woven cedar basket filled with candy and walnuts sitting in front of me, some of the candy wrapped individually and some stuck together—Christmas candy in bright reds, greens, and yellows.

Aunt Rita handed me a nutcracker from the table and pushed the basket toward me without saying anything, then went over to the stove, where a kettle sat with the lid rattling upon the growing pressure of steam. She looked inside and turned off the burner. The smell of salmon rushed into the air. Then she went back to the sink and picked up her knife again. "I got some salmon heatin' up for you. It'll be ready in a minute."

"Great," I said.

She smiled. "Were you wishin' for some?"

"Yeah, I was." I began cracking and eating walnuts.

Aunt Rita was now an elder with children, grandchildren, great-grandchildren, nieces, and nephews. It is the Indian way to drop in and visit, to eat, to just sit and talk with the family. She probably had as many visitors in a week as there were pictures on the walls. But having visitors didn't mean she had to quit going about her business. The fact that she sat me down and was throwing some food in front of me like any other nephew felt good, like the time elapsed didn't matter; what mattered was that I was there.

"What are you doin' down there in Seattle these days?"

"Well, I graduated from the UW, and now I'm working in the

social services for Indians in the Seattle area. It's called Urban Native Support Services."

"Oh, that's good," she said. "I like to see you kids go to college and use the education you got in a good way like that. How's your mother doin'? I think about her at times."

"She's doing alright," I said. "Keeping busy, working, that sort a thing."

"That's good. Everyone liked her. So smart and polite, she fit right in with us, ayyee! And yer sister?"

"Good. She's still goin' to school in New York."

"Yer mom stopped bringin' you kids around. I haven't seen Tia since she was just tiny."

The mason jar was almost full, and she was putting the huge necks into a separate bowl. My grandma used to make fish head soup, with salmon heads and backbones simmering in broth with potatoes, macaroni, onions, salt, and pepper. My dad and I loved it. My mom put up with it to be respectful. She had a psychological difficulty with the severed heads bobbing around in the kettle, the eyes going from death-vacant to milky-white. Deer and elk, crab, frybread, and strips of smoked salmon—these things were always served, depending on which had been brought over by relatives.

"I don't suppose you ever hear from my dad?" I gave no thought to the question before asking it.

Aunt Rita turned from the sink, resting her wet hands on the drainboard with her arms in a straight, locked position, her shoulders up under her ears. She looked me directly in the eye and shook her head. "No, I don't see or hear from him. Some folks seen him around here at times, years ago, but rarely then even. Last I ever heard he was headin' up to Canada."

I picked at the crushed walnut in the palm of my hand. "Canada, huh?"

Aunt Rita went over to the stove and shoveled several big flaky chunks of steaming fish onto a plate, then brought it over to me. "Are you lookin' for your dad?" she asked.

"No, not exactly. Well, maybe in a way. I'd like to know what became of him. If he's even alive."

There was a loaf of white Oven Joy on the table, a box of pilot bread crackers, and a tub of margarine flecked with breadcrumbs and globs of jam. She scooted each item toward me several inches to let me know that they were there.

I thanked her and began to eat, buttering the bread and crackers, then putting pieces of salmon on top. I remembered my father saying that the food always seemed better out here—so simple but so good. And it was true.

"What have you been up to?" I asked.

She was putting a tea kettle on the stove. "Oh, I had a busy couple days this week. Some people came over to place orders for wool hats. You know when they become dancers they get the wool hats, and a bunch just became dancers so they needed a few made."

"Smokehouse dancers?"

"Yeah, Smokehouse."

"Do you go there much?"

"I still go," she said, "but I don't stay too late anymore. I don't want to catch a cold and have you guys bury me." She gave a loud laugh at this, her mouth remaining open in a wide smile.

We had gone to the smokehouse one time. About a mile off the road, down a narrow snake of ruts and potholes, it was a tall building of old gray planks, surrounded by tangles of slender alder, maples, and blackberry bushes. I remembered deer hoof rattles and hand drums, shaking and pounding with a force and power almost frightening to me as a child, grabbing the center of my body with such heavy thumps of energy I found myself holding my breath, opening my eyes wide with an experience not fully understood but recognized for the respect that it demanded. I recalled hearing voices chanting and listening with my heart and the marrow of my bones—as I was listening here now in Auntie Rita's house.

Aunt Rita brought the tea kettle over and set it down on a pot holder. She poured herself a cup and offered me one. "This is an herbal tea from a plant that grows here called Xex mein. It's medicine, good for everything."

"Sure I'll have some," I said, holding up the cup she had given me, which she filled with the dark liquid.

"You dry the leaves out and burn a little bit of 'em when you're afraid, and it helps you not to be afraid no more," she said matter-of-factly, her face in repose as she watched me take the cup.

While I ate and drank the strong tea, she talked about my relatives and what they were doing, who had gotten married, who had had children, and who was going to school, each time explaining their relationship to me. When I finished my tea, she poured me some more. As she did, I watched her hands, which were as expressive and as wise as her face—lined, calloused, powerful hands, each contour telling of the guidance she had given, all the lives she had touched, all the mouths she had fed, and all the young Indian faces she had held in them.

"So you want to sing a few songs?" she asked when she'd seen that I was done eating.

Feeling a bat-sized butterfly flap through my full stomach, I took a deep, nervous breath. She noticed, and it made her smile. "Yeah, I would," I said.

She walked slowly into an adjoining room, where I could see her sewing machine and sewing materials, and a supple ragged-edged piece of deer hide, about the size of a small tablecloth. She got her hand drum, its yellowish-brown, mottled surface appearing almost translucent toward the center, where uncountable beats from the leather of the drumstick had buffed and worn the hide.

She eased down onto the couch, and I turned my chair out to face her. "What kinda songs do you want to learn?"

"Anything, I guess," I answered, awkwardly. "I'm not really sure."

"Okay," she said, looking at a spot somewhere on the floor, a place for her eyes to stop while her mind searched for a song. "Levi, I'll do each song a few times for you. When I sing, try to sing along. It doesn't matter if you don't know the words or sounds. If you try to sing with me, you'll learn them."

I gave a nod and waited. She was bouncing the stick gently off the taut surface with just the slightest sound, then she closed her eyes and began to beat the drum. Her song opened up softly at first, then gradually grew louder, the old Indian woman's voice dancing with the heartbeats of the drum, the high and almost undetectable vibration of age carrying the sound, her far-reaching connections with the songs showing like both a sadness and a smile on the chants.

I started by humming, then began to form syllables, trying to let myself go but not being able to completely shake the touch of anxiety and self-consciousness that impinged upon my comfort with the sound. Slowly, I began to recognize the repetition and the circular movement of the songs as she repeated them.

After each song, she told me its name: "Dance of the Whirlwind," "Dance of the Maiden," "Dance of the Little Man," "Dance of the Mother Earth," and "Dance of the Salish Warrior." On and on she sang for about thirty minutes. The last song was "The Spirit of Sla Hal," a lamenting song that was strong and fast. I could see the dark expanse of huge waters, and smell cold wind and salt; and there were islands towering in the sky, their backs bristling with trees like the hackles of wolves, huge animals crouching and sloping down to drink from the lapping waters; and canoes cutting the surface like tiny water bugs beneath the awesome slope of rising firs, cedars and snowcapped mountains. The song moved through a low chant vibrating on the quick hard palpitation of the drum, then climbed to a wail that rose off the sharp valiant cry of Coast Salish words that were foreign but struck me as mine, and I felt the hot pressure of tears. Aunt Rita's dark eyes moved over mine, and she nodded her head, telling me that we were going to bring the song around one more time. And we sang.

When it was over, she placed the drum across her knees like a dinner plate and watched my face for a while. Then she spoke. "There's no excuse for what yer father did. He left and didn't come back. I'll tell you something. In the smokehouse there are black paints, and there are red paints. You know, the people paint their faces either black or red, depending on which type they become. Black paints are more group-oriented, and red paints are more solitary. Your grandmother was a red paint, very insightful and strong. We thought your dad would be one, too, but he wouldn't go into the smokehouse to get his song and find out if he would be a red paint or a black paint. He was sick inside and he needed to go in, but he wouldn't. I think that's what happened to him. When you get sick that way, like he did, you need to go in. If you're lookin' for him and you find him, Levi, don't expect too much."

"I'm not gonna go look for him," I said. "I wouldn't know where to start."

"You're not going to look?" She leaned in a bit like she were telling me a secret. "It's part of why you're here, enit? You're lookin'."

I held still and listened. "I see your scar," she said. I glanced down at my right hand where it rested on my knee, as it instinctively withdrew like a scolded animal. "Why are you lookin' at your hand?" she asked. "I mean here." She reached out, and touched her wise old index finger to my chest. "He's a part of you, Levi, in your blood. But beyond that I don't think you know much else. I don't think you got the chance." She straightened up and pointed at the picture of our family on the wall. "You don't have to find him to know what you are. You're findin' out right now—by comin' here. I know what yer dad was like, with you folks I mean. Your grandparents were real disappointed in him for the things he done. But you, Levi, you're the one to make sure that the way he was as a man doesn't move on into the future. You can carry the good things, like this." She softly tapped the drum one time with the stick and smiled. "Knowing the way he was because of his pain will help you to not be that way. You must carry the good things instead and heal this." She reached forward again, touching her finger to my chest.

"I'm gonna try," I said.

"I know," she assured me. "That's why you came back here."

I looked down at my hands. "Yeah, it is."

"You got a good start then. So, do you got 'em all?" Auntie Rita asked, raising the drum and the stick again, indicating the songs. Then she smiled, her cheeks balling up beneath her eyes like smooth apples.

"I think I need to hear them again."

She dismissed this with a wave of her hand, chuckling, and said that her voice had had it. Then she went into another room, and I could hear her opening a drawer and scraping around for something.

She came back out with a cassette tape. "They're all on here," she said, and handed me the tape. "This is me and your cousin Joe singin' all them songs. Oral tradition, eh?" She laughed again.

I stayed for a while longer, talking to her as she went back to canning geoducks, occasionally taking a few minutes to sit down with me at the table. When I told her about my dad not being able to enroll us when we were kids because of the mixture of three tribes, she looked very surprised, then shook her head and said, "You go down to the tribal enrollment and have 'em go into the records. You got plenty in you for enrollment. Yer both Lummi and Klallam, but that won't make no difference. That wouldn't have kept you out. Sounds like a mistake was made. I'll tell you what, you bring Tia back here, too, and we'll all go down there to the office. We'll get you both enrolled." She smiled and shook her head. "I thought you were enrolled at the beginning." It sounded so easy. I wondered what kind of effort my dad had made way back then.

When I left, I took the tape with me, three jars of canned salmon, and two frozen crabs. As I stood at the doorway, Aunt Rita also handed me a small baggie. It was the Xex mein. "Take this and burn it when the need comes," she said. Aunt Rita extended her hand, and my fingers closed around the herb in a confluence of her world and mine. "I will," I said. Then I also promised to come back and bring my sister and mother with me.

On Lummi Shore Road, on an impulse I pulled over at the casino and parked in front of the grocery store. Two men had their pickup truck parked by the pay phone, an older Indian man and a middle-aged one. The older man was sitting on the open tailgate, while the younger man was putting air in the rear left tire. Rust had eaten away at the fenders. The older man was talking—calling over the side of the truck bed to his friend. He stopped when he saw me. "Hey, brother," he said.

I thought he was going to ask me something so I stopped. "Hey," I answered, but he was just saying hello. He resumed telling his story, while I went to the pay phone and dialed my sister's number in New York. I wanted to tell her that we were going to be enrolled, adding two members to the tribal head count—two members long overdue. Now if the federal government ever wanted to check up on me, I'd come up on the computer screen as Levi Shea, card-carrying American Indian with the right to fish and hunt in the usual and accustomed places, and not pay taxes when buying potato chips at any convenience store on tribal land.

I let the phone ring eight times. There was no answering machine.

The older man was talking about a woman they both knew: "Nora got fitted for her dress nearly three months before the wedding. Then she went and gained fifteen pounds."

I dialed again in case I'd gotten the wrong number the first time, again letting it ring eight times.

The man continued his story: "When she came down the aisle, squeezed in that dress, the organ was playin' 'June is bustin' out all over'—hah, hah, hah!"

Then the old guy's friend rose up from the side of the truck, with dark glasses, sparse mustache, and a wide grin, the air hose dangling from his fingers. "Kinda the theme song, eh, uncle?" They both laughed.

I hung up the phone and got back into the car. I looked at the bag of Xex mein on the car seat next to me. It was awfully small.

17

I hadn't heard anything about Nicki for a while. I knew she had been coming in every week for counseling, and since her aunt was able to bring her in I didn't have to. I had seen her only once since visiting the graveyard. One day when I was on my way out she was just walking into Becky's office. When she saw me, she stopped in the doorway for a moment as if she were going to come out and talk, but she didn't move and looked very serious, as though my encouraging presence just wasn't what it used to be. "Come by my office sometime," I said. She nodded at me with cool affirmation, then gave a big smile.

The next week I came back from a transport to see that she had stopped by, and we had missed each other. There was a note on my door that said: "Are you ever here?"

It was a few weeks after the visit with my Aunt Rita when I finally spoke with Nicki again. It was late February, and it had gotten nearly too cold to rain. On my way out of the office Luke stopped me and said, "Guess what?"

I knew it was about Nicki. He always seemed serious when he was going to tell me something about her, taking special care to be sensitive about something that was maybe a little more difficult than all the other rough crap.

"What is it?" I asked.

"Nicki wasn't there when her aunt and uncle came home from work, Levi. She gets home from school at about three o'clock. Frieda is usually there before Nicki because she works part-time in the mornings, but today she ran some errands, and when she got home—no Nicki."

I glanced up at the wall clock above Vicky's desk. There was a browning half of an apple on her desk calendar. "It's only five," I offered. "Maybe she went somewhere with friends."

"No, that's not it, Levi, Frieda checked her room. A bunch of her stuff was gone. She left most of it but a couple of her bags were missing." Luke had taken off his tinted glasses and was tapping them methodically against the desktop.

"The rest didn't fit her," I said absently. "she's outgrown it."

"What?"

"Some of the clothes were from when she was smaller; they didn't fit so she left 'em."

"Yeah, well I reported her as a runaway," Luke said. "At this point that's all we can do, unless you got any ideas about where she might be."

"What about her dad? Maybe she's going home."

"Yeah, I thought of that. I called him and told him that if she shows up to call me immediately, and he said, 'She shouldn't be out on the streets at her age, you people should find her.'" Luke shook his head. "Dumb shit, enit?"

"She's pissed at him," I said. "She wouldn't go there."

"He's still her dad," said Luke. "You never know."

"Remember what I was tellin' you about her mom calling her, about Lydia sending Nicki a bus ticket?"

"I don't know," said Luke, "I'm thinkin' there's the possibility of her meetin' her mother somewhere here, in the city. Maybe her mom had a bender in Yakima, she's sobered up, and now she's back in town to get her daughter."

"But maybe Nicki's going out there," I said.

"I doubt it. Twelve-year-old girl with no money or know-how travelin' around; I doubt it."

"She's got plenty of know-how," I said. "Probably too much."

"Yeah, I suppose it's possible," said Luke. "If the cops find her, she'll go to CPS after hours; they'll get a hold of Nicki's auntie and uncle." Luke put his glasses back on and stood up. "I'll give my home number to Frieda. That's all we can do for now. Let's just hope she makes it through the night, okay? Hell, she'll probably show up on Frieda's porch tonight, cold and hungry."

Luke moved past me and stood in the doorway. "I gotta lock up," he said. "Let it go for now."

"Why don't I give you my home number in case you get word," I said suddenly, "like if you need me to go talk to her." I felt immediately uncomfortable, like I was not presenting healthy boundaries, and I wondered if my eagerness had thrown a surreptitious, possibly even perverse cast over my relationship with this twelve-year-old girl. "We got some things in common," I added, trying to clarify my seemingly desperate commitment to the case.

"Do you know what transference is?" Luke asked me.

"Sure," I answered glibly. "Something being moved from one place to another." I felt angry and embarrassed at the fact that I was feeling angry and embarrassed.

"Put up some boundaries, kid," Luke said, slapping me on the shoulder with a stiff arm and open palm, like a trainer telling me I was taking too many shots to the head. "Don't bend over backwards 'cause you mighta been through similar stuff as this kid. You don't need to waste your night worrying about it."

"Well, this is really shitty," I whispered, facing Luke's empty chair near the window. It was already dark outside. The window was a shadowy mirror with the faint sounds of rain on the other side. I could see Luke waiting in the doorway.

"This kind of shit was happening before you got here," said Luke's reflection, "and it'll be happening when you leave." The finality of this statement silenced me.

Back at my apartment I turned on the TV and wiped the gray film of dust from the screen with a dirty sock. It sounded as if Arti was dragging cumbersome objects across the floor upstairs, possibly moving more furniture around the entertainment center. I thought about calling him and maybe going out for pizza and beer.

Luke's comment had propelled me into an alienated, dejected place—a place for wound licking and brooding, a place where a child goes with his cheek still stinging from a heavy-handed swipe across the face. How did Luke's sense of boundaries serve Nicki? How did it serve me as I gathered speed in a piecemeal unearthing of the reasons why I scrambled alongside Nicki's path, hands outstretched with melancholy anticipation, waiting to catch her when she stumbled and save her from the fall?

In my fridge there was some cheese and salami. I made a sandwich with no condiments and found a lone can of beer that had gone unnoticed behind a browning hunk of broccoli. For about a half hour I sat in the stolen easy chair, chewing, swallowing, sipping, and watching sitcoms I didn't recognize. Then suddenly I brushed the crumbs from my shirt, turned off the TV, and dug through the drawer in the kitchen where I had put the Xex mein. I crumpled the dry stalks and leaves into a tiny blackish ball and burned it on the base of an inverted coffee cup. When the last wisp of smoke had drifted to the ceiling, I put my shoes back on and headed to the Greyhound station, where I sensed that Nicki either was or had been.

I drove past the line of yellow cabs waiting for fares along the front of the building, past the wall where the Tall Fighters had been eating the Cheez Whiz, and found a space one block from the station. When I entered the building, I didn't really expect to see Nicki. If she had planned to take a bus to Yakima, then I had no reason to believe my timing would be right. I just felt that I had to check. The interior smelled of dead air and urine like the stagnant confines of alley doorways. From the loudspeakers in the ceiling, a voice squawked with a pitch so high and metallic the words were nothing but irritating gibberish. The voice blurted the announcement three times before I could make out what it was saying, "Bus from Wenatchee has arrived."

The glass doors swung open, and the passengers ambled in, their faces a combination of aimlessness and urgency as they did a visual scan for their rides. Three young Mexican boys dressed in black from head to foot bumped into one another, appearing somewhat stunned by the light of the station, as if they had just crawled out of a box and into the sunlight. One of them was lugging a maroon suitcase that probably held the possessions of all three.

I scanned the hard plastic chairs welded together in rows like egg cartons. The lights were out in the ticket office, which was recessed beneath an overhang, shielding it somewhat from the long fluorescent bulbs lining the ceiling of the station and giving it a gray cast. The only sign of intelligent life was the yellowing plastic backs of two computer monitors visible atop the long counter. On the glass divider was a paper clock reading "will return" with the fat red hands set for 7:30.

There, about three rows back from the ticket counter, I saw Nicki, with her serious profile facing the "will return" clock, waiting for its promise to come true. She was wearing a green baseball cap, and her hair was pulled into a hurried ponytail with some loose strands tucked behind her ears.

I walked up to her and stood at her side with my hands in the pockets of my long ski jacket. She felt me standing there but didn't turn right away; I saw her eyes narrow, staring at the thick glass along the ticket counter but focusing on her periphery.

"Nicki," I said. She looked up at me without surprise, seeing an old acquaintance whom she would have preferred to avoid. "We need to talk about a few things, Kid. This place for starters. I'm afraid I gotta put my foot down and take you back home."

She sighed heavily and gripped her knees with her hands. "That's where I'm goin', Honey," she said, tension shifting the smooth flawlessness of her face.

I sat down next to her and leaned forward, looking straight ahead as she did. "Well, that's not what I meant. Home for the moment is with your aunt."

The corners of her mouth turned upward in an icy mock smile. She shook her head but said nothing.

"Nicki, why don't you talk to me about what's going on. Take your time and just tell me what happened." I noticed she had her rust-colored gym bag pushed partway beneath her seat; it was overstuffed, and the seams were pulled flush with the vinyl material of the bag. It looked like a huge sausage, its swollen contents straining against the thin membrane.

"I talked to my mom. She said to be at the station by 6:00—said she'd wire me a ticket from Yakima. We're gonna live there."

I looked at my watch. "Nicki, it's 6:30. Did she send it?"

She winced and shot me a look of exaggerated hurt, her eyes rolling toward me scornfully. "No, not yet. I'm going to check again when the guy comes." She gestured towards the ticket counter with her chin.

"Look, Nicki," I said pointing at the paper clock, "it says he won't be back until 7:30." I looked up at the schedule board and found the bus to Yakima set for a 6:45 departure.

"No, that thing's not right," she said shaking her head. "He's been comin' and goin'."

"Nicki, the last bus to Yakima is 6:45."

"I know. We still got fifteen minutes."

"Nicki, you can't be here by yourself. It's dangerous for you to pull this kinda stuff, got it? You can't be doin' this crap anymore. It's time to go home."

She looked up toward the ceiling and settled into her seat, getting a firm position for the battle. "You mean I'm not allowed to be with my mom? What's home, Levi? What are you talking about?"

It did sound a little crazy. "Nicki, it's not that you can't be with your mom. But she left you, and it sounds like she's drinking a lot. Now, Luke has to figure out if he can recommend you go over there, and if he does then we can work out the trip; but you can't just go runnin' off. It's dangerous, and if anything happens to you I won't forgive you."

"But I'm already here," she said, after thinking for a few moments, "and nothin' has happened to me. Now you can make sure I get safely on the bus. And besides, there's a security guard—a great big black dude walking around here. If anything happened, I woulda started screamin' for him."

"Nicki, I can't let you go. This is something that needs to be decided by Luke and Wilma."

"Look!" Nicki said, pointing at the ticket counter, "he's back again."

A young black man stepped into the office from an unseen door and began poking around behind the counter.

"Just check and see if she sent it," said Nicki. "Maybe he's puttin' me off 'cause I'm a kid."

"Okay," I said, "we can check."

A white man with his hair hanging in his face dove in front of us and slid to a stop at the ticket window, the sound of sand and Formica grinding under his battered loafers. He flung the oily strands out of his eyes with one hand and jabbed the other over the glass divider with an old dollar bill sticking out between two fingers.

"I need some change, man, I got a program comin' up."

The black man looked at the dollar. "I don't have any change."

"C'mon, I only need four quarters for your TV."

The employee glared at the man, opened a drawer beneath the counter, and scooped out four quarters. He snatched the dollar from where it hovered a foot or so away from his face and slid the quarters through the slot at the bottom of the window. "That's all. Don't ask again."

"Thanks man, I appreciate it." The white man shambled off to the row of chairs with small black and white TVs growing up out of their arms, plopped down, and fed his quarters into the plastic growth.

The employee at the ticket counter turned his attention to us for the first time. "Can I help you?"

Nicki pointed at me. "Yeah," I said on cue, "I'm checking to see if her mother has wired her a bus ticket to Yakima. Her name's Nicki Sanders. The ticket would be from Lydia Sanders."

Nicki pressed her hands against the glass.

"Yeah, she was checking on that awhile ago." He punched a few buttons and studied the screen.

I suddenly became aware that I was holding my breath. Maybe I wanted to see her mother come through just for one small triumph.

"Sanders?" he said. "Nicki Sanders—no, nothin' here for her, sorry."

I put my hand on her shoulder and guided her away from the window. "She's probably not ready for you yet," I said. "C'mon, let's go sit down for a minute."

Nicki sat down and wound her hand up in the carrying straps of her bag to anchor herself.

"Nicki, your mom's in a lot of pain, too. She loves you, and I'm sure she wants you with her, but she isn't ready. She's sick right now, but we'll talk to her and let her know what she needs to do to get you back."

"You're going to take me back, aren't you?" Nicki was looking me straight in the face, trying to touch that place of kinship, the source of turmoil and ambivalence within me, appearing confident that it existed. Her eyes scintillated with demand, waiting for me to commit to the jagged direction that she had steered me in months ago.

"Nicki, I can't physically stop you. I'm not gonna carry you outa here, but I'm tellin' you, you don't know what's waiting for you out there, maybe nothing, maybe just another bus stop. You know what I'm sayin'?"

She smiled a little, and her eyes moved around the room, seeing through the walls, staring into her mind. "Hey, that's a good name for a poem," she said. "Just another bus stop."

"Go ahead and use it," I said. "Now let's go home."

"Can you just call her for me," she begged. "Call out to Yakima and see why she didn't send a ticket. See if she's there."

"I don't know where she is, Nicki. I can't call her."

She reached into the pocket of her jeans, pulled out one of my cards and turned it over, revealing a phone number with area code 509. She handed me the card. "It's long distance," she said, "so I couldn't call."

Why hadn't she called collect? She was too bright not to think of it. She was afraid. Afraid to hear a drunken voice at the other end with no recollection of the promise. Afraid to face one more rejection. And so was I. Maybe it was time to draw the line.

"There's no point in doing that now," I said, dismissing the idea hastily. "I'll have Luke talk to her first thing tomorrow. We know there's no ticket, now let's get some sleep, and we can look for answers and solutions tomorrow."

She loosened the carrying strap from her hand. "Please call. I wanna know."

It was getting unbearable. It was beyond the ticket now. She was seeking an answer with some finality, no doubt thinking something like, Did you forget to send the ticket? Do you remember my birthday? Do you want me back? Do you give a fuck? "I'm going to give her another chance, Levi," Nicki announced. "If she blows it, then I'll leave her and move in with my auntie and uncle and live there 'til the end of my goddamed days! I'm not a little kid. I'll decide where I'm going."

The security guard shuffled past, looking from side to side. Just as Nicki had said, he was a huge black man, his neck swelling out of his collar and exceeding the diameter of his head. His whole body was a series of bulges through his dark navy uniform, cinched at intervals with belts and seams binding him into an uncomfortable short-stepped gait. "See," said Nicki, "he's been watchin' out for me." Finally the security guard exited the other side of the building. "Are you gonna make the call?"

I walked to the pay phone, and Nicki didn't follow. I could've punched a bunch of numbers and mouthed a phony conversation to the dial tone, but she knew I wouldn't do that. She knew that I was going to make the call. I picked up the receiver and dialed the number off the card. I was standing between two people in a line of three pay phones—a man bitching to his ride for not picking him up on time and a bag lady. I plugged my other ear with my finger but could still hear the conversations next to me. The phone at the other end began to ring. On the third a man grunted hello, his voice sounding rough and put out, as if getting to the phone had exerted him.

"Hi, is Lydia there?" I asked.

"Liddy? No. She was, but she took off. Who's this?"

"Levi. I'm calling from Seattle. I'm sort of a friend of Lydia's family," mainly Nicki, her daughter."

"Oh, yes, Nicki! How is she?"

"You know Nicki?" I asked, slightly surprised by his sudden enthusiasm.

"Oh, yeah," he said, with affection in his voice. "She's a great little girl."

"Yeah, she is," I agreed, "but she's not doing very good. We're trying to find her mother."

"Well, Liddy took off yesterday, drinkin' you know. We don't drink no more, so she didn't want to be here, I guess. She's probably still around, but we ain't seen her since she left. But I'll tell her yer lookin' for her, if I see her, eh?"

"Okay, I'd appreciate that. Hey, do you know if she sent a bus ticket to Nicki?"

"No, I don't know nothin' 'bout that. Does Nicki need a ticket out here? She could stay with us 'til her mom shows up if she needs to."

"No, that's okay," I said. "Thanks, though." I gave him Luke's name and number, as well as mine. He told me to tell Nicki that Dave and Emma had said "hi" and that they'd look for her mom. I thanked him and hung up.

The security guard was back, escorting a bum out of the bathroom, the scrawny transient's zipper still down, the front of his shirt covered with vomit. One of his hands fumbled at the zipper while the other thrashed the air around his head as if he were being set upon by horseflies.

Nicki was watching me, sitting very still like a painting of something beautiful surrounded by chaos and impurity, sitting in a place where she didn't belong, strong and sad and sublime. I walked over to her and sat down. "When did you talk to your mom? When did she tell you there'd be a ticket here?"

"Yesterday."

"She's gone, Nicki. She left her friend's house yesterday."

"I knew it. I could tell."

The employee who had been working the counter came out from a door next to the ticket windows with a black leather jacket over his blue coveralls. He pointed at me and Nicki as he passed. "Good luck," he said, and hurried out into the night.

"Nicki, it's 6:50."

Nicki picked up her bag. I could see that it was very heavy.

"Let me take your bag for you," I said, holding out my hand.

"No, that's okay," she said. "I'll carry it."

It was late by the time I dropped Nicki off at her aunt and uncle's place. Her aunt hugged her for a long time, pulling the girl's head to her breast and surrounding her tightly in her arms. Her uncle put his hand gently on top of her head. "We want you to stay here as long as you need to," he said.

Nicki stared hard at me before I left. As she looked at me, the piercing intensity of her eyes faded, as if strength and freedom had been relinquished. It was an ancient expression reflecting both pain and wisdom. It made me think of the eyes from pictures I had seen in books, like the Apaches waiting to board the prison train to Florida. I had seen this expression on Nicki before, in the dream I'd had the night after first meeting her—the dream in which her face was being painted with bands of deep red, like a mixture of rich soil and blood. When I left, there were crows in the trees outside the house, cawing in the darkness.

When I got home, I called Wilma and told her that I had acted on intuition and had found Nicki, and that I had taken her back to her aunt and uncle's home. Then I asked her if I had done the right thing. Wilma sounded excited that I had found Nicki, but she became somber as she listed the things that we had to do to bring some stability to Nicki's life. I could hear she was washing dishes, and while she was speaking, she dropped a dish and it smashed to bits in the sink. "Shit!" Wilma cursed. "You did the right thing, now get some sleep, and I'll see you tomorrow."

18

After hanging up, I called Arti. We hadn't gotten together in a couple of weeks, only occasionally crossing paths entering and leaving the building. Now we walked to one of our usual spots several blocks from our apartments with a mutual stooped posture and mood, feeling no need to talk, plodding toward our destination as if out of ritual.

Arti was a detached support. Throughout the last year, I had spent many hours at the table with Arti, staring into the blank space before me that reflected my condition. But Arti's presence served as a sort of anchor to keep me from floating completely into nothingness. He stayed rooted there just off the highway of my concerns, not wanting to know too much about the traffic. But this time I felt I might bounce a few thoughts off Arti to see what came back.

For a long time, we sat in silence with a pitcher of beer. There was a bowl of peanuts on the table along with a bowl for the shells. Arti had a box of Hot Tamales, and he periodically threw a few into his mouth, chewed them lackadaisically with horse-like rhythm, then washed them down.

"So how's the job?" he finally asked after a half hour or so of fractured conversation and a couple of preparatory pints. "You sounded kinda bummed on the phone, and you look like you've been awake for a few days."

I exhaled and offered the first comparison to my condition that came to mind. "Have you ever thrown a gunnysack full of kittens into a river?"

"Is that your analogy of the job?" He frowned and took a sip of his beer.

I shrugged and popped a whole peanut into my mouth, shell and all.

"What's that all about?" Arti asked, arching an eyebrow up into a severe angle.

"I like the salt on the shell," I said, grinding it up and swallowing.

"That's one way of getting fiber, I suppose." He raised his glass and took another sip. "Now, you were asking me about the kittens. No, I've never done that, but I think I might see what you're gettin' at. Why don't you give me some specifics."

I looked at him for a moment with a premonition of only partial perception on his part, resulting from a gradual rift in our experiences over the months, fearing that maybe he wasn't going to come close to understanding.

"Man, I haven't drank since I visited my auntie," I said, stopping my glass in transit to my mouth and staring at it with mundane wonder.

"What auntie?"

"My grandma's sister on the Lummi Reservation."

"I bet it'd been a long time since you'd been up there." Arti's words were garbled by Hot Tamales.

"Yeah, it had been," I said, picking a few grainy splinters of peanut shell off the end of my tongue. "I threw a sack of kittens in the river," I blurted, "and now I'm responsible." I was suddenly irritated by the obtuse longevity my analogy was taking on.

Then I took three long gulps, determined to make Arti understand what I'd been through. "In my job I assist people in getting services—intakes, outreach, referrals. The main purpose of our program is to divert families from the system and help them get around when they're in it. I have a caseload of people, but most of my contact is with the kids. I'm usually the one who makes initial contact with clients before the counselors take over. The idea is to eliminate the need to remove the kids, and to keep them from getting hurt."

I fell silent and stewed over my explanation so far, feeling a little anxious. It was colorless and distant; verbalization had sucked the power right out of it. But I kept trying to explain.

After taking another long drink and wiping the foam from my mouth, I said, "You meet a kid, and you make a connection. You know what's been going on at home for this kid's entire life. You meet them and you become responsible. You want to right a bunch of wrongs, and you find that sometimes there's nothing you can do. And you know what's coming in their future."

Arti was resting on his elbows, holding his glass against his cheek. "You're letting everything be so damn dark, obsessing over that job, holing up in your apartment, breaking your bathroom mirror. And by the way, just 'cause I almost majored in building construction doesn't mean you can rely on me to keep fixing all the furnishings you smash. You need to start bringing some positive stuff into your life, you know? Like maybe get a girlfriend. For example, I'm still seeing that girl I was telling you about when you were heavily medicated at my apartment awhile back, and things have gotten a little better for me since we started dating. She brought something of value into my life to help offset the burdensome load of crappy stuff."

Arti's words hardly registered as he played a shoddy devil's advocate to keep the interrogation of myself going out loud. "I'm not emotionally ready for a girlfriend at this juncture," I responded. "I think that only a prostitute would have me at this point—that is if my salary permitted one, which it doesn't."

"Jesus! Get a grip," Arti said, glancing to the table next to us where three young professional-looking women sat, rolling his eyes to show them that his sensibilities had been injured, just in case theirs had been. Then Arti sat for a moment with his mouth open, waiting for my next words.

"The term you hear the most is 'the cycle of abuse,'" I continued, determined to stay with the only subject that I could discuss. "It's the shit that happens to these kids, the shit that their own parents and relatives are doing to them because the same shit happened to them when they were kids, and it goes on and on. Do you know what I'm sayin'?"

"Of course. The cycle of abuse and violence is a human issue, not just an Indian thing." Arti drained his glass and refilled it with enthusiasm from a newly arrived pitcher. Foam gushed over the sides and he attacked the lip of the glass with his mouth, sucking at the foam like a dehydration victim.

"The goddamned system comes in too late," I mumbled. "After turning the Indians inside out, the system comes in to clean up a little of its embarrassing mess."

Arti was silent for a half a minute, gazing around the bar.

Arti's eyes moved down to the table top then back up to me, and he said, "This whole thing is personal, isn't it? But Levi, you can't undo the past." Arti's eyes took on a flicker of discomfort. Then he thumped the tabletop with the knuckle of his index finger and said solemnly, "Is it maybe that you can't figure out how to handle being Indian? I mean, were you not really thinking there'd be this much shit when you got into this job, or did you know there was, and you felt you had to get into it 'cause there's no way around facin' it? Quit talking about the kids, Levi. Say a little something about yourself. That's who's on the rack here. Let's hear about you." He stopped and took a drink, pain reflected in his eyes.

"Yeah, Arti, I know," I said, somehow relieved that he understood. I continued. "Arti, that girl I told you about, Nicki, made me remember things about my life when I was her age. It's like when I hear about her grandparents or parents, I see my family reflected in the stories. Nicki's following the same path that I am. My dad was like her dad. She's been dealt the same cards that I was dealt way back when, and I did my best to ignore them. Then I met that kid, and I see where I'm coming from. I've found out what I am, and there's so much ugliness and so much beauty that there's this knockdown-drag-out battle ragin' between the two sides, and that can break a person. You know?"

"Yeah, I gotcha," said Arti. "Now go get some counseling, you basket case!" He thrust a knuckley finger at me, holding it there for a dramatic few seconds. "Embrace and heal that inner-snot-nose! Here, have a Hot Tamale."

"No thanks, I hate those things."

"Do you think I'd insist if I didn't know what was best for you?" Arti persisted.

I grudgingly took one of the capsules and ate it with displayed disgust.

After I swallowed the thing, Arti raised his glass in a toast and said, "To our children's future of pavement and extinction." We clinked our glasses. "Do what you can," Arti said. "You know what's right, now do what you gotta do." I nodded and took a drink. After a couple drinks you can feel better about life's difficult journeys into the self. But after a few more, this resolve begins to warp, you become immersed in a counterproductive fog, and soon you're rebelling against the comfort you had momentarily obtained, rebelling against your own best interests, and perverting the healthy progression that you almost had attained.

"Shit," I hissed with inebriation. Suddenly something dawned on me in a resolute flash of rash defiance with a corresponding failure of rational thought. "Then that's what I'll do. I'll do what I can. I'll see this one through—just this once. The system failed her, and I owe her, goddamnit!"

"Owe her what?" Arti shook his head rapidly like a bug had flown into his face.

I ignored Arti as he tried to maneuver his head into my wandering field of vision. "Transference? Okay Luke, what if it is? You detached, pompous, psychoanalytical...Shit on the boundaries! What's worked so far anyway? Nothing, that's what!"

"What the hell are you talking about?" Arti interrupted.

"Destiny, Arti," I said for lack of a better word. "I think that's what I'm talkin' about."

Arti slumped down in his chair. "Don't do anything you'll regret, whatever it is you're yakin' about."

I realized that it wasn't about satisfying the dictates of my job, bound within the confines of an eight-hour workday—it never had been. It was about doing right by Nicki, doing right by myself. Just doing right. If no one else would stand by her, I would, as I would for my own sister, and as my sister would do for me. It was about loyalty.

"Arti, I'm going to take one last action on gut feeling and then step away. I think I've gotten the picture. I'm so goddamned right I can barely stand it."

"Well, whatever you're talkin' about doin', I ain't drivin' you there."

We didn't talk much anymore. When a third pitcher was empty and there were another three inches of beer left in his pint, Arti said, "I'm fading, and I'm hungry. I think I'm going to go home and make myself a great big thing of stuff. Meeting adjourned until next time."

I acquiesced. "Yeah, sure."

"Are you coming?" he asked.

"I'm feeling kinda heavy and introspective," I said. "I might need another beer to deal with it. You go ahead."

"I'm not really in a position to say anything," said Arti, "but you can't use that as a crutch forever." He pointed at the empty pitcher.

"It's more like a wheelchair," I corrected, "and you're not in a position to say anything. Just wait 'til your relationship falls apart. You'll be beggin' for a pull off the overflow bucket after last call."

Arti nodded with theatrical resignation at the troubling portent of my words. Then his face became serious. "Look, I didn't want to upset you when I kinda went off on you a minute ago. But you need to face it. That's all."

"It's okay. I know what's goin' on in here," I said, smiling and tapping my temple.

Arti nodded and walked out into the night. I hurried through another beer, sipping mechanically. I laid down my money and walked into the bathroom. As I stared at the wall above the urinal, inches from my face, I saw that some drunken clod trying to make the most offensive and inflammatory remark that he could exhume from the bowels of his intellect had scrawled, "I fucked your mom." Just below it, some pragmatic smart-ass had responded in a smaller more unobtrusive hand with "Go home Dad, you're drunk."

I chuckled with appreciation and left the bar. It had begun to drizzle, with icy mist falling. I drove downtown to the Greyhound Bus Depot, which was empty except for an old woman asleep in her chair, a bonnet fashioned from a plastic produce baggie. I went to the ticket counter, where an East Indian man asked if he could help me. I laughed a weak, ironic seizure of a laugh riding on a short expulsion of tired air. "Yes, I think so," I said merrily. "You can fix me up with one ticket to Yakima for Nicki Sanders, leaving anytime tomorrow afternoon."

The man banged on the keyboard and examined the screen through thick glasses with a rose tint. "How about a 2:00 P.M. departure, Mr. Sanders?"

"That's perfect, but Nicki Sanders is my little sister. I'm her brother, sending her to a place where she can stop, where she can feel."

"Good," said the man. "That's twenty-one dollars and fifty-two cents." After I paid, he handed me my ticket—my ticket across the healthy boundary into the far reaches of unacceptable conduct and poor judgment, rallying behind the belief that if a kid wants to be with her mom, despite how unraveled and incapable her mom might be, then she should have her.

When I woke, my resolve was still intact, though weakened slightly without the bolstering of booze. The first thing that I saw after the blurry, pale expanse of the ceiling was the bus ticket placed on the milk crate next to my bed. I showered, got dressed, and went to work with the ticket tucked in the inside pocket of my jacket. In my mailbox at the office, accompanying several invitations to trainings that focused on healing and justice, was a note from Connie LaForce that read:

> *Levi,*
> *I need you to do an intake. Go to the address below and see Kristen LaGuardia, a Chippewa woman from Minnesota, 21 years old. Don't have many details. I get the impression she's thinking about going home. Wants to talk to someone here to tell her about the program. She split with her husband. It's a domestic violence case, but she said she doesn't mind a man coming out. Could be better anyway in case her husband shows up. Do intake and just find out what's happening. See if we can offer any help. She's got two little kids. She'll be home all morning. Call her if you can't be there before 12:00. 636 East Fir St. #202 (about a mile or so from here), 328-7064.*
> *Thanks,*
> *Connie*

I fastened the note to my clipboard then thought again about Nicki, deciding I would call her and tell her about the ticket. I would implore an oath of silence as to its actual origins. Then I would drive to the Chippewa woman and do the intake, allow her experiences to coalesce with mine, take her by the proverbial hand and run away, pump a few bullets into her husband, and live happily ever after, or at least until new, unseen and horrific discoveries of ugliness rocketed me into a violent mood crash, sending me fleeing for an exit to another path. Probably not. Instead, after a brief intake I would rendezvous with Nicki and send her away like she wanted, to Dave and Emma, the clean and sober friends of the family, so she could continue her search for her drunk mother. I would instruct her to call me if it didn't work out, and if not then I would get her on another bus back to Seattle. And then I would focus on positive change for myself, face my own questions and embrace the answers. I would perhaps quit my job, realizing that it had served its purpose, and move, enlightened, on to something else, having learned an important lesson the hard way. I would move on, stronger, a better person for all the experiences of the last year.

I dialed Nicki's number at her aunt's, assuming, feeling that she would be home, having refused to go to school in the interest of recovering from a recent and intense bout of betrayal. I was right. She answered the phone. "Yeah," she croaked. Her nose was plugged, and her voice was hoarse. I figured she'd been up smoking and crying all night.

"Nicki, it's me, Levi."

"Levi." She repeated my name with particular deadness. "What's up?"

"How are you?" I asked, awkwardly.

"Forsaken and fucked."

"Watch your language. Are you still packed?"

"Why?"

"I'm going to swing by your place this afternoon. I have something for you. I'm doing you a favor of the kind that's never going to happen again. So wait and don't go anywhere."

There was a long silence on the other end, the inert air of

understanding.

"Keep the bags packed. Do you still have Dave and Emma's number? Are you listening?"

"Yes."

"Do you know them well?"

"Very well."

"Then you'll wait?"

"Yes, I'll be waiting." She suddenly sounded like a very small child, and I was struck with visceral, incapacitating guilt.

"Okay," I said. My voice faltered, and I thought about how nice it would be to drop dead still clutching the phone.

"I'm not mad at you," Nicki whispered. "Just so you know."

"Okay," I said again, and hung up the phone with a click that struck me as very final sounding.

I put on my jacket and headed off, with the information about Connie's task fastened to my clipboard, to Nicki's destiny—and mine.

I parked across the street from the apartment where Kristen LaGuardia was staying, walked up the stairs from the open courtyard, and knocked on the door of her unit. The peephole went black as someone on the other side peered through at me, then the door was flung open by a tall, slender Indian girl.

"Are you Levi?" she said, as I was getting ready to introduce myself.

"Yeah," I said, lifting up the clipboard with affirmation, "and you're Kristen?"

"Yeah, c'mon in."

She had light brown hair and dark, frantic, angry eyes, darting rapidly about and locking onto all new stimuli in her environment, prepared to guide her body in a gush of instinct in accordance with any encroaching threats she sensed. Her wide mouth had red chapped lips that she pulled in tensely between sentences. She was wearing a thrift store combination of white jeans and a shirt of striped pastel shades of orange from a previous decade, her breasts small and squeezed in the tightness of the shirt, her torso and waist straight and adolescent looking.

She spun on her heel with such suddenness that her long brown hair swept around her shoulders in a centrifugal fan, as she plunged back into the apartment. I figured that perhaps something was burning on the stove or that she had an important person from across the continent waiting on the phone. I followed in her harried wake of agitation into the cramped apartment.

She definitely intended to leave. There were packing boxes, heaps of clothing, and toys scattered around the floor. I moved to the couch on the far side of the room, the only piece of furniture other than a sagging, tattered armchair and a coffee table, and sank uncomfortably into a deep, yielding cushion.

She was picking her way through the flotsam when she stubbed her bare toe on one of the boxes. With an attempt at great force, she shoved heartily at the box with a long, skinny leg and managed to drive it across the carpet and up against the wall.

I took the pen out of my shirt pocket, preparing to commence the intake.

"I plan to go back to Minnesota," Kristen began, as she located the stack of children's clothing that she was apparently looking for and stuffed it into a Naugahyde suitcase. "My asshole of a husband is still around, and he's going to be back. He explodes, he pouts, he crawls home—that's the pattern."

"Are you expecting him soon?" I eyed the door with mild dread.

"God, I don't know where he is or what he's doing. He started raisin' hell two days ago and pushed me into the wall right there." She gestured off to my right, where the drywall was cracked and concave in the rough shape of a human head and shoulders.

"Shit," I said squinting at the wall. "Are you okay?"

"Yeah, it didn't hurt—these walls are flimsy. The asshole is paying for it, though, I'm gone. Jerk's got nothin' we want or need. All he's got is a nice truck, snakeskin boots, and a bunch of big belt buckles. Other than that—zero."

"Did you call the cops, file a police report?"

"Nope, I'm sick of all that crap. Besides, he left because I hit him with a hammer. He's out drinking right now, and I'm loading up and leaving."

Her two kids, a little boy and a little girl, were on the floor of the recessed kitchenette, dabbing up what looked to be spilt sugar and licking it off their sticky fingers. Apparently, they had been at it for a while, as evidenced by the rug lint stuck to their faces like five o'clock shadows.

"Hey! That's enough you two! Get up and go play in your rooms—c'mon!" Kristen shoed the kids out of the kitchen. They stopped a few feet from their mother's waving hands and stared at me. "I'm doing it this time. I don't have to take this anymore. I'm gone." Kristen stared into my eyes, then looked down at the clipboard, where my hand and ink pen hung over the paper like a wet towel drying on the line.

Overwhelmed, concerned, and amused, with vacant obligation I scribbled, "Girl bouncing off walls. Kids eating sugar off floor."

"How old are they?" I asked.

"Five and three," Kristen said, flinging open the freezer door and hoisting TV dinners, chicken pot pies, bags of vegetables, and a whole chicken into a box. "You can take this food. You have families who could use it, don't you?"

"Yeah, sure. I can do that."

Next Kristen advanced on the cupboards, piling canned goods, Raman noodles, and spaghetti into another box. She stopped abruptly, clutching a can of creamed corn, and strode out to the living room and stood in front of me with her legs spread shoulder width, her hip cocked out to one side. "We'll see if that bastard tries to follow me," she threatened, shaking the can of corn menacingly. "We used to live back on the reservation together. We've only been in Seattle for six months. I just found out a little while ago that right before we left, he stole my grandpa's fly rods and paint compressor—my grandpa was a painter—and sold it all for drinkin' and drugin'."

"He uses drugs?"

"I don't know what he does anymore."

I looked past Kristen to see that the kids had crawled into the kitchen and were back at the sugar. "They're back at the sugar," I said.

Kristen whirled around and escorted them out by the collars of their pajama tops. "To your room, please!" They exited the kitchen and took up their previous positions several feet away.

"Now, Kristen," I said, determined to bring some structure and coherency to my presence. "I understand that you plan on leaving in a hurry, so what exactly do you need from us?"

"Advice. Legal stuff, I guess. I was going to get a restraining order, but that doesn't matter now because I'm goin' for sure. I've made my decision. My family can't stand him. He wouldn't dare follow us."

Kristen began picking through the toys, shoving the bigger ones into a pile against the wall and tossing the smaller ones into another suitcase, this one red with an imitation lizard-skin pattern. "You can take some of these toys, too, if you want. I imagine you have families in need of 'em."

"Yeah, maybe," I said. "You know, Kristen, it sounds like you're in danger if he should come back before you're outa here. Maybe you should think about calling the cops."

"Well, you're here," she said, as though her summoning me had obviated any further concern for security.

"After you hit him with the hammer," I pressed on with increasing misgiving, "is that when he left?"

"Yeah, I hit him in the forehead after he started shoving me around again, and while he was stunned I just backed into a corner and waited. The kids ran to me and held onto my legs. After standing there rubbing his head for a while like a dumb ox, he kicked a hole in the wall"—she gestured to the wall opposite the one with her imprint, to another ragged hole that I had not noticed before—"Then he stormed over to the cupboard, grabbed my bowling ball of bourbon, and stomped out."

"Your bowling ball of bourbon?"

"Yeah, it was a collector's item. It was a bottle of bourbon in the shape of a bowling ball with a pin connected to it for the handle. I don't even really drink, but the thing's been sealed up for about twenty years I think, and I wanted to save it."

"That's understandable," I said absently.

"Look, Levi. I'm leaving and it's final. What exactly do you guys do, anyway?"

"Well, we're a social services agency for Indians. We have a counseling component, a foster care component...."

"Do you have travel vouchers—money for Greyhound tickets, anything like that?"

"Well, yeah, we do, but you gotta be a client for three months before you're eligible for any of the financial assistance."

"Oh, well, that's okay. We'll manage." She glanced over to the kids. They were sorting through the garbage pile, discreetly rescuing some of their toys, and transferring them to the simulated lizard-skin suitcase.

"Kristen, I haven't really had the chance to ask you many questions, but it sounds like you're doin' the right thing. There's no reason you should put up with him hurting you."

She had squatted down to enter the same space as her kids. Because she wasn't wearing any shoes or socks, her bare toes were gripping the dismal green shag of the carpet. She smiled, and her face and body relaxed at the same time, like she was suddenly really looking at me. The trepidation in her eyes was dispelled for a few moments, and they were strong and young and bright. I wanted the image of her crouching there among the boxes with her two small children to burn in. As chaotic as the last few minutes had been, I recognized in that instant of her smile not only her own sad deviation but a painful evolution that had laid its hands on all of us—me and Kristen, Nicki and her parents, all of us.

I was returning her genuine and truthful smile, when a very bad thing happened. There was a loud crack that seemed to shake the walls, its origins a startling, heart-stopping mystery for only the most infinitesimal fraction of a second before my senses converged as if sucked into a vacuum, a vacuum created by the front door as it exploded inward, the jamb tearing and popping off into two splintered strips as the cheap hollow door slammed into the wall, the knob punching yet another hole in the drywall.

It was Kristen's husband—a young Indian man inflamed with drunken rage. While he paused briefly in the doorway, strangely my eyes first focused on his huge silver belt buckle, as big as a postcard.

Then, dumfounded, I saw the object in his hand—the goddamned bowling ball of bourbon. His lips trembled, shining with spittle as he tried to form words, his face twisting up balefully with pain and fury. There was a bulging red contusion on his forehead. His hand spasmed, jerking twice toward his mouth, as he struggled with the impulse to take another drink. And then in a decisive explosion of focus he stepped forward and hurled the cumbersome collector's item at me. Impulsively I ducked, though it was hardly necessary, since the ball toppled awkwardly above my head, striking the wall about five feet to my left, shards of glass and a fine powder of dry-wall exploding with a heavy crash, the smell of bourbon rushing over me, screams from the children erupting like sirens.

"I can't believe it. You already got some guy here!" he bellowed, coming at me, growing larger with his approach, his face tomato red and swelling, his belt buckle bearing down on my face, now as big as a license plate.

With considerable effort, I freed myself from the soft embrace of the couch and rose to my feet, holding up my clipboard with two hands. He was on me in three strides, each step punctuated by my entreaties—"Hold on! Hold on!"—and Kristen screaming, "Get out, you bastard!" Then he swung quickly with a strong right deliberately at the clipboard, as if it were hateful and tormenting like the red flash of a matador's cape. His fist passed through the particle board and carried through to my shoulder, having just enough force to sit me back down into the couch. With pieces of clipboard still in the death grip of my fists, I fought back, bouncing around spastically in the cushions, as he descended upon me, our fists and arms clashing between us, his knuckles glancing off my forehead and my right cheekbone. My fist connected with one of his front teeth, and a tremor rocked through his head and neck. I flung the two halves of the clipboard aside, and in a maelstrom of self-preservation, indignation, and rage, I dove up and forward beneath several of his drunken haymakers, driving my head into his abdomen, penetrating and pushing with my legs. He folded and stumbled back, feet digging in for balance, his calves pinning against the coffee table, then he went down hard, the legs of the table cracking as it flipped partially up on its side, grudgingly allowing his body passage, then settling back on all fours, broken. I straightened up and took a half step back, then wound up and kicked at him with unbridled adrenaline, missing his body as he squirmed to the side, the instep of my charging foot catching the lip of the coffee table, sending it over and onto its back like a stranded turtle. Then Kristen entered the tunnel vision of my senses, pointing from me to him, back and forth erratically with great vigor and condemnation of the whole scene. She shrieked, "Stop it, right now, goddamnit!" In nearly the same instant that I perceived her advance, a lukewarm mist blew forcefully into my face, filling the space between me and her husband. I could still see my target in the cloud, and raised my foot to stomp, with such enthusiasm that I nearly leapt off the ground. Then I brought my foot down with all my weight toward his head as he raised himself up with his arms, pulling his legs in toward his body to rise. My boot crashed into his head just as an amazing pain bit into my eyes, lips, and every pore on my face. My vision fled the burning sockets as the thick rubber sole of my boot connected with his skull. The impact was more felt than seen, as my weight and momentum rode his head and shoulders to the floor, pinning him to the carpet, his neck twisting, my ankle twisting, my foot sliding down the side of his face, my balance sliding away with the rush of inertia as I blindly buckled and fell, reeling forward into the side of the stove bordering the entrance to the kitchenette with a hollow metallic boom as the thin sheet metal bowed and creased before my weight. I was on fire and almost fully blind. It was mace; Kristen had hosed the two of us down good.

"Aw shit!" I bellowed pressing my eyes pointlessly into the crook of my elbow. I tore my arm from my face and forced my eyelids to blink open, catching a hazy acid glimpse of the space before me. Kristen's husband was hunched over with his knees tucked under his stomach, his hands poised and trembling ten inches from his face.

I lunged for the exit, my arms bent before me, my face tight and swelling like a giant beesting. I slammed into a wall and rebounded towards the door that was wide open, its handle stuck in the plaster. I forced a blink for the next direction, and beheld a huge woman in a voluminous muumuu, back-peddling from my approach in horror. "Call the cops for christsakes!" I howled, stumbling down the concrete stairs, grabbing at the railing and groping for my footing. I made it down and jogged through the courtyard, hunched over and stealing tortured glances ahead to my car. There was a mud puddle by the passenger door, and I dropped to my bruised knees and pushed my face into the cold, silty water, swilling the puddle like a madman. I thrust my hands in and splashed in a frenzy, mud and silt running thickly down my cheeks, chin, and neck.

When the pain had dropped one increment below pure agony, I struggled to my feet and shouted at the heavens, "How much more can I give, goddamnit?" But the unbearable swell of self-pity demanded more expression, and I wound up with my uninjured foot and lashed out violently, finding unexpected purchase. Although fleeting and obfuscated by my pain, I had a brief awareness of the fact that I had just kicked and severely damaged the panel on my passenger door. Finally, I guided myself around the front end of the car, got in, and rolled slowly over the two miles or so to my home.

Once there, I yanked the car to the curb and ground both tires into the concrete. I bailed out, jumping the four stairs down to the door of my basement apartment, my eyes and lips now the two remaining areas where the pain had dug in tenaciously and was only slowly, reluctantly, letting go. I unlocked the door and went inside, swinging the door savagely shut, but the trapped air of the small foyer slowed the door and cushioned its impact against the jamb. So I tore the door open again and flung it shut with everything I had, slamming it with the desired crack of metal and wood.

Panting, I cranked on the faucets in the bathroom sink and engaged the plug. As the sink filled, I squinted my way into the bedroom and pulled open my sock drawer. As I took out the baggie of Nicki's Valium, I realized that I was growling, each exhale a primal rattle of powerless defiance. There was nothing inside me but rage and defeat, the oxygen drawn off the surface of my brain with each rumbling snarl.

I tore into the bag, my fingers grasping at one of the tiny pills, the others scattering and bouncing lightly about the carpet as the bag burst open. I threw the one pill into my mouth then dropped to my knees and grabbed another, swallowing both.

In the kitchen next to the sink was a bottle of rye whiskey with about four inches left. I swept away the obstructing mass of dishes, which clattered to the floor, shards of glass and ceramic sliding across the linoleum. I uncorked the bottle and pulled at the alcohol with disdain and disgust at the overwhelming and nauseating strength that seared its way down my throat to my stomach. Still clutching the bottle, I returned to the bathroom, where the sink was nearly full. I grabbed a breath and plunged my face into the cool water. I stayed there for a long time, still and blind in the water's embrace. I could hear the hum of pipes and currents, like the murmur of a seashell. I took another breath and returned to the water, moving my face from side to side. After repeating this several times, I stood up and faced my dripping, red-eyed reflection. The front of my shirt was stained with dirt from the mud puddle in an uneven brown ring. I tipped the bottle one, two, three times, the slosh of amber growing less and less until it was a thin film of foam running translucent down the sides of the bottle.

I threw a towel down over my pillow, not wanting to dry my face, and lay there curled up on my side, breathing anxiously. "Well, Dad, you would've loved that," I said to the ceiling, already drunk. "Right up your alley. But I understand you have adventures of your own to live, while I need to hang out here for a while right in the thick of it. I know you. I got you figured out. Gimme a few minutes on that bus ticket thing, Nicki. I've done enough for the moment. I need to call Wilma, probably should call the cops. All in a day's work. Here I am, Levi Shea, my father's son. Bastard explorer of the American frontier and the dynamics of the broken home. Just gimme a couple of minutes, and I'll get right on the rest of my duties." I mumbled my promise to the darkness of my eyelids and was gone.

19

I slept without waking for the rest of the day and through the night. I left the heater off, and the cold came through the walls and into my bed. I woke fully clothed and rolled over to look at the neon numbers of the clock radio. It was 7:15 A.M. Rolling onto my back and staring into the leaden darkness above, I could hear the creak of my leather belt with each rise and fall of my stomach. I was awake and alone once again with reality, guilty of taking flight to escape it. The weight in my chest made me feel like crying, but I was dry, empty. I went to the bathroom, leaving the light out and climbed into the shower, where I bathed and washed my hair. Then I curled up on the floor of the tub in the concealing darkness and let the hot water run over me for nearly an hour.

When I entered the building, Verna's head jerked to attention with the rattle of the glass door as it opened, as if I had snuck up on her in some private place. Wilma was standing next to her, but her head came up slowly as though she dreaded what was coming through the door. At first I thought the mood was related to Kristen LaGuardia, for surely the police had been called about the violence. For several seconds they both communicated with me only through the expressions on their faces, then Wilma's eyes welled with tears.

"Come on," she said and stepped toward me. Her hand moved across my back until her arm was round me and she was guiding me into her office. Verna was the only other person I could see in the silent building. I could feel Verna holding her breath, I could feel the pain of her gaze, and I knew it wasn't about Kristen.

There are things that a look can tell you. You have no details, but you know the basic story. Because of this, the news was not shocking, it was only words, confirming what Verna and Wilma communicated through their eyes.

Nicki was dead. I couldn't hear anything else because of the weight; it blocked up my ears and filled my limbs, and my chest swelled with it. I could see Wilma's lips moving. Her face was leaning forward very close to mine. She was holding one of my hands in both of hers, away from me as if it were someone else's limb. She shook my hand up and down, I could see she had to make great effort because the hand was so heavy.

Then I vaguely heard her say something about the program shutting down for the day out of respect. She also said something about a talking circle and a ceremony for the staff. Her voice was hoarse and distant, drifting across a great canyon where the winds from below blew most of her words away. She had asked me if I wanted to talk, but I was mute. Finally, she said "Go to your family. Go home." I was getting up out of the chair; I was standing. She rose with me as though I were a decrepit elderly man who might fall.

In the gathering space by the coffeepot, I could see into Luke's office and he was there, his profile framed in the doorway, leaning back in his chair facing out the window. I floated toward him on a gathering swell of consternation, with Wilma still behind me, waiting to catch me if I fell.

Luke spoke, without turning from the window. He sounded like a storyteller, his voice rumbling low and introspective. They had found her in a park overlooking the bay. She was curled up on the grass atop a bluff that sloped thirty or forty feet down to the lapping water below. It had been raining lightly. She had drunk over half a fifth of whiskey, and in the dreamless sleep of an alcohol coma she died during the freezing night in a pair of jeans and a sweatshirt. I had been to the spot before—the place where she died. The rain must have touched her face when she looked skyward, it must have turned her beautiful new skin cold. But I knew that the poison in her body could not touch the magnificence of the Indian girl it had taken. I knew that she was beautiful and powerful, and that nothing could take that away. The water below her was the Puget Sound. And there were islands. I could see them far away.

I was moving toward the front door. My feet on the carpet then the street was the only sound, the padded ticking of time passing.

The sky was the color of ice and I was driving.

The months moved on, one after the other, unemployment checks announcing their approaches and departures. I stayed with my mother off and on for a few days at a time, sitting on the porch, my brain not doing much beyond the base interpretation of the unchanging scenes in front of my eyes.

My mother talked a lot, and sometimes I listened and sometimes not. But I suppose it helped just to hear her voice. She talked about her job, our family, and the trivialities of the day. Occasionally she talked about what was going on with me and the things that had happened. If I wasn't too tired, I'd try to talk, but mostly I listened, if not always to her words, at least to the tone and fluctuation of her voice, reassuring me that there were parts of my world—good things—that were still alive and not so damaged, and that I could see them if I looked with the right perspective.

Other times my mother sang the old songs like, "Good Night Irene." I think that her mother sang them to her when she was a child, and maybe it was her subconscious way of trying to make me feel like a safe little kid.

Tia would be home fairly soon, in mid-July. We had spoken briefly on the phone several times. She kept the conversations simple and didn't push for specifics, simply saying that she couldn't wait to get home to see me, and we would talk then.

After a couple months I had finally spoken to Wilma, too. I called her up to apologize for not coming back to work, and for not returning the messages she left on my neglected answering machine during the first couple weeks after Nicki went away. She told me that it was understandable and that everybody was taking it very hard. The ceremony they had held had been positive, and she wished I had come. After the ceremony they had had a sweat for any of the staff who wanted to attend out at the cultural center where the sweat lodge was. Every employee who had been in any way connected with Nicki went, except me.

Wilma said that the organization would pay for a counselor for me and that I could come back when I was ready if I decided that it was the right choice. Then she told me that I had "hard shoes to follow."

"Hard shoes to fill," I said, and heard myself laugh for the first time in a long while. "Hard shoes to fill or a hard act to follow," I repeated. "You got to pick one of 'em."

"On second thought," Wilma said, "maybe you should consider another field, aayee!"

I almost didn't want to ask about Lydia and Charles Sanders, but I had to.

"Lydia's staying with her sister," Wilma said, "and she's doing real bad emotionally. But she went into treatment, and she and her sister are going to start coming here for groups when she starts aftercare. We got a loss and grieving support group startin' up, and we'll get her in it. Charles has been calling her, I hear. He wants to come in, too, says he needs to. Goddamn, it's gonna be rugged."

It was too much. I didn't ask or say anything else about it.

Before we hung up, Wilma told me to take care of myself, and there was an edge of loving threat to her words.

"Okay," I said. "I'll try."

I talked to her again about a month later to let her know I was alive and to see how things were going. A new worker had been hired to replace me. I made Wilma promise me that she would pass a note to the new worker telling her to find Jerry Reeves's kids. As yet they still had not been retrieved. It was a sunny day, spring was coming to life, and things had begun to grow. Wilma told me about a powwow that was going on that weekend. As I was saying good-bye, Wilma interrupted me. "Wait, Levi," she said. "There's one more thing."

I could hear her rustling some papers around on her desk. "What is it?"

"Well, there was a note that Nicki left on her dresser. I never told you about it because I wasn't sure what it meant, and I thought it might upset you more."

I dreaded hearing it. I dreaded the part I might have in the note, my portion of the blame. "Oh," I said, moaning involuntarily.

"It's okay, Levi," Wilma said, reassuringly. "It was written towards the end, but we don't think she wrote it on that day. It's not a suicide note, it's something else. It was on top of her journal. I think you should hear it now."

"Go ahead," I said, swallowing hard and waiting. Wilma's voice trembled slightly as she read:

Where are you taking me, anyway?
You got someplace for me to stay? You got a place for you?
Just a friend is all you are, walking with me in the dark
not thinking it would be this tough.
An Indian friend, and that's enough.
I think sometimes you know less than me
Madchild Running, do you see?
Madchild Running, run, go free.

I had her read it another time. Then when I asked her to read it yet again, she said my name with a grave, sudden force, as though she were snapping me out of a dangerous trance.

"I'm writing it down," I said. "It's mine, after all."

"Yes, I guess it is," she agreed, and read it one more time. "She held nothing against you, Levi. Do you know that?"

"Yeah," I said. "I think so." I told Wilma to give my regards to everyone at the office for me, and we said good-bye.

20

It was a big powwow. They had risked having it outdoors and lucked out on the weather; although it was late June, weather-wise that meant nothing in Seattle, it just happened to be sunny and warm. I parked about a quarter of a mile away and walked along the rows of cars that packed the fields around the park. That morning I had had the oil changed in my car, had gassed it up until the needle was pegged past the full line, and had thrown two stuffed travel bags in the backseat.

I walked into the park towards the sound of drums and singing. Over the crush of bodies I could see the eagle feathers and porcupine hair roaches, and a blur of bright colors—eagle feather bustles and fans, buckskin and ribbon shirts. It was an intertribal powwow, with dancers wearing regalia of many different nations, advancing around the arena. I heard the clacking of wooden paddles, of claws, talons, and deer hooves; the tinkling of hundreds of small metallic bells sewn onto the regalia of more than a hundred dancers, their music traveling along the surface of the earth with the thumping of the drums.

Vendors surrounded the far side of the grounds in a semicircle of stands with blue tarps stirring in the wind. The smell of fry bread and chili wafted upon the afternoon heat. Shouts of children and the crying of babies mixed with the singing and the pounding of the drums. In the crowd I saw faces of people who were familiar but no one I knew well enough to approach. I had been half expecting to run into coworkers and would have welcomed seeing them now.

I stood watching on the fringe just beyond where the crowd became thick. Finally, the intertribal ended, and the MC announced a competition for the Women's Traditional. At that moment someone tapped me on the shoulder. I turned around and found myself facing a young woman. When our eyes met her tentative expression relaxed into a wide smile with a slight overbite of large white teeth.

"It is you," she said with a nervous laugh. It was Reyanne. She was flanked by two small children, a boy and a girl.

I didn't say anything, but I smiled.

"This is Teren and this is Theresa," she said, putting a hand on each child's shoulder and easing them forward. They both simultaneously rolled their eyes up at me like little marionettes.

"The twins!" I said. "You got 'em."

Reyanne nodded, still grinning.

We stood there nodding for what felt like a good four or five seconds. Then her kids got antsy, and Teren started poking at Theresa's ribs with a corn dog stick. "Well, we're going to walk around," Reyanne said, deftly swiping the stick from her son. Then looking me squarely in the eyes she said, "Thanks, Levi."

I smiled again, and said, "No problem."

When they were gone, I maneuvered through the crowd and up to a bleacher, ten feet from the drummers, who were singing for the Women's Traditional. There was room at the end of one of the planks, so I took a seat two rows up from ground level. Out on the field, about ten women danced slowly in a circle, straight-backed with their heads erect and proud, all with one or two eagle feathers pointing skyward from the firm clench of their hair, their braids lying heavily against their dresses like strong dark ropes. Eagle feather fans held in front of their breasts, they stepped with graceful certainty over the grass, their eyes fixed somewhere beyond the wall of faces that surrounded them. In silent resolve, they danced, their moccasins touching the earth before them, moving in the circle, upon the pounded yellow grass, their movements uniform with one another...all except for one.

A little Tlingit girl, six or seven years old, cloaked in her black and red tunic and cape, moved with wide stalking steps, her delicate face and intense gaze set squarely forward, her small form hunched and advancing beneath skinny outstretched arms so that her cape spread wide and fell about her—surrounding her like the wings of a soaring bird, and from her leading hand a fan of eagle feathers splayed in an arc of iron gray symmetry, pointing the direction of her movement. Abalone buttons were stitched along the borders of her cape, and a bright green frog was emblazoned in its center, covering the narrow expanse of her back and stretching across the cape in proud announcement of her clan. She moved just outside of the others, her circle a larger one than theirs, like a tiny orbiting star. Her brow lowered with intensity, searching an earth miles below her, her mouth pulled in tight, brown cheeks slightly puckered with concentration. Around and around she danced, never relaxing the power of her movements, the fire of her spirit burning strong.

I began to cry without sound and could not stop. Tears streamed down my face as I followed the girl with my eyes, wiping the tears so that I would not lose the clarity of her image. I had never been so proud of anything before as I was of that little girl, watching her feet connect with the dry solidness of earth, offering the gift of her dance with the strength of an enormous heart and open eyes, shining with intensity, around and around, her feet and her spirit moving her over the field, alive, young, and Indian.

When the dance ended, I left the powwow, going somewhere I had not planned to go. It was only 1:30. There was plenty of daylight left, and the measure of time for me was now as simple as the rising and setting of the sun.

I stopped at a convenience store and bought a cup of coffee and a small red rose from the white bucket next to the cash register. The ferry was about to leave as I pulled into the terminal, purchased my ticket, and was hurried on by the attendant. I was already humming the songs of my Auntie Rita, not aloud but somewhere inside. I could only faintly hear the progression of their rhythm, not remembering all of their titles or words, as if someone were singing them to me from very far away so that I would not have to work to remember them. They started quietly, then grew louder, as if they were forming and wandering like tributaries seeking to fill the larger body.

As I left the car and mounted the slight incline of matted grass into the graveyard, the sight of the gray stones and the green field shimmered before the film of tears in my eyes that had been coming off and on during the trip. I saw the images of faces laughing and faces frowning in the defiant expressions of pride from the depths of sorrow. I heard the words of poems, and the voices of those who had fought and of those still fighting.

I walked right to where Wilma said that it would be, two down from her grandfather's. The dirt had already turned the color of ash under the sun and the wind, and blades of spring grass had grown up from the moist ground beneath. There were two white couples in their mid-forties taking pictures of Chief Sealth's grave. I could hear their voices but not their words. For a while, I thought about speaking to the freshly turned ground at my feet. And then I heard myself singing, the first that grew loud enough in my memory for me to sing it. It was a song for warriors going away. I sang what I remembered several times through, and then began another, "The Dance of the Maiden." I remembered Nicki running through the snow; I could see her laughing at me, and I could hear myself singing "The Spirit of Sla Hal," the one that made me see islands. I remembered my Auntie Rita's voice announcing its name softly on the tape in a dry and reflective whisper, in the darkness of my car on the way home from the Lummi Reservation.

I squeezed my eyes shut, and my voice carried out to the thicket of blackberries that encircled the graveyard in a high gnarled wall of leaves and thorns. It moved over Nicki's grave and all of the others, over the white tourists and the church behind me, and into the air over the water and the trees. And I hoped that it was heard. I hoped they were in a place where they all could hear me.

When I was finished, I took the little flower that I had been holding and placed it at an angle on the grave. "I tried to get the ticket to you," I whispered. "But it was the wrong thing to do. I was wrong. I'm sorry." I wiped my eyes for the last time. "Don't come back," I said out loud. "I'll be okay."

As I walked from the grave, I noticed that the two couples were also moving on, and I knew that our paths would meet when we reached the opening in the low wooden fence. I could see in my peripheral vision that they were all looking at me, and one of the women was several hurried strides ahead of her companions, as though she were trying to head me off. We reached the gate at the same time, and I looked into her face, she staring earnestly into mine. She leaned in toward me and I came to a stop. The solemn look that etched hard crow's feet around her eyes was maybe a little too strained, like she were about to break some bad news to me and wanted me to see beyond a doubt that she as sympathetic and did not want to offend in any way. Her hair was mousy and graying evenly, cut just below her ears. She was wearing dark green shorts, a polo shirt, and large pearl earrings.

She blinked rapidly several times, her eyes probing mine as if to ascertain whether or not I was ready for a heavy question, then she licked her lips. "That was very beautiful," she said. "Was that an ancestor of yours? Were you singing to an ancestor?"

We looked at each other for a few more moments as I processed her question. "She was a child who died in the Indian wars," I said. I wasn't being sarcastic. It was all that I felt at that moment.

She cocked her head, and the sympathy in her eyes heightened and became maudlin, then settled into mild confusion, freezing into permanency. I turned and left the graveyard, and I could feel the woman standing at the gate, watching me leave. At the side of my car I removed the baggie of Xex mein from my pocket and placed a full pinch of it on a small, flat rock. I used the car lighter to ignite it, gently pushing the hot coil over the herb, occasionally looking up to behold the green stillness of the graveyard through the thin ribbon of smoke that rose before me, up into the sun.

Nicki was gone. Now it was only me and my graveyard of skeletons, a rattling of bones, deafening and demanding. I had tried to save her, save her from becoming me. I had tried to save her from the dull persistent battery of pain that pulses its way through forgetfulness, pain that I knew would keep coming for her, just as it came for me. And I thought that if I could save her, maybe it would all be okay, I would be okay. But now it was just me and my past. Me and my future. And the bones were like rattles, their pounding message neither good nor bad, waiting for me to take them in my hands and decide the rhythm for myself. When I made choices, when I took action, I would try to make them in honor of Nicki. I would try to live in honor of what she represented, all that she was and could have been, in honor of the enduring spirit of the Indian child, alive and breathing, an energy that would grace the earth forever.

I crossed Puget Sound and jumped I-90 heading toward the mountain pass, and beyond toward eastern Washington, Arlee, Montana, and the Flathead Reservation. In a while I would come back and would take my mother and Tia to visit Auntie Rita. Then we would eat, and we would talk, and we would laugh. But for now I would drive a ways.

Two hours later, as the day began to slip away, I was east of the mountains and speeding smoothly down the straight stretch of highway that flowed before me, turning into a thin line and disappearing into the sky.

At a place where the brown prairie hills moved out to all horizons, I breached a small rise in the road where it cut through two low bluffs of rock and stunted brush and pitched me down a long gradual stretch of highway into an expanse of plains so huge it was as though the world had opened like a flower and pushed itself up until its body met the sky. And the sky along the horizon was a fiery red-pink, like the wild blaze along the body of a steelhead as it breaks the white churn of the river; and at the edges of the burn where the heat of day dimmed and disappeared, and washed itself into the whole of the sky, came the color blue in strokes the size of clouds, soft like milk dyed with the juice of blueberries, over my head and behind me and away.

I'm out there, man.
Somewhere.
Looking for a place to stop.
Looking for a place to feel
Looking for a place.
Somewhere.

Epilogue

Mother told me, she was talking about some of her relatives and a man who was sick for a long time; and seems like nobody knew what was the matter with him. His grandmother would come everyday and sit by his side and sing songs and she came to a certain song, and he began to sing that. This man said it seemed like he was on a high bluff, way up, on some island. And when he looked down, way down to the beach, he saw nothing but human bones, bleached by the sun. All on the beach. It was in his mind all the time, that was making him sick. He began singing.

—Aurelia Mary Celestine, 1886-1982